THE LAWMAN: MANHUNT

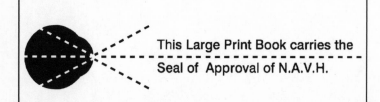

This Large Print Book carries the
Seal of Approval of N.A.V.H.

THE LAWMAN: MANHUNT

LYLE BRANDT

THORNDIKE PRESS
A part of Gale, Cengage Learning

GALE
CENGAGE Learning

Detroit • New York • San Francisco • New Haven, Conn • Waterville, Maine • London

GALE
CENGAGE Learning™

LIBRARY OF CONGRESS CATALOGING-IN-PUBLICATION DATA

Brandt, Lyle, 1951–
   Manhunt : the lawman / by Lyle Brandt. — Large print ed.
     p. cm. — (Thorndike Press large print western)
   Originally published: New York : Berkley Books, 2010.
   ISBN-13: 978-1-4104-3028-1
   ISBN-10: 1-4104-3028-6
   1. Large type books. I. Title.
PS3602.R364M36 2010
813'.6—dc22   2010021286

Published in 2010 by arrangement with The Berkley Publishing Group, a member of Penguin Group (USA) Inc.

For Bill Munny

1

"They're late," said Jimmy Beck.

You couldn't silence Jimmy by ignoring him, so Ethan Frain replied, "Have you got somewhere else to be?"

Beck blinked at that, looking confused, and spat tobacco juice into the dirt before he answered, "Me? Uh-uh."

"Then stop complaining," Frain commanded.

"Right. Okay."

That set the other men to snickering, Creed Sampson with that snuffling sound that passed for laughter since his old man punched his nose flat one too many times. Tom Dahlquist knew the trick of laughing silently, his shoulders jiggling, while Dick Eyler snorted once and let it go.

They had been waiting for the best part of the morning now, having arrived soon after dawn, and Frain's other companions would be getting antsy soon. They wouldn't quit on him — none of them had the guts to challenge him, alone or all together — but he wanted them with all their varied wits about them when the *Katy Flier* finally arrived.

And Beck was right. The train was late.

Not that its passengers were likely to complain.

This time around, the *Flier* was an abbreviated "special," consisting of a locomotive, its tender, one passenger car, and a standard caboose. The passengers included thirty men in chains and eight with guns, assigned to watch the others while the *Katy Flier* was en route from Huntsville, Texas, to Fort Leavenworth in Kansas.

After Leavenworth, the prisoners would be dispersed to federal lockups in the North and East, beyond Frain's reach. He had one chance to stop the train, with any reasonable prospect of success. Failing that, he might not see his brother again for the rest of his life.

The *Flier*'s route meant that it had to cross the Oklahoma panhandle. Instead of wasting time and energy to build a town where none existed when the track was laid, some genius had gone dowsing and discovered water in the midst of nowhere, sunk a well, then built a water tower with a windmill standing by to keep it filled. Now trains could stop and fill their thirsty boilers without passengers debarking, roaming off, and getting lost.

Not that the *Flier*'s current occupants would be allowed to leave their car, while there were slop buckets available. Their guards would see to that.

The water tower and its windmill had no competition in a flat landscape where trees were few and far between. Nearby, a gully undercut the tracks, and they were braced with timbers to create a trestle that concealed Frain, his companions, and their horses. Frain supposed the gully would be prone to flooding during heavy rain, but it was bone-dry now and offered shade.

It had cost Frain a fair amount to get the *Katy Flier*'s schedule and the number of armed guards aboard. His party was outnumbered — maybe two to one, if members of the *Flier*'s normal crew were packing guns — but he was counting on surprise to tip the odds.

Surprise and pure brute force.

His four companions might not be the smartest outlaws in the business — hell, some might suspect they didn't have one decent brain among them — but there was no doubt concerning their ability to follow orders or their willingness to get their hands dirty. Sampson alone had killed at least two dozen men, not counting Indians, and if you'd added all their scores together, it was pushing sixty. Ropes were waiting for the lot of them, if they were ever taken into custody.

But there would be no risk of that today.

It had been seven months and thirteen days since the Frain gang had blundered into an ambush trying to hold up a mail train. Ethan had taken a slug in his hip but remained in his saddle, while his brother Evan tumbled from his horse, scalp grazed, and lay unconscious on the field. The choice came down to death or leaving him behind, and it had been a close call, even then.

There'd been no chance for Frain to liberate his brother prior to trial, nursing his own wound in the bargain, but he had a chance today. Before it was too late.

And this time, it was do or die.

"You gonna eat that biscuit?"

Evan Frain turned from his window, toward the hulking convict in the seat beside him, meeting tiny, ratlike eyes set in a florid, hairy face. The hulk, one Drake "Mad Dog" Bodine, had finished off his beans with one sad biscuit on the side and ogled the remains of Evan's meal as if he'd never seen a finer feast.

"I'm done," Frain said and passed Bodine his metal plate. The shaggy giant made a piglike snuffling sound in lieu of thanks.

"Don't mention it," Evan replied.

He didn't have much appetite these days, ate only for the sake of keeping up his strength, in case he saw an opportunity to brain one of his guards, pick up a gun, and make a fight of it. Frain knew that it was tantamount to suicide, but in his melancholy moments he preferred that to the slow death waiting for him at his journey's end.

Frain wished that he could reach the judge who'd sentenced him to thirty years and snap his scrawny neck. What was the old man thinking? Thirty years for an *attempted* robbery and giving one slow guard a flesh wound that they called *attempted murder?*

Okay, he'd tried to lift the U.S. mail. So what? Was that worth thirty goddamned years out of his life?

Frain would be fifty-six years old when he got out, too old for anything but scut work, living hand to mouth and thinking of the old days when he'd swung a wide loop with his brother and the rest.

Thinking of Ethan stoked the anger in his gut. Frain hadn't seen his brother ride away

11

and leave him, being knocked out cold and all, but he assumed there'd been some pressing reason Ethan couldn't help him. Then, in custody, his reputation worked against him, making sure there were too many guards on hand for any kind of raid against the county jail or courthouse.

As for Huntsville . . . well, his brother might act crazy sometimes, but he wasn't stupid. Anyone who tried to crack the worst prison in Texas might as well bed down with rattlesnakes and spare himself the ride.

Now he was on the *Katy Flier,* bound for Leavenworth and God knew where beyond it. There'd been talk of someplace in New York, maybe a prison camp in Florida, where alligators took the place of human guards. It hardly mattered, either way.

Frain knew he couldn't last three decades in a cage.

He wasn't sure that he could last three years.

What did a lousy biscuit matter, in the scheme of things?

They had him chained three ways: his ankles shackled, left wrist handcuffed to his window seat, and tethered to his porky neighbor with a belly chain. Frain couldn't stand upright or move about the car unless one guard unlocked him, while another held a ten-gauge shotgun leveled at him, well beyond arm's reach. It was humiliating when he had to use the slop bucket, but there would be no rest stops on his last trip north.

Where are you, Brother? Evan asked his grim reflection in the mirror, silently. *Where are you when I need you?*

Marshal Burt Alford checked his pocket watch and guessed that they were twenty minutes from the no-name water stop, where he would have to shift himself and disembark. It was routine, scouting the landscape while a prison train was stopped, no matter if the nearest town was forty miles away.

Security was Alford's personal responsibility, no shifting it to deputies with thirty convicts in his care.

Some of the bunch were types a man could turn his back on without getting knifed or strangled for it. Simple thieves or swindlers, bootleggers who'd peddled liquor on a reservation, and an idjit who'd believed he could impersonate a U.S. senator to get free room and board in Houston.

On the other hand, he had some hard-core bandits, one convicted rapist who'd been spared the noose because his victims had been Mexicans — and Drake Bodine. The law suspected *him* of seven murders, but the bodies hadn't turned up yet, so he was facing fifteen years for rustling army cattle. Alford wondered why somebody hadn't shot him, when they had the chance, but now Bodine was his responsibility.

At least until they reached Fort Leavenworth.

Buford was armed with a Winchester model '73, chambered for the same .44-40 cartridge as his Colt Single-Action Army revolver. Three of his deputies also carried rifles, while four packed double-barreled ten-gauge scatterguns loaded with double-ought buckshot. The shotguns circulated, passed around to those assigned to watch the shackled prisoners at any given time, where they could unleash bloody havoc at the first sign of an uprising.

Sleeping and meals rotated for the deputies, with four on duty at all times and Alford supervising all concerned. It was his third run to Fort Leavenworth in eighteen months, without a major hitch so far.

Ten years behind a badge for this? he thought, then shrugged it off.

It could always be worse.

The train was slowing down for its approach to the lonely water tower, stuck in the middle of no-man's-land. At least the open plains surrounding it made watching for an ambush simple. No one could approach the train unseen.

Unless . . .

He'd have to check the gully, just in case.

Alford had nearly missed it on his first trip, feeling foolish when he saw a buzzard lift off from below ground level as the train was almost ready to roll out. He hadn't made the same mistake again, and never would.

An easy job could get a lawman killed, if he let down his guard.

In preparation for their stop, Alford passed through the prison car, telling the shackled jailbirds, "We'll be topping off on water, up ahead. Nothing to see. No reason anybody needs to leave his seat. If you have any pressing business, hold it till we're on the move again and someone brings the pail around."

There was some grumbling at that, but Alford didn't care. What could his charges do but grouse and mutter, while he had them all immobilized?

Topping the locomotive's boiler off took fifteen minutes, give or take. Alford could let one of his deputies investigate the gully, but he liked to do the job himself. Break up the drab monotony and stretch his legs a little. Feel the sunshine on his face.

Rifle in hand, he cleared the car and stepped onto its rear platform, three feet from the caboose. Outside, the speed and rocking motion of the train seemed more exaggerated, even as the brakes began to whine.

Alford leaned out, gripping the rail with his free hand, and scanned the empty landscape to the north and west.

It seemed as lifeless as the surface of the moon.

Ethan Frain was mounted on his bay mare as the *Katy Flier* hissed and rattled to a halt, its locomotive panting just beside the water tower. Flanking him, his men were saddled up and clutching guns, Dick Eyler leading the spare horse they'd picked up for Evan outside of some tiny burg, fifty miles back.

The piebald gelding's former owner wouldn't miss it.

He was punching cows in Hell.

Ethan spurred his mare along the gully, to the point where its west bank had broken down to form a ramp of sorts. He took it at a gallop, leaning forward in his saddle, reins gripped in his left hand, a Colt Thunderer in his right. Cresting the gully's lip, he swung back toward the *Katy Flier* with a silent snarl, hearing the others close behind him.

Ethan saw the *Flier*'s fireman lowering the water chute to fill the locomotive's boiler, still oblivious to danger closing from behind him. Midway between, plodding toward the cut, some kind of lawman saw the riders bursting into view and raised a lever-action rifle to his shoulder.

Ethan Frain was faster, with the Colt already in his hand. He didn't even have to cock it, since the Thunderer was double action, firing with a simple trigger pull instead of thumbing back the hammer first. Aiming across his mare's neck, Frain fired once and saw his .41-caliber slug strike his target an inch of so left of his badge.

The lawman lurched and staggered, tripped over his own feet, and collapsed facedown, his rifle falling out of reach. Ethan considered shooting him again, on the fly, but his first shot had alerted the train's other guards all scrambling now to defend their little Alamo on wheels.

One down left seven fit to fight, but Ethan was in no position to start counting heads, as gunfire echoed from the passenger car and caboose. Rifles and shotguns blazed away from open windows, Ethan and his men returning fire and ducking lead.

He'd warned the others to be careful, shooting at the main car, since he couldn't say where Evan would be seated, but the harsh reality of battle vetoed caution. Galloping and shooting while the train's guards tried to kill him, Frain himself could not place any of his shots with true precision, or expect the others to surpass his skill.

If he had been a praying man, this would've been the time to ask God's mercy and protection for his brother, but the notion almost made Frain laugh, after the hell they'd raised together in their time.

And if that time ended today, well, it had been a decent run.

Approaching the caboose, Frain saw a deputy crouched on the rear platform, pumping the lever action of his Henry rifle. Taking time to cock the weapon spoiled his aim, and Ethan seized the opportunity to slam a .41 slug through the lawman's throat.

It was the opening he'd hoped for, suddenly dismounting in a leap, trusting his bay to stick around and answer when he whistled later, if he still had breath to whistle with. A short run brought him back to the caboose, mounting the platform, pushing past the corpse to make his way inside.

He caught another lawman turning from an open window, shotgun sweeping toward him. Frain fired twice and saw the bullets hit, dropping the lawman to a crouch as spastic fingers clenched around the shotgun's triggers. Pain lanced through Frain's eardrums as the double blast, confined, came close to stunning him. But it was angled toward the ceiling as the lawman fell, his wasted buckshot opening a ragged skylight overhead.

A noise behind him brought Ethan around, pistol rising, but it was only Jimmy Beck invading the caboose, grinning to beat the band.

"Ready?" Beck asked.

Instead of pausing to reload his Colt, Frain holstered it and claimed the fallen marshal's Smith & Wesson No. 3 Schofield revolver for himself.

"Ready," he said and pushed on toward the passenger car.

The first shot made Evan Frain blink, then smile. He turned to Drake Bodine and said, "Duck down, if you want to keep breathing."

"What the hell?"

Evan ignored him, bowing forward, twisting in his seat to make himself invisible below the windowsill. He wasn't sure the side wall of the railroad car would stop a bullet, but it was the only cover presently available, since Frain was cuffed and shackled to his seat.

Guards scurried through the car, ducking to peer from the windows, cocking their weapons.

"Where's Alford?" one of them asked.

"Went outside," said another. "Can't see 'im."

"Goddamn it!"

Now Frain heard the throb of hoofbeats, followed by more gunfire, and he had to bite his tongue to keep from crowing. Something in his gut told him that this was Ethan's doing, but if he was wrong, it still gave him a chance to cut and run.

Assuming he could ditch his chains.

"What's funny?" Bodine challenged, squinting at him through a veil of greasy hair that spilled across his forehead.

"Wait and see," Evan advised.

The guards were firing now, forced by the layout of the car to lean across their shackled captives, angling shots through open windows where they could, or simply blowing out the glass. Frain's ears rang with the din of it and echoed with his pulse, besides.

He wished one of the deputies would come and lean across his seat and give him a chance to reach a holstered six-gun with his free right hand. One shot to drop the lawman and another for his left-wrist manacle would leave three or four live rounds, depending on whether the deputy kept the hammer on an empty chamber. Blast his shackles, grab the dead man's Winchester or ten-gauge, and he'd have no trouble with the belly chain.

And if Bodine tried to obstruct him, claim one of the weapons for himself, Frain would be pleased to put a bullet in his fat, misshapen head.

But no one came to use Frain's window. Even in the heat of battle, it appeared the guards were mindful of the risk posed by Mad Dog Bodine. Frain waited, fighting the impulse to raise his head and glimpse the riders as they galloped past, whooping and hollering.

Was that a voice he recognized or just his damned imagination playing tricks on him?

Somewhere behind him, Evan heard a door bang open, followed by more gunfire. It was almost close enough for him to taste the grit of gunpowder, this time. One of the deputies let out a howl of pain, and then all hell broke loose, the convicts shouting, lurching in their seats and rattling their chains, as bullets flew around them, zinging up and down the car.

Bodine half rose, bawled, "Give 'em hell!" — and then collapsed, as a shotgun blast shattered his skull. Warm blood speckled Frain's prison uniform, staining the white stripes crimson.

The shooting only lasted half a minute longer, maybe less. Frain heard boots clomping toward him, along the car's center aisle, and sat upright, steeling himself for whatever came next. A shadow fell across him, and he looked up into his own grinning face.

His twin dangled a ring of keys and asked him, "Are you ready to get out of here, or what?"

Aside from Drake Bodine, four other convicts had been shot in the confusion. Two were dead, the others touch and go. Ethan and Evan freed the others, for the hell of it and to confuse manhunters who were bound to come along, sometime within the next few days. They left the prisoners to deal with two surviving marshals and the *Katy Flier*'s three-man crew as they saw fit.

They lasted all of sixty seconds, as the convicts vented their accumulated rage. Unless some of the prisoners knew how to run a train, the *Flier* wasn't going anywhere.

Evan was quick to swap his bloodstained

uniform for clothing packed inside the piebald gelding's saddlebags and to don the gunbelt that his brother offered almost as an afterthought. It felt good, being in the saddle after months in chains and cages, knowing that he had a choice of where to go and what to do when he arrived there.

"I wondered if you'd make it," he told Ethan.

"Ye of little faith," his twin mimicked their father's voice, sounding exactly like the old man did when he was reading scripture. Just before he started working on them with his razor strop. It sent a sharp, uncomfortable chill down Evan's spine.

"Hey, now!" one of the convicts called out to them, from his place beside the locomotive. "Where's the horses for the rest of us?"

Frain's chill became a tingle, almost pleasant, as he turned to face the prisoner.

"Can't help you," he replied. "You've got some time before a posse gets here. I was you, I'd use it making tracks."

"On foot?" the convict challenged. "Out here, in the middle of nowhere?"

"We could've left you chained up," Ethan offered, putting in his own two cents. "You don't like freedom, go on back inside and fasten up your chains."

"Says who?"

The twins exchanged a smile. It felt like coming home.

"Be sure you want to do this," Evan told the red-faced convict.

"Oh, I'm sure," the man in stripes replied, stooping to grab a lawman's shotgun lying at his feet.

Two bullets struck him in the chest, a hand's width apart, and punched the convict over backward in a boneless sprawl. He shivered once and then lay still.

"Who else feels like an argument?" asked Ethan Frain.

"Somebody? Anyone at all?" said Evan, goading them.

Their men had weapons leveled at the convicts now, prepared to blaze away, but none of those still wearing stripes made any hostile moves. Some made a point of showing empty hands, while others turned away and started walking.

"Not as stupid as they look," said Ethan.

"Sure they are," Evan replied. Then smiled again and said, "I needed that."

"Figured you might. Do you remember how to ride that animal?"

"You want to wager on it?"

"Maybe later," Ethan said, and reined his bay mare off toward the northeast. "Right now, I feel like getting out of here."

"And going where?" his brother asked.

Winking, Ethan replied, "As if you didn't know."

2

Half past noon at the Arcade saloon, Jack Slade was holding queens and treys, hoping to make a full house on the draw. Two pair wasn't the worst of hands, but he'd been leaking money slowly since he joined the game and needed something to persuade him that his luck hadn't run out.

"One card," he told the dealer, tossing in a useless four facedown.

The dealer, seated opposite, the thirteen-dollar pot between them, echoed his request and skimmed a card across to land between Slade's waiting hands.

Slade let it rest there for a moment, while the deal went on around. The player to his right — a cowboy from the Rocking R, outside of town — had called for two cards and looked disappointed with the pair he'd drawn. There were two players on Slade's left, one standing pat, the other joining Slade to take a single card.

"Dealer takes one," said John Muldowney, one of Enid's seventeen attorneys, as he palmed one off the top and set the deck aside.

"Your bet," Muldowney told the cowboy seated to his left, Slade's right.

"Check," said the cowboy. Meaning that he'd missed whatever combination he was hoping for, to take the pot.

"Yours, Marshal," said the dealer.

Slade picked up his card and saw a rotten deuce. Keeping his poker face intact, or trying to, he tossed some chips into the pot and told the table, "Fifty cents."

"Ernie?"

"Too rich for my blood," said the player who had drawn a single card. "I fold."

"Johnson?"

Before the player who stood pat could speak, Slade saw Hec Daltry enter through the Arcade's bat-wing doors. Hec scanned the sparsely populated room and spotted Slade facing the door. He raised a hand and started toward the table, as Muldowney's voice reached Slade.

"Marshal?"

"Sorry?"

"Your bet, if any," said the dealer.

Damn it!

"I blanked out for a second there," Slade

answered. "Sorry. What's the bet, again?"

"Johnson raised you a dollar, and I called."

His two pair probably weren't worth another buck, but Slade had reached the point where he'd feel foolish if he didn't see the other hands.

Almost as foolish as he'd feel when Johnson or Muldowney claimed the pot.

"I'll see it," Slade replied and dropped more chips atop the growing pile.

Hec Daltry reached the table, standing to Slade's right.

"Two marshals," said the cowboy who had folded. "We're in trouble now."

"Fear not," Muldowney said. "You've lost enough, nobody's gonna claim you cheated."

"That's hilarious," the cowboy groused.

"I aim to please," Muldowney told him. Then: "It's down to you, Marshal."

"The old man wants to see us," Daltry interrupted.

"I'm just finishing my lunch, here," Slade replied and fanned his cards out on the tabletop.

"Two pair," said Muldowney, just in case somebody couldn't see. "Queens over treys. Ernie?"

Another hand slapped down.

"Two smaller pair," the dealer said. "Jacks

over deuces. Johnson?"

Johnson beat Muldowney to it, speaking as he faced his hand. "Three sixes. Ain't they purty?"

"And they beat my fours," the dealer said, sounding amused despite his loss. "The pot's yours."

Slade rose as the chips retreated, caged by Johnson's arms. "I'll leave you to it, gentlemen," he told them. "Duty calls."

"Come back and lose your money anytime," said Johnson, chuckling.

Slade let it go and followed Daltry toward the exit. When he reckoned they were out of earshot from the poker table, he told Hec, "I hate a cheerful winner."

"Sure," Hec said. "Who doesn't?"

"What's doing with the judge?" Slade asked.

"Can't say. His boy caught me doing a head count on the cells and told me both of us were needed, right away."

The judge was Isaac Dennison, whose word was law throughout the western half of Oklahoma Territory. He'd been at the job for ten years now, starting in 1882, when it was still Indian country. Before that, Dennison had occupied a federal bench in Kansas. Going even farther back, he'd been a judge in Reconstruction-era Mississippi — a turn that had recently come back to haunt him, nearly costing his life.

The judge's "boy" was Aidan Finn, new on the job. His predecessor had been murdered in the very courthouse where Finn had his tiny lair, adjacent to the judge's quarters, by the same men who'd come gunning for Judge Dennison. So far, Slade thought that he was holding up all right, with no sign that it troubled him to fill a dead man's shoes.

"Some kind of an emergency?" Slade probed.

Hec shrugged. "You know what I know, son."

Slade cut a glance at Daltry, swallowing his smile. He didn't think that Hec was old enough to be his father, but the weathered face made estimating Daltry's age a futile exercise. He definitely had more time in as a deputy U.S. marshal, but Hec didn't talk up his past the way some did, making it sound like he'd been everywhere and seen everything.

Enid's main street was crowded as the noonday hour slipped away. The lawmen took their chances, dodging wagons and horsemen to cross at the main intersection, approaching the federal courthouse. Slade couldn't see the judge, with sun glare on the upstairs windows, but he could imagine Dennison pacing his chambers, grumbling impatiently.

Bad news for someone, when Dennison summoned two marshals at once, on the run.

Slade wondered who was dead, this time.

Finn wasn't in his office when they got there, so the marshals passed it by. Slade hesitated for a second, then rapped lightly on the judge's door and waited for the summons.

"Enter!"

Slade let Hec go first, trailed him, and closed the door behind them. Dennison was standing on his little balcony that overlooked the partly walled-off courtyard, offering a God's-eye view of the imposing scaffold built to handle six condemned defendants at a time.

It seldom came to that, but every now and then the hangman had a full lineup, requiring him to test each rope with varied weights. Slow strangulation or beheading weren't what Dennison envisioned when he sentenced a convicted prisoner to death, and he'd dismissed his share of executioners for clumsiness. One who'd received a second chance, then botched another hang-

31

ing, had received a six-month sentence for contempt of court, followed by banishment from Oklahoma Territory.

"Gentlemen, please sit," the judge instructed, turning from his view and moving toward his own chair with the aid of a familiar walking stick.

Slade saw that Dennison was still in pain — no great surprise, after he'd been shot twice, barely two months ago — but he was healing, putting less weight on his cane these days, with fewer grunts and grimaces. The grim expression on his face today, Slade thought, had more to do with recent news than aching bones.

"I got a telegram this morning," Dennison began, once he was seated. "From Fort Leavenworth."

He paused, as if waiting for Slade or Daltry to inquire about the cable's contents. When they didn't, Dennison pushed on.

"They were expecting thirty prisoners on Tuesday," Dennison explained. "A special train from Huntsville prison, down in Texas." Leaning forward to consult the message on his desk, he said, "The *Katy Flier*."

"That's a prison train?" Hec asked.

"Not ordinarily," said Dennison. "They run a special now and then. The convicts pass through Leavenworth, which is a military lockup, then go on to other federal prisons, north or east."

"You say they were expecting prisoners," Slade interjected. "Meaning that they never made it?"

"That's correct. The train did not, in fact, arrive. The officer in charge of prisoners at Leavenworth — a Colonel Bryson Handy — wired back down the line to check the *Flier*'s progress. What he learned, last night, is that the train was stopped by unknown persons west of Woodward, in the panhandle. Most of its convict passengers were liberated."

"*Most* of them?" asked Slade.

"Five were shot on the train, and another outside. That makes nineteen dead, including ten deputy U.S. marshals and the *Flier*'s three-man crew."

"Jesus!" Hec muttered.

"And twenty-four on the run," Slade observed.

"Eighteen, now," said Judge Dennison. "Four have already been captured, with two others shot by a rancher who frowned on them robbing his home."

"Still, Judge," Hec said, "eighteen's no picnic, running all over the countryside to who knows where. If it's just me and Jack —"

"You won't be chasing all eighteen of them," said Dennison. "You're only after one . . . plus the one who broke him out of custody."

"Who's that?" Hec asked.

"I don't know if you'll be familiar with him," Dennison responded. "Evan Frain?"

"Can't say it rings a bell," Daltry replied.

"I've heard the name," Slade said. "But it was farther south and west."

"That fits," said Dennison. "He's better known in Texas, westward through the territories of New Mexico and Arizona. Presently, he owes the U.S. government thirty years of his life for attempted mail robbery. Unofficially, Frain and his gang are suspects in at least a dozen murders, several times that many robberies, and other crimes less savory."

"How many in the gang?" Slade asked.

"It's flexible. I have some posters on the scum most frequently reported riding with him. You can take them with you."

Slade cleared his throat and asked, "Why are we focusing on him, Judge?"

"Frain's gang staged the breakout," Dennison replied. "I mean to hang them for the murders of ten marshals in my jurisdiction."

"But if everyone was dead when help arrived —"

"Not quite," said Dennison. "Hec, you'll remember Burton Alford."

"Burt? Sure, Judge," said Daltry.

"Alford was my first deputy marshal, when I took this job," the judge told Slade. "He transferred out to Texas, back in '86. I won't pretend we've kept in touch, but I get word of him from time to time. He was an upright, decent man."

"One of them on the train," Slade guessed.

"In charge of the delivery," said Dennison. "Apparently, he was the first man hit when Frain's men rushed the train. Somehow, he hung on till the posse found him and described the man who shot him to a tee."

"And that would be . . . ?" Slade prodded.

"Ethan Frain," said Dennison. "Another worthless cutthroat. Evan's brother."

"So, Burt recognized the brother?" Daltry asked.

"No way to help it," Dennison replied. "He had an eye for faces, as you may recall. And there was Evan, riding with him all the way from Huntsville."

"Judge, I still don't follow you," Hec said.

"You see one Frain brother, you've seen them all," said Dennison. He shifted in his high-backed chair, leaned forward, planting elbows on his desk, and met Slade's gaze.

35

"They're twins. Identical."

"You were a twin, right?" Daltry asked him, when they'd left the judge's chambers.

"Right."

His brother's murder was responsible for bringing Slade to Oklahoma and the job he held. If Jim were still alive, Slade wouldn't know Judge Dennison and wouldn't have a badge pinned to his vest. He wouldn't be assigned to track a group of men whose latest crimes included something like a dozen murders.

And he likely never would've met Faith Connover.

"Does that feel odd?" Hec asked.

"Does *what* feel odd?"

"Hunting a couple twins, when you *are* one?"

"Feels like another job," Slade lied.

"I guess it would feel odd to me."

"You mind if I hang on to these and look them over while I'm getting ready?" Slade asked, showing Hec the rolled-up posters Dennison had given them.

"Feel free."

They had agreed it was too late to leave that afternoon, preferring to begin their manhunt with an early start. It gave them time to pack, say their good-byes, and cover up to fifty miles with any luck, their first day on the trail.

"I'll meet you out at Miz Connover's place, then, after breakfast?" Hec confirmed.

"I'll be there," Slade replied and started back toward his hotel.

In his third-floor room, before Slade packed his saddlebags, he sat and spread the wanted posters out in front of him. They numbered six, but he was drawn first to the pair depicting the Frain brothers.

No surprise, there.

Ethan Allen Frain — a patriotic twist — was born on August 2, 1866, which put him four months short of twenty-six years old. He was a native Texan, six foot one, black-haired, and had a small scar on his left cheek, though the drawing on his poster didn't show it. Various authorities suspected him of murder, robbery, arson, and rape — presumably the crime Judge Dennison had found "less savory."

Evan Arnold Frain quite naturally shared his brother's birthday, height, and hair color. His poster listed no scars, which would help Slade tell the two of them apart, assuming that he ever found them. Charges filed or pending against Evan Frain included murder, robbery, horse theft, and kidnapping. No rape, which made Slade wonder whether Ethan had been acting on his own, in that case, or the victim hadn't managed to identify accomplices.

Assuming she'd survived.

And, then again, the posters could be wrong.

Some outlaws, grown notorious, were blamed for anything and everything that happened in the areas they frequented. Slade personally knew of one case where a bandit had been blamed for robberies in Wichita and Kansas City, executed on the same day, within half an hour of each other. Legends traveled fast, and there was no outrunning them.

It made no difference to Slade. He would be tracking the Frain brothers for their latest murders and escape from federal custody. Whatever else they'd done, or been accused of falsely, they would stretch rope for the *Katy Flier* massacre.

As for their sidekicks . . .

Slade went through the posters, finding that Judge Dennison had placed the rest in alphabetical order. First up was James Thomas Beck, alias "Jimmy Boone," "Jed Brown," and "Jack Bannerman." Always the "J.B." initials, as if straying far from his birth name was too much for Beck's brain to handle.

Beck was twenty-three years old, a blond, left-handed native of Louisiana, who had served a year for theft in Arkansas and seven months in Tennessee over a shooting scrape. Since then, he'd been a known accomplice of the Frains in robbery and murder, plus a rape claim that might — or might not — be connected to Ethan Frain's case.

Next up, Thomas Dahlquist, with no middle name. He was a thirty-one-year-old from Utah, out of Mormon stock, described as "portly," crowned with thinning reddish-colored hair. He wore a mustache, to conceal the childhood scar of a cleft lip, and favored two guns over one. At age nineteen, in Provo, he had shot the father of a girl whom he'd been courting, then escaped from jail before he could be tried and hanged for murder. Since then, he'd been linked to half a dozen killings and a slew of robberies spanning five states and territories.

Richard William Eyler was the youngest of the gang, at nineteen, a Missourian who'd likely grown up listening to stories of the James and Younger brothers, cast as heroes by some die-hard rebels in the Show-Me State. He was described as tall and thin, with brown hair and gray eyes. He had been serving time in Amarillo, on a charge of vagrancy, when he met Ethan Frain in jail and they broke out together, crippling a guard in the process. That had been two years ago. Today, the law regarded Eyler as a seasoned murderer and bandit, eligible for a noose if he was caught alive.

The last poster belonged to Creed J. Sampson, no apparent name to go with the initial. He was twenty-two, half white and half Cherokee, born in the Indian country before it became Oklahoma. Sampson wore his black hair long but sometimes tucked it underneath his hat when scouting targets for the gang. His first known victim, knifed to death when he was just thirteen, had been a drifter who'd imposed himself on Sampson's mother in her husband's absence. Since then, he had claimed eleven lives on record, prior to joining in the slaughter of the *Katy Flier*'s guards and crew. The other charges filed against him — rustling, robbery, escape from custody — were small-time by comparison.

Six killers, maybe more. Slade wouldn't know for sure until he found them. *If* he found them, which was far from being guaranteed.

He packed the posters with his other gear, picked up his guns, and locked the room behind him when he left. The clerk downstairs wished him the best of luck, as always, and Slade thanked him.

He would need it.

For the moment, though, he put the Frain gang out of mind.

And thought of Faith.

The Connover spread lay five miles outside Enid. Slade had made that ride so many times, by now, he thought that he could do it in his sleep, trusting his horse to find the way.

And yet, it still felt special, every time.

Faith Connover had been his brother's fiancée when Jim was murdered. Jack didn't know her — hadn't even known Jim was engaged — when he received the telegram informing him that Jim was dead. They'd fallen out of touch, mainly because Jack's lifestyle as a gambler kept him always on the move, outrunning letters that he never even knew were sent. He'd *missed* Jim, in a way he guessed that only twins can really miss each other, but the gulf between them had grown wide and deep, no doubt increased by Jack's unhappy memories of childhood.

The rest of it, all that had happened after Jack arrived in Oklahoma, still reminded him a bit of falling dominoes. Sometimes he felt as if the years of wandering, living from one deal to the next, had been some kind of preparation for the life that he was truly meant to lead.

And then again, sometimes he thought that notion was ridiculous.

Long story short, he'd come to bury Jim and settle his estate, whatever that might be, but found out that his brother had been murdered — and engaged to marry, when he died. Faith was a widow in advance, and while Jack tried his best to comfort her, he felt the stirrings of attraction that went far beyond mere sympathy. He'd fought it, but it didn't seem to matter.

And in time, he'd learned that Faith could feel it, too.

Meanwhile, there had been murderers to find and punish. Slade had bridled at Judge Dennison's first warning to stay off the case, unless he meant to solve it legally, but soon he'd donned the federal badge that still adorned his vest. It hadn't ended well — at least, not for his brother's killers — but the job he'd taken simply as a means to vengeance wouldn't let him go that easily.

Neither would Faith.

Slade marveled, sometimes, at the changes he'd been through since stepping off the train in Enid for the first time, nearly two years back. He'd never craved a home before, at least not consciously, but now . . .

Now, what?

He wasn't riding out to ask Faith for her hand in marriage but to tell her that he'd soon be leaving on another manhunt, going who knew where, in search of men who'd gun him down without a second thought and laugh about it afterward. If he returned alive, there'd likely be more bloodstains on his hands.

Slade knew that Faith was bothered by his job. Not irked or miffed, but deeply troubled by the violence, unsettled by his frequent absence. Slade had finally explained what nearly happened with Kate Bender in the middle of another case, some weeks ago, and even though Faith understood that it had been against his will, he'd still seen pain flicker behind her eyes.

I should've kept my mouth shut, Slade reproached himself, for something like the thousandth time. But living with a silent lie had tainted everything between them. It had eaten through his guts like acid, till his heart and tongue took over from his brain.

Faith understood. She'd put the almost-incident behind her, but Slade still kept searching for recriminations in her tone, her glance, even her touch. Having confessed, *he* couldn't let it go.

How was he any better off?

I still have Faith. That's how.

And now, he had to say good-bye again.

The house was quiet when he reached it, supper still an hour off, Faith's two farmhands still busy at their jobs. No one was on the porch to greet him as Slade stepped down from his roan, but by the time he finished tying off the reins, he heard her footsteps on the boards behind him.

"Jack."

Smiling down at him, she didn't make it any easier.

"Sorry I have to do this," he began. "I know I've only been in town a couple days, this time, but now —"

"I know," she interrupted him. "The jailbreak. Or the *train* break, I suppose it is. Word gets around."

"It seems so. Anyway, I have to leave first thing tomorrow."

"Come inside then," Faith replied, taking his hand. "We don't have any time to waste."

3

Breakfast was eggs and ham, with fried potatoes and the kind of coffee Slade could never get in town, for some reason he didn't understand.

"Is there a trick to this?" he asked Faith.

"To what?" she asked, before Slade raised his mug. "The coffee? Not that I'm aware of."

"Not some special recipe?"

"No, Jack. We buy the beans and grind them. End of story."

"Hmm. I thought maybe you were a coffee witch."

"Not me," she said. "You cast the spell last night."

Slade felt the color rising in his face, cheeks warming as she laughed.

"I've never seen you blush before, Marshal."

"I've never heard you talk about . . . um . . . you know."

45

"Guess I'll have to remember that, next time I want to get your blood up."

Slade ducked his head and forked another slice of ham. Faith reached across to squeeze his free hand, then released it, fingertips trailing across his knuckles.

"You'll be careful, won't you, Jack?"

"I always am," he said.

Not that it always helped.

"These men sound extra dangerous. I can't help worrying."

"I know." Slade met her gaze and held it. "I'll be *extra* careful. And Hec Daltry's coming, too, remember."

"That's a help," Faith said. Her tone wasn't convincing.

"There's a chance that we won't even find them," he suggested. "If they're smart, they should be back in Texas, halfway to New Mexico by now."

"Won't officers be hunting them in Texas?"

"They'll be hunted everywhere, after the mess they left behind."

The words were barely out before Slade cursed himself, regretting them. The last thing that Faith needed was a fresh reminder of the *Katy Flier* massacre.

Instead of going quiet, though, she shifted to another subject and surprised him.

"Will it feel strange, hunting twins?" she asked. "I mean, because of Jim and —"

"I'm not sure," he answered, honestly. "I feel *something*, but I can't put a name to it. Not sympathy. They're outlaws, plain and simple, when you strip the rest of it away."

"I only thought it might be . . . difficult," Faith said.

Slade shrugged and pushed his eggs around the plate.

"So far, I've only seen the drawings on their posters. Or, I should say, *drawing*. It appears they used the same one twice, just changed the names above it, and the charges down below. It may be different when I see them. *If* I ever do."

"Jack, promise me." Her face and tone were stern. "Don't let it slow you down, in case you need to . . . do something. Just don't."

"I won't."

"Promise."

"You have my word."

"God, listen to me. Am I jinxing you?"

"If I believed in jinxes," Slade replied, "I'd be a fortune-teller."

"You could work at home," she told him, smiling.

"Anyway, until my first prediction flopped

47

and people started showing up with pitch-
forks."

"You could always put a curse on them."

"Curse *at* them, maybe."

"Hit them with your crystal balls."

"It's normally just one," he said.

"Is it?" she teased.

Slade was considering a quick trip back to
bed, when Faith's housekeeper, Mamie
Tomlin, came into the dining room.

"Sorry. Excuse me, ma'am," she said to
Faith. "But there's another marshal just arrived, outside."

"That's Hec," Slade said.

Faith gave a wistful smile. "It is, indeed."

Slade gathered up his gear and led the way
outside, to find that someone had already
saddled up his roan gelding and brought it
from the barn. He turned to Faith, one
eyebrow raised.

"Now who's the mind reader?"

"I didn't want to make it any harder," she
replied and smiled again.

"Uh-huh. Too late."

She stepped in close to kiss him lightly on
the lips and whispered, "Just a little something for the trail. Be sure to bring it home
with you."

"Count on it."

As they separated, Faith addressed herself

to Daltry, lounging by his gray, one elbow resting on the hitching post.

"Jack's promised that he'll bring you safely back," she said.

"And I aim to return the favor, ma'am."

"See that you do."

"Top of my list," Hec said, grinning.

"And you," she said to Slade.

"I know, I know."

"All right, then," she replied and went inside before she had to watch him ride away.

"It's nice," Hec said, as they passed through Faith's gate. "Having someone to worry, I mean."

"It can be," Slade granted. "It gets heavy, though."

"Yeah, I can see where it might. You prob'ly don't know I was married once."

"I never heard that."

"I don't talk it up, you know? It was in Kansas. Little town called Jetmore, north of Dodge. I was their marshal for a while, back in the eighties. Lots of trouble, then. It worried Kate a lot. We used to fight about it, then she left me for a peddler, passing through."

Slade glanced at Hec to see if he was joking, but his solemn face betrayed no humor.

"Hec, I'm sorry," he replied.

"Don't be. She gave me fits about my drinking, anyway. You want to know the funny thing?"

"What's that?"

"She left, I quit. You know, I'll have a beer from time to time, like anybody else. But slugging down the red-eye, no sir. That went out the door when she did. Can you figure that?"

"Too deep for me," Slade said.

"Yeah, screw it. How about our odds of catching up with these bad boys we're looking for?"

"I couldn't tell you," Slade replied. "If it was me, I wouldn't hang around the territory any longer than I had to."

"Same here. But you never know."

"You never do," Slade readily agreed.

They rode in silence for a mile or so, before Hec asked him, "Do you figure you can get inside their heads? These twins? Because you *are* one?"

"Doubtful," Slade replied. He could already see that angle getting old. "Some twins supposedly know what the other's thinking, but I don't remember anything like that with Jim and me. Not after we were out and on our own, at least. Our parents didn't play it up, like dressing us the same or anything. I never heard of one twin reading minds inside a different family."

" 'Course not," Heck said. "I wasn't thinking about any kind of magic. Nothing supernatural. But if it helps to be a twin, and figure out the way they think . . ."

Slade thought about it for a moment, then said, "If they're close, it could give them an edge. Two heads are better than one. They could have little tricks and signals they're not even conscious of, like when to make a move in an emergency."

"So, watch 'em close, you're saying."

"If we even get the chance."

"That's right," Hec said. "I understand we have to do it, but I'd guess our odds are fifty-fifty, if we're lucky."

"It'll disappoint the judge, we come back empty-handed," Slade observed.

"You're telling me. I kept expecting him to tell us that we can't come home without them."

"He won't ask the impossible," Slade said.

"Only the next best thing. You want to pick up where they left the *Flier*, then?"

"Unless we stumble onto something in the meantime," Slade replied. "The judge's friend —"

"Burt Alford."

"Right. Before he died, he saw them

headed off northeasterly. That's headed our way, more or less. Could be we'll cross their trail."

"Or, maybe they rode off that way to fool the prisoners they left behind. That way, no one can sell them out."

"There's always that," Slade said.

Slade wasn't sure that visiting the *Katy Flier* murder site would tell them anything. Would any tracks from the escaping horsemen still remain? It struck him as a last resort — but at the same time, it might well be all they had.

"Don't get me wrong," Hec said. "I *hope* we find them. Still, six men."

"Six posters," Slade corrected him. "I didn't hear a count from Marshal Alford in the judge's story."

"Meaning that they could've picked up more along the way?"

"Or lost some and replaced them," Slade replied. "No way to tell."

"That's what I love about this job," Hec said. "It keeps you guessing to the bitter end."

"Which, hopefully, won't be this trip," Slade interjected.

"Amen, brother!" Hec came back. "Amen to that."

■ ■ ■ ■

Hec Daltry understood Judge Dennison's desire to catch and hang the men who'd killed Burt Alford. He had traveled down the vengeance trail a time or two, himself, starting with rage that later turned to something cold inside, like he imagined it must feel to have a belly full of stones. He still recalled how good it felt to drop the hammer on a man you truly hated.

For about five seconds.

After that, he'd started wondering about his motives and his actions, thinking that he might have lost something along the way. Not certain what it was, but pretty damned sure that he couldn't get it back again.

That didn't matter in the present case, of course. Hec had no special grudge against the Frain brothers or those who rode with them, beyond the fact that they were cutthroat scum. His job demanded that he hunt such men, day in, day out, and there was nothing personal about it. If Judge Dennison had come along, wanting to meet the killers on the trail somewhere, that would have been another story altogether.

But the judge was back in Enid, with his cane, his bum leg, and his grief. Even his vengeance, if he got it, would be by the book.

The law said those who'd killed the *Katy Flier*'s guards should hang. Daltry had seen enough executions to know that he'd rather go down fighting, gut-shot, than to feel a rope around his neck. He wondered if the Frains and those who rode with them would feel the same.

They'd all served time, of course, but that could reinforce a man's desire to stay outside a cage at any cost. The bold escape, with no survivors on the law's side, told him that the fugitives weren't likely to surrender peaceably.

And that was why he'd brought a second pistol, in addition to his normal Winchester rifle and long-barreled Colt Single-Action Army revolver. The hideout piece was a Dolne Apache pistol, named for the European gunsmith who created it, a trick number designed for saloon and street fighters. The .275-caliber six-shot pinfire revolver had no barrel per se, and was inaccurate as hell beyond six feet or so. It had a hinged knife blade that folded back beneath the cylinder on its left side, and its folding handle was a solid set of knuckledusters. In a pinch, you could shoot with it, stab with it, or use it to bash in a face.

Hec had confiscated the Apache from a whore he had arrested, five or six years earlier, and kept it as a conversation piece. He'd never planned to carry it, but now he found its solid weight in his pocket a comfort.

And overnight he'd honed the blade to razor sharpness.

Just in case.

A part of Hec's mind hoped they wouldn't find the Frains at all — and that, in turn, made him feel guilty. Nothing that he couldn't live with, but it was embarrassing to think that he was scared of men he'd never met.

Embarrassing . . . but maybe true.

They'd killed ten marshals on the *Katy Flier*. Not a couple. Not half a dozen. *Ten,* for God's sake, and all armed, fighting back. What chance did two more badges have against such men?

Hec wasn't doubting Slade, of course. With barely two years on the job, Jack had the makings of a reputation that would follow him for life. First thing, he'd nailed the men who killed his brother, playing hard against long odds, then he'd gone on to tackle other challenges that would've cowed a lesser man. Within the past four months he'd brought the bloody Bender clan to justice and had hunted down the men who'd tried to kill Judge Dennison, unmasking — and, from what Hec heard, annihilating — a criminal secret society.

Jack Slade could pull his weight.

Hec Daltry's doubts concerned himself.

He wasn't *old,* but he had twenty years on Slade, at least. The little aches and pains of so-called middle age had settled in, reminding Hec that there were faster guns around, and some of them would plug a lawman for the simple hell of it.

Hec hadn't shot a man in nearly two years, now, and hadn't killed that one. It was a record he'd grown proud of, in a quiet way, but when he caught a job like hunting down the Frains it made him wonder whether he was good enough.

Not that he'd ever voice such doubts.

Hell, no.

He'd been a lawman for the better part of thirty years, beginning as a sheriff's deputy in Fort Scott, Kansas, at the relatively tender age of twenty-one. It paid better than cowboying, and he'd enjoyed it for the most part. Killing his first man, the week before his twenty-second birthday, hadn't put him off the job, and there'd been several more since then. It all came with the badge.

But he'd been thinking of retirement,

lately. Not this year, but maybe soon. Hec had some money put away, enough to carry him if he was careful with it, didn't fall in love, or pull some other silly stunt.

Now this.

To hell with it, he thought.

As Jack Slade said, "Looks like a farm."

It was. Not much of one, so far, but someone had been working at it, putting time into the house and barn, clearing the land, plowing enough to get a fair crop started. Slade saw corn and something else just sprouting, which he couldn't name by sight.

They didn't hurry the approach, wary of spooking anybody in the house. A wisp of smoke was rising from the chimney, which meant that someone must be home. The shutters on the windows Slade could see had firing slits cut into them for home defense. They would be killing-close before the farmhouse occupants could see their badges, and Slade didn't want to die because he galloped up to someone's doorstep in a needless rush.

"You think they're buttoned up in there on purpose?" Daltry asked.

"No telling," Slade replied. "Living out here, it pays to be leery of drifters."

"I supposed. You feel the itch yet?" Meaning the sensation some men claimed to feel when they were being tracked by gun sights.

"Hard to tell," Slade said. "I'm sweating some."

"Yeah. Me, too."

With fifty yards to go, Slade called out to the silent house. "Hello, inside! We're lawmen passing through. No need to fear. We'd like to ask some questions, if you wouldn't mind."

"Here's hoping they aren't outlaws," Daltry said.

Slade had considered it but didn't think that criminals would bother planting corn. Of course, somebody like the Frains could be inside the farmhouse, having killed the rightful occupants or taken them as hostages. Where were their horses, then? Inside the barn?

"Here's hoping," he replied and stealthily released the hammer thong that held his Colt securely in its holster.

When they'd closed the gap to thirty yards, the front door of the farmhouse opened and a man emerged, holding a rifle at the ready. Someone closed the door behind him, and a shorter gun barrel poked through the shutters on his left.

"Not good," Hec said.

"Let's wait and see," Slade cautioned.

"I'm obliged to see your badges," said the rifleman.

"We're wearing them," Slade answered him. "Might be too far for you to see."

"Come closer, then. Real careful-like."

"Careful it is."

When they were near enough to speak without raised voices, he performed the introductions. "I'm Jack Slade, and this is Marshal Daltry. As I said, we're passing through on business, and we're hoping you can spare a bit of time."

The rifleman could see their tin, now, and he visibly relaxed. "Ben Morrisey," he said. "That's Ellen on the scattergun. My darlin' wife."

"We're pleased to meet you both," said Daltry, as the stubby shotgun barrel was withdrawn. A moment later, an attractive redhead stood beside her husband on the porch, a small boy peeking out around her skirts.

"You're here on business, you said?"

"None that pertains to you or yours," Slade hastened to assure him.

"Well, you'd best come in and sit a spell," said Morrisey.

The house was clean and cozy, filled with cooking smells that pricked Slade's appetite. He sat with Hec on one side of a rough-hewn dining table, facing the farmer and his son, while Ellen Morrisey poured coffee, dark and strong.

"So, what's this business?" Ben inquired, after a quick sip from his coffee cup. "We rarely see a lawman out this way, and never two."

Hec Daltry kept it short. "There was a breakout from a prison train," he answered, "maybe two days west of here. We're looking for the men who got away and wondered whether you'd seen any of them passing through."

"Convicts?" There was a note of fear in Ellen's voice.

"Yes, ma'am," Slade said. "A few have been reclaimed, already, but the rest are likely scattered far and wide by now. We're after one man in particular, with those who staged the break."

"Well, sir," Ben Morrisey replied. "With that in mind, I'm pleased to say that you're the first strangers we've seen in . . . oh, three weeks or more."

"Closer to four, now," said his wife. "The last one was a tinker, on his own."

"Well, that's good news for you all," Daltry said. "But not the best for us."

"How will we know them, if they happen by?" asked Ben.

"The leaders of the bunch are twins," Slade said. "Identical. The rest are just your basic trash. We've got some posters you can look at, if you like. No photographs."

"So, if a pair of twins come calling —"

"Don't try to take them into custody," Slade said. "It looks like five or six of them, at least. All dangerous."

"I'd welcome them with open arms," Daltry advised. "*Fire*arms, that is."

"It's like that, then."

"With any luck, you'll never see them," Slade suggested. "If you do, protect yourselves."

"I will," the farmer said. "Now, could you use a bite to eat?"

"Nice folks," Hec said, when they were on the move again, their bellies full of stew and apple pie.

"I'd say so," Slade agreed.

"You don't reckon the Frains came this way, then?"

"It's hard to see them passing up a homestead, if they needed food."

"Or missed a woman," Daltry said.

"Or that."

"You think they'll be okay?"

"I hope so," Slade replied. "I'm worried someone else won't."

"Yeah." Daltry was quiet for a moment, then said, "Jack, you know we can't be everywhere at once."

"Feels like we should, though."

"Sure. I used to feel that way. Still do, sometimes, I guess. It doesn't help, though. When you strip it down, the nature of our job is cleaning up somebody else's mess."

"I'd like to get ahead one time," Slade said. "Prevent the mess."

"We stop the Frains," Hec said, "and we'll be heading off a world of hurt for folks we'll never meet."

"We'd best not miss them, then," said Slade.

"And if they're gone? What, then? They could've cleared the territory, easy, in the time they've had."

"I guess we follow them, if that's the case," Slade said. "It's why we've got the 'U.S.' on our badges, right?"

"Sure, sure. But we can only follow solid leads."

"We need to find some, then, I guess," Slade said.

"And if we run across them, by some chance . . . what, then?"

"We do our jobs," said Slade.

"I'm thinking, though. They've killed ten marshals, and I'd hate to make it twelve."

"Same here."

"So I say, if we get a shot, we oughta take it. Skip the shit about surrendering and make it easy on ourselves."

"Just gun them down, without a call?"

"They're goners, either way," said Daltry. "What's the diff? We could be doing them a favor, anyhow. Who wants to hang?"

"I'd like to find them, first," Slade said, "before I carve a strategy in stone."

"Yeah, sure. You're right. Don't mind me, anyway. I'm just thinking out loud."

"No harm in that."

"You won't hold it against me, then? Wanting to live, I mean?" Hec forced a short, strained-sounding laugh.

"Not likely," Slade replied.

"If we decide they've left the territory, I suppose we'll have to go someplace and wire the judge. Tell him we've left the reservation, so to speak."

"Makes sense."

"I reckon he won't mind," Hec said.

"Not if we do the job right," Slade replied.

"That's what I'm saying. Do it right, so no one has to come along behind us, doing it again."

Slade understood how Daltry felt. He didn't plan on taking any chances with the Frains, either, but he wouldn't commit to executing them on sight. It ran against the grain, somehow, in spite of all they'd done and still might do.

But if they raised a finger to resist arrest, all bets were off. With Faith in mind, he'd absolutely do what must be done.

And do it right.

4

"Smell that?" asked Ethan Frain.

Riding beside him, Evan caught a whiff and said, "Wood smoke."

"Somebody cooking," Ethan said.

"I'm getting hungry, now you mention it."

The brothers urged their horses to a trot, the others coming on behind them. Still not rushing it, until they saw what lay ahead and where the smoky scent was coming from.

Five minutes later, they were lined up on a rise that overlooked a farm. Spread out before them was a smallish house, smoke wafting from its chimney, with a modest barn, good-sized corral with two fair-looking horses in it, and a privy in the back. Chickens were busy pecking in the door-yard.

"You reckon they'd invite us for a sit-down meal?" asked Jimmy Beck.

"Who says they got a choice?" Creed

Sampson sneered.

"Now listen up," Evan commanded. "All these little homesteads are like forts. We spook these people going in, we could be all day killing them and lose a few of you, besides. We ride in slow and easy-like. Ethan and I will do the talking."

"Meaning," Ethan interjected, "that nobody else should say a goddamned word."

"We *do* still get to kill 'em, though?" Dick Eyler asked.

The twins exchanged a glance. Evan could see his own dissatisfaction with the others mirrored in his brother's eyes, but what were they supposed to do about it? Certified killers weren't easy to come by, much less the reliable kind who took orders without too much bucking against it. Evan didn't mind the thought of cleaning house and starting fresh, building another gang with new recruits, but that would have to wait.

Meanwhile, his stomach had begun to growl.

"What do we watch for, going in?" he asked nobody in particular, knowing that Ethan wouldn't bother answering.

Sampson answered, "Guns and dogs."

"Women," Tom Dahlquist added, and the others laughed along with him until they felt the weight of Evan's glare.

"We're a quarter mile out from that house," he informed them. "Plenty of time between here and there for whoever's inside to get ready and greet us with lead. Now, I plan to get through this alive, so I'll make you a promise. The first sumbitch who tips our hand will die by mine. Questions?"

Nobody answered, but a couple of them shook their heads.

"All right, then. From the minute we move out until I tell you otherwise, your traps stay shut. I don't care if a troupe of naked dancing girls runs out to meet us doing cartwheels. No one says a word. You hear me?"

Bobbing heads along the line.

He spared another glance for Ethan, saw his brother shrug, and nodded in return. No words were necessary. Both knew there was still a chance that someone in the group, although forewarned, would find a way to screw it up. But Evan meant what he had said, about killing the first man who spoke out of turn.

Before he kicked his piebald gelding into motion, he released the hammer thong that kept his pistol in its holster, getting ready for whatever happened next.

He could already smell fresh blood.

Gene Bollinger was mucking stalls inside the barn and getting tired of it when Sally called him from the farmhouse.

"Gene! There's riders coming!"

Bollinger immediately dropped his rake and bolted for the yard, saw Sally on the front porch, pointing, and faced to the northwest from there. He spotted half a dozen men on horseback, closing at a slow trot, and fast-walked toward the house.

Don't let them see you running.

Halfway to the porch, he started giving Sally orders.

"Close the shutters and get out the extra ammunition."

Moving to obey, she asked him, "Do you recognize them?"

"Not from here. They're too far off."

He didn't have to tell her that their closest neighbors lived six miles away, off to the east, and only two of them were male.

That made the horsemen strangers.

Being strangers made them dangerous.

There was no law to speak of in the Oklahoma panhandle — or none you could rely on in a hurry, anyway. Surprises in the form of strangers riding past were apt to mean trouble, and trouble sometimes led to killing.

They'd been lucky so far, avoiding any major problems, stopping short of bloodshed on the few occasions when a drifter happened by, looking for handouts. Bollinger believed in being civil, to a point, without displaying any hint weakness to outsiders. And it never hurt to let the strangers see a gun or two.

Sally finished closing the shutters while Gene fetched his Winchester model 1866 rifle from its place about the mantelpiece. He kept the hammer on an empty chamber, but it only took a second with the lever-action to prime it with one of the tubular magazine's seventeen .44-caliber rimfire cartridges.

By the time Gene reached the front porch, Sally had finished latching the shutters and stood inside the door, nearby but out of sight from the yard, with his Colt Dragoon revolver gripped in both hands. Little Peg was in her place under their bed, clutching her rag doll. Being brave.

The riders were two hundred yards away by then and showed no sign of slowing down. Gene figured they could see that he was armed, and if they recognized the Winchester they'd know that he could aim and empty it before they closed to pistol range. He wasn't any kind of trick-shot artist, but survival in the territory meant hitting a target more times than you missed it. Bollinger judged his marksmanship to be above average.

Start shooting, then, said a voice in the back of his mind. But he stalled.

It was one thing to kill in defense of his home, an idea he'd accepted before moving west. Squeezing off at a stranger before he could speak, though, felt more like an ambush. Suppose he got lucky and took out all six before one of them dropped him, then found they were innocent cowboys. What, then?

Then you plant 'em, forget 'em, and get on with life, said the voice in his head.

Not so fast.

Without turning, he told Sally, "Close the door, sugar, and get to the window. Don't take your eyes off them for even a second."

"I won't. You be careful," she said, and the door shut behind him.

"I will be," he promised the afternoon's breeze.

At a hundred yards, Gene could make out their faces. Hard men, by their looks, which proved nothing. Soft men didn't last long out here, whether farming, droving, or drifting in search of adventure. You weathered life's hardships or fled, if the land didn't bury you first. The reward was freedom; its price, eternal watchfulness.

At eighty yards, he called out to the six, "That's far enough. There's nothing for you here."

One near the middle of the line called back to him, "We don't want any trouble, mister. We're a posse out from Elkhart, looking for some fugitives."

"Elkhart's in Kansas," Bollinger replied. "You've strayed across the line."

Their spokesman answered back, "I failed to mention that we're lawmen. All we want is information and a little water for our animals."

Gene thought about it. Took a chance.

"Come closer, then," he told the man who seemed to be in charge. "Just you. Nobody else."

Evan Frain didn't mind riding up to the farmhouse alone. In fact, after months under guard in a cage, the risk gave him a thrill. Frain didn't have to sell his story all the way, just get in close enough to drop the farmer, then deal with whoever was watching his back.

A woman, most likely, and Frain hoped

that he wouldn't have to kill her outright. Not that he would flinch from it, but seven months was too damned long to go without a woman, and they hadn't run across one since he'd fled the *Katy Flier.*

When Frain had cut the hundred yards in half, the sodbuster piped up again. "I'll want to see a badge," he hollered.

"Got it right here for you," Frain replied.

Nor was he lying. He'd lifted a star from one of the *Flier*'s marshals, as a memento of their time together, and had pinned it to his shirt, beneath a buckskin vest. Frain hadn't thought much of it, at the time, but now the smallest thing could be interpreted as Providence assisting him.

Amen!

At thirty yards Frain stopped and drew the left side of his vest back, letting sunlight catch the star.

"See that?" he asked.

"I'll need a closer look," the farmer said.

"My pleasure," Frain replied, fighting an urge to smile.

He kept the vest pulled back, holding the gelding's reins loosely in his right hand. Right now, a soothing voice was more important than a fast draw. There'd be time for that when Frain had closed the shrinking gap between him and the homesteader and found the perfect place from which to make his move.

"Hold up right there," the farmer ordered, when some twenty feet still lay between them. Calling to the farmhouse, then, he said, "You got him covered, Sally?"

"Got him!"

Sally. Frain couldn't resist a smile, now.

"I don't know whether you can read it, standing back there, but the badge says 'U.S. Marshal.' "

In fact, it read "United States Deputy Marshal," but what difference did it make? By the time this hick was close enough to check it for himself, he wouldn't be reading Frain's tin.

"I didn't catch your name," the farmer said.

Frain used his own. Why not? "And you are?" he replied.

"Gene Bollinger."

His host was moving closer, one sidling step at a time. Careful not to cross his woman's line of fire from the window on Frain's left, he circled to the piebald gelding's right. His rifle wasn't aimed at Frain. Rather, its muzzle bobbed somewhere between his waistline and the ground.

"Well, Mr. Bollinger, as I already said, me and my men are down from Kansas, chasing bad men."

"Must be bad," said Bollinger, "to bring you all this way."

"The very worst," Frain said.

"What did they do?"

"You name it, sir. Murder and robbery, for starters. Then, there's rape," he said and cut a sly glance toward the house.

"Well, we ain't seen them," Bollinger replied. "You all are the first strangers we've laid eyes on for a month or more."

"So, you don't get a lot of traffic out this way?" Frain asked, reins shifting from his right hand to the left.

"Not much," Gene Bollinger agreed.

"That's helpful," Frain replied.

And shot him squarely in the chest.

"Come on!" snapped Ethan Frain, spurring his bay mare down the long slope toward the farmhouse.

He'd been watching the windows when his brother took the farmer down, then vaulted from his saddle in a leap they'd practiced for occasions such as this one. At the same time, someone fired a pistol from the window to the left of Evan's gelding, missing him but shattering the horse's hip joint.

The gelding went down, thrashing and

squealing in pain, its forelegs and the right rear raising dust clouds in a vain bid to escape. Evan was in position to relieve its suffering, but he'd be saving all his bullets for the home's defenders, taking full advantage of the wounded animal as a distraction.

Halfway to the house and closing, Ethan heard a woman cry out from inside. "Gene? Can you hear me?"

Gene was down and out, done twitching now and cooling on his way to worm bait. He must've taught the little missus how to shoot, though, which would be a problem. One they'd solved, with variations, in the past.

He rode straight in until they reached the hundred-yard mark, then veered left and took a couple of the others with him, forcing them to follow when he cut across their path. One of them — Dahlquist? — yelped a curse, but didn't make it personal by adding Ethan's name.

Another gunshot sounded from the house as Frain rode toward its northeast corner, where the shooter couldn't track him without changing windows, maybe changing rooms. He didn't hear the bullet pass him, knew it even might have been his brother firing, but his job was still the same: circle

75

around behind the house and storm it from the rear.

Distraction was the key, but if he had misjudged the situation — if, say, Farmer John had several kinfolk in the house, all armed — Ethan's flanking tactic might rebound against him, leave him bleeding in the dirt. It was a risk he took for Evan's sake, and for the hell of it.

More shots behind him now, as Ethan charged around the farmhouse, counting windows as he passed and looking for a way inside. No back door on the dwelling, which was bad in case of fire. No open windows anywhere that Frain could see.

Hold up a minute, now.

In case of fire . . .

Frain didn't want to burn the farmhouse, if he had a chance to loot it first. But they already had a fire burning inside, and Frain thought he could make use of it, with a little help.

Grinning, he wheeled his mare around to meet Dahlquist and Eyler, blocking them and calling out for them to stop. They reined in short of a collision with Frain's bay, their faces flushed with the excitement of a battle.

"Ethan, what the hell?" Eyler demanded.

Frain dropped from his saddle, landing

lightly on his feet. "Get down here, both of you," he ordered. "Boost me up onto the roof."

The pair dismounted and left their horses standing while they hunched and formed a cradle with their hands. No questions, which was wise. Frain planted one foot in their palms, pushed with the other, while his two compadres straightened up and launched him past the eaves onto the farmhouse roof.

Whoever still remained inside would hear him crossing, might try shooting at him through the roof, but Frain was ready for them, clutching his pistol right-handed, removing his hat with his left. Four long strides brought him to the chimney, where he dropped his hat over its opening and pressed it down, trapping the smoke inside.

Creed Sampson sat astride his sorrel, twenty paces from the house and out of line from any nearby windows. No one in the place could reach him with a bullet where he was, and Sampson felt no inclination to become a target for the sake of Evan Frain or anybody else.

Not that he was scared of fighting. Hell, no. Sampson had been killing for a decade, give or take. His gunbelt bore two pistols and a bowie knife, but he was counting on the lever-action ten-gauge shotgun braced across his pommel if it came to shooting in the next few minutes.

He'd already fired one buckshot charge into one of the house's front windows, blowing the shutters to pieces, before Evan told him to quit it and get the hell back. Which was fine, too, he reckoned. Less chance of a slug with his name on it finding him there, hiding out in the blind spot.

It surprised him to see Ethan on the roof, appearing out of nowhere. Sampson watched him clomp across and squat beside the chimney, capping it off with his Stetson. A few curls of smoke still escaped, worming out from under the hat's brim, but most of it had to be penned in the chimney and looking for somewhere to go.

Sampson smiled to himself. That was smart. He gave credit where credit was due, and the twins had their fair share of brains. Not like some he could mention, with no wits about them to speak of, who shambled through life and were lucky to see the next sunrise.

In the dooryard, Evan's piebald gelding kept on rolling, kicking with its three good legs, trying to stand. It was pathetic, getting on his nerves, and Evan must've felt the same, because he finally squeezed off a pistol shot to silence it, then edged back toward the window Sampson's shotgun blast had nearly cleared.

Scratch pity. Evan needed silence now, for *listening.*

No more shots came from inside the house. In their place, Sampson heard someone coughing — a woman? a kid? — as the smoke curled around them, fouling the air. A couple minutes later, it was bleeding through the window shutters and around the door, seeking release.

It could go either one of two ways, now. The folks trapped in the house would make a break for it, or they would stick, keep breathing smoke, and pass out on the floor. In that case, it was fifty-fifty they'd be dead when someone reached them. On the other hand, if they should come out shooting, they'd be dead damn for sure.

Sampson tugged his sorrel's reins to turn it slightly, found an angle that he liked, and held it there, raising the shotgun to his shoulder. The ten-gauge kicked like an ornery mule, but he liked watching triple-ought buck shred a target on impact and scatter the leftovers wide.

And he was ready when the front door opened, moments later, to expel a smoke cloud that contained a woman *and* a child. The woman had a pistol in her right hand, clinging to the little girl's right with her left, and Sampson was about to blast her with his ten-gauge when Evan Frain ran up behind her, grabbed the piece out of her hand, and sent her sprawling with a shove between the shoulder blades.

"You won't be needing this," Frain told her, as he tossed the gun aside. "But I've been needing you."

Later, Tom Dahlquist lurched out of the house, grappling suspenders over meaty shoulders, and asked Evan Frain, "You want another go?"

"Not now," Frain said.

His answer seemed to puzzle Dahlquist, twisting up his face as he tried to make sense of it. "So, what?" he finally said. "Are we stayin' the night here, or what?"

"They've got two decent horses in the barn," Frain answered. "One for me, the other for Miss Sally."

Frain couldn't remember when or how he'd learned the widow's name. That part of it was hazy, blurred like looking through a dirty window in the rain.

Dahlquist had grasped the concept of the horses. "Okay, sure," he said, scratching himself. "Let her carry the kid?"

"The kid stays here," Frain answered.

"Huh? Oh . . . right. I hear you."

There were some things that no child could absorb and still go on to lead a normal life. Frain was an expert on such matters, schooled by personal experience. But, then again, he hadn't done so badly, overall.

He wasn't at Fort Leavenworth, for one thing.

And he'd never see the inside of another prison cell.

That was a promise to himself that Evan meant to keep. If necessary, he'd enlist his brother's help, but they could wait a while before discussing it. Why ruin what had come to be a special day?

Frain heard a gunshot from the farmhouse, followed by a wail like someone's ghost trapped in the rafters, desperate to escape. Such screams had moved him, once, but that was long ago, lost somewhere in a life that barely registered in Evan's memory.

He looked off toward the barn and saw his brother coming, leading a palomino stallion and a dun mare. Both were saddled, ready for the trail. Evan had always fancied palominos but had never stolen one before. He took it as another omen that his recent bitter luck had changed.

He shifted toward the open doorway of the farmhouse, looked inside, and and saw the woman hunched over the small, crumpled figure of the child. Creed Sampson stood beside her, reaching down to tangle fingers in her hair and lift her head.

Frain snapped at him, at all of them, "We're leaving in ten minutes. Get your damned pants on and look around for anything you want to take along."

"Will she be needin' any clothes?" Dick Eyler asked. He had been grinning when he said it, then saw Evan's face and sobered in a hurry. "Awright, then. I'll get her some."

"Nine minutes, now," Frain said, turning away.

Ethan had reached the porch. "You want to torch the place?" he asked. "Confuse the law a bit?"

Evan considered it, then said, "Smoke's likely to attract the neighbors, if they have any. Let's leave it."

"Right."

"I like the stallion."

Ethan turned, eyeing the palomino. "He's all right. We won't know if he's built for speed until you break him in. Like her," he added, nodding toward the house.

"I thought we'd bring her," Evan said, not

82

asking for permission.

"Think she's smitten?" Ethan teased him.

"We can always drop her off somewhere, along the way."

"And have her point the law in our direction?"

"Did I say she'd be alive?"

"Ah. Well, then. That makes all the difference."

On impulse, Evan blurted out, "I'm never going back inside."

"The house?"

"Prison, for Christ's sake! Can't you —"

Ethan's smile caught him before he got wound up and made him shake his head. "Goddamn your joking."

"Some say it's my finest quality," Ethan replied.

"I'm not one of them. And I mean it, Brother. Do you hear me?"

"Absolutely. Neither one of us is ever living in a cage again. I promise you."

"I'll hold you to that," Evan said.

"Back at you."

A scuffle behind them brought both heads around, to find Miss Sally struggling feebly between Jimmy Beck and Tom Dahlquist. They'd wrestled her into a calico dress, without shoes.

"Are you ready, then?" Evan demanded.

"Ready!" Beck answered, snapping a salute that stopped just short of mockery.

"Okay, then," Evan told Beck. "You're in charge of her. If she gets lost, you take her place tonight. Now, saddle up!"

5

"The nearest town is what, again?" Slade asked, as they were breaking camp their second morning on the trail that might lead nowhere.

"Amity," Daltry reminded him. "Means friendliness, or some such. I was through there once, a couple years ago. I don't remember anybody being all that friendly."

"Maybe it was you," suggested Slade.

"It could've been, I guess. I went in looking for the mayor they had then, on some kinda fraud deal. He was gone and took the money with him. Everybody else was in a funk about it."

"Did you ever find him?"

"Nope. We got word later, he was out in California, somewhere. Got mixed up in something like the first deal, and they shot him."

"Who did?"

"Beats hell outta me. You ready?"

"As I'll ever be," Slade said.

"You want to stop in Amity and ask around, then?"

"Might as well. Look on the bright side, Hec. Maybe they've all forgotten you."

"Wouldn't surprise me. Try to help some people, and you may as well forget it."

"It's a crazy world," Slade said, mounting his roan.

"You got that right."

Slade had enjoyed a full night's sleep, if he could use that term for lying on the hard ground in a thin bedroll. At least the night was fairly warm, and no coyote serenade had roused him from his now-forgotten dreams.

"How far to Amity from here?" Slade asked, when they were on the move.

"The best I recollect," Hec said, "we ought to be there in late afternoon. For supper, anyway."

And after that, say half another day before they reached the stretch of track where Frain's gang had dispatched ten deputies to their rewards, whatever those might be. Slade hadn't prayed since childhood, but at times he liked to think there might be something more, beyond the life he led each day.

The trick, in his profession, was to put the

great transition off as long as possible. Do unto others, right, before they did it unto you.

They rode another silent mile before Hec said, "A penny for your thoughts?"

"You wouldn't get your money's worth," Slade told him.

"I was thinking of a little gal I used to know in Amarillo. Ever been there?"

"I played cards there, once or twice," Slade said.

And on the second visit, won two hundred dollars from the snotty son of a state senator, who'd called Slade out for cheating when he couldn't win it back. It might've come to shooting, but he'd knocked the brat unconscious, then spent three days dodging trackers sent out to redeem the legislator's so-called honor.

"Did you play the Paradise Saloon?" asked Daltry.

"That, I don't recall."

"Well, you'd remember Emma Carson if you'd ever met her. Spunky little carrottop with green eyes. Had a mouth on her to shame a teamster."

"That's not ringing any bells," Slade said.

"We had a good old time, I tell you," Hec went on. "I was a Potter County deputy, back then, for Sheriff Vardaman. Big Dick, they called him. Must've been because his name was Richard, though. I seen him in the bathhouse, once."

Slade tried to change the subject, asking, "What put you in mind of Emma Carrot-top, just now?"

"Carson," Daltry corrected him. "I dreamed about her, overnight. Man, dreams are funny things."

"They are that, for a fact."

"We weren't in Amarillo," Hec continued. "In my dream, I mean."

"Where were you?"

"Tombstone, Arizona. Do you find that strange?"

"Depends. You ever been in Tombstone?"

"Never in my life."

"How did you recognize it, then?"

"I was with Emma, takin' care of business in her room, over some bar they had there, when the Earp brothers came knockin' on the door."

"All of them?" Slade tried not to laugh.

"Wyatt and Virgil, I believe it was. Or maybe Morgan."

"No one that you ever met, though."

"Well, I've seen their pictures."

"Sure. What did they want?"

"They cussed me out for bein' late to the O.K. Corral."

"And what did you do?"

"Well, what *could* I do, when Wyatt Earp comes calling? I got dressed and went off with them."

"To the gunfight? Ten years back?"

"That's when I woke up," Daltry said. "Reckon I'll never find out how it went."

"The good news is that you were on the winning side."

"Funny. It didn't feel that way."

Slade's pocket watch said it was nearly three o'clock when they rode into Amity, a wide spot in the road, no more than three or four blocks long. Its single street was bustling with foot traffic, people clustered on the wooden sidewalks, breaking off their conversations as they spotted Slade and Daltry riding in.

At first, Slade thought the gawkers seemed hostile, but he adjusted that assessment when they'd cleared the first block.

"Looks like something's got 'em agitated," Daltry said.

"Or scared," Slade offered.

"Christ, I hope it's not some kind of epidemic," Hec replied. "The damn near last place that I'd want to be in quarantine is Amity."

Slade saw no symptoms of disease on any

of the faces that were tracking them, no signs announcing quarantine on any of the buildings.

"No," he said. "It's something else."

As if in answer to his words, a man detached himself from one of the groups to his right, midway along the second block, and moved to intercept them in the street. He wore a gray suit and a bowler hat to match, relying on a crimson vest for color.

"You're the U.S. marshals?" he inquired, while staring at their badges.

"Deputies," Slade said.

"We didn't think you'd be this quick to get here."

Slade exchanged a glance with Daltry, then replied, "You were expecting us?"

"Well, not specifically. Our riders went out yesterday. One up to Liberal, the other back to Enid. I suppose one of them met you on the way?"

"We must've missed 'em," Daltry said.

"But then . . . I mean, how did you know?"

"Know *what?*" Slade asked.

"About the murders and the kidnapping!"

Slade felt his stomach do a lazy roll.

"Is there a lawman here in town?" he asked.

"Yes, sir. Constable Atterman's the one you want."

"Why don't you lead us to him, then," Slade said, "and we can start from the beginning on this thing."

"You mean . . . ? You aren't . . . ?"

"The constable?" Hec urged.

"Yes, sir! Just follow me."

The bowler hat led them across Main Street, another half block to the west. Slade hadn't thought to ask his name and didn't bother now, preoccupied with the uneasy feeling in his gut.

Murder and kidnapping.

It could be unrelated to their mission. People killed each other in the territory every day, and while true abductions were thankfully rare, Slade had investigated several since he donned the federal badge. His first such case, in fact, involved Faith Connover. She had come out of it all right, but as a rule . . .

They stopped outside a tiny office with the legend CONSTABLE painted in black and gold across its door. Amity's lawman was discussing weighty matters with two other men as they dismounted, leaving Bowler Hat to interrupt their conversation.

When he registered their presence, Constable Atterman hurried to meet them, pumping hands and telling them, "Welcome! I'm Jubal Atterman. Thank God you're here!"

They introduced themselves before Hec said, "We understand you sent for help."

"Amen to that. We never thought you'd be so quick about it, though."

"They're here for something else," said Bowler Hat, intent on being part of it.

The constable appeared to sag. "Oh, yes?"

"Hunting some convicts off the *Katy Flier*," Daltry said. "But since we're here, what's going on?"

"Let's step inside my office," Atterman suggested. Waving off the other men, he told them, "Gentlemen, I'll see you later."

Bowler Hat tried slipping in behind Slade, almost stepping on his heels, but Atterman stuck out an arm to block his way. He said, "Thanks for delivering the marshals, Virgil. We can carry it from here."

"Oh, sure. I'll just go back to work, then."

"That's a mighty fine idea."

Atterman shut the door and cocked a thumb over his shoulder. "Virgil Stark," he said. "Town barber and a first-rate busy-body. Now, then, to business."

The constable circled his desk and sat down in a tall, creaky chair. Slade and Daltry found two more and sat facing him, while Atterman rolled and lit a cigarette.

"Your barber mentioned kidnapping and

murder," Slade remarked.

"A double murder, that would be," said Atterman. "One of the worst I've ever seen."

"Well, then, if we can help. . . ."

"I hope so." Blowing smoke plumes toward the ceiling, Atterman sat back to tell his tale. "Ride fifteen miles northwest of town, you'll find the Bollinger place. Well, it *used* to be. Gene and his wife, Sally Ann, with their little girl Peggy. Nice folk. Made the long ride to church Sunday mornings, the weather permitting. No trouble in town or with anyone else, that I ever heard of."

"They're the victims?" Slade asked.

"That's the word," said Atterman. "Yesterday morning, comes a neighbor passing on his way to town, stopping to jaw a little. He found Gene dead in the dooryard, shot, and Peggy in the house. No sign of Sally Ann, except a tore-up dress somebody left behind."

"The girl was shot, as well?" Slade asked.

Atterman nodded, grim-faced. "Close enough for powder burns. Took off a quarter of her skull, I'd say. At least she wasn't *interfered* with, if you want to count small blessings."

"So, what did your searchers find?" Hec asked.

"Searchers?"

"Yes, sir. You've got a kidnapping, the lady out there somewhere with whoever snatched her. Are you telling me nobody went to look for her?"

"You've had a look at Amity," said Atterman. "My jurisdiction ends one step beyond its boundary. On top of which, I can't go riding off and leave the people unprotected, with a killer on the loose."

Slade swallowed his contempt and said, "You mean to tell me *no one* volunteered to form a search party?"

"These people," Atterman replied, "they're decent folk, but they're not fighters. Not the way us lawmen have to be."

"You've done a lot of fighting, have you?" Daltry asked him.

"My fair share," the constable replied, defensively.

Slade let it drop, saying, "We'll need to see the farm and look around for evidence. Someone will have to show us where it is."

He stopped short of adding, *Whether you like it or not.*

"No problem," Atterman agreed. "But do you want to see the bodies, first?"

"They're here in town?"

"Just up the street there, at the undertaker's."

"May as well do that, then," Hec replied.

"I'll just escort you over there," said Atterman.

Slade let him take the lead, hung back with Hec, and whispered, "I feel safer now."

Hec snorted. "Hey, what did I tell you about Amity? They oughta change this rat hole's name to We Don't Give a Damn."

The undertaker was a beanpole of a man named Silas Black. It suited him, from his demeanor to the standard mourning suit he wore. Once Atterman had introduced them, he hung back and let Black take them on from there.

"I've seen them," he explained. "Once was enough."

Black led them through another door, into his workroom. The undertaker's parlor had one operating table, but he'd rigged another using sawhorses and wooden planks. A man lay on the table, while a smaller form, sheet-covered, occupied the makeshift slab.

Gene Bollinger had clearly died from one shot to the chest, piercing his heart or coming close enough to do the job and drop him without much resistance after he was hit. Various scavengers had spent some time with him before his neighbor came along, and likely more after the startled farmer rode for help.

"You should prepare yourselves for this," Black said, before he raised the sheet on Peggy Bollinger. "Closed caskets for the pair of them, you understand. But this . . ."

Slade couldn't claim it was the worst thing he had ever seen, but it was high up on the list. Being a child's corpse made it worse, he guessed, because protecting children was a basic impulse, geared toward the survival of the species. Young life interrupted.

"Jesus!" Daltry muttered. "Cover it, already."

It, not *her.*

The child that Peggy Bollinger had been was gone. Whatever their beliefs about an afterlife or lack of same, only the husk remained.

"The constable says that she wasn't tampered with," Hec told the undertaker, not quite making it a question.

"Both were fully clothed upon arrival," Black replied. "I found no evidence of any further . . . improprieties."

"You think the Frains did this?" Hec asked.

Slade shrugged. "I wouldn't put it past them. Ethan and another of them, Beck, both had rape charges on their records."

"No rape here," Hec said.

"You think the wife was taken off for

ransom?"

"No. Good point."

"We won't know any more until we've seen the farm and tried to find a trail," Slade said, as they emerged from Black's workroom. He spotted Atterman and told the constable, "We'll need to see the farm next, if you'd rustle up that guide we talked about."

"Today? Right now?"

"Enough time wasted, as it is," Hec answered, gruffly. "Any more would be a crime, itself."

"You won't get there and back ahead of nightfall," Atterman informed them.

"Then we'll camp out," Slade replied. "Won't be the first time."

"Well, then . . . if you're sure. . . ."

"Dead certain," Hec insisted. "Ticktock, Constable."

As Atterman clomped off along the sidewalk, Daltry turned to Slade and said, "I've got a bad feeling about this thing."

"Same here. If it's the Frains, they're hunting. If it's not, they could be up in Indiana, somewhere, by the time we clear this up."

"That's *if* we clear it up," Hec said. "You ever notice that the scum we're sent to wrangle always has a long head start?"

"Seems like it," Slade replied. "Speaking of which, we need to find a livery and feed our animals."

The stable wasn't far away from Silas Black's deadhouse. They'd almost reached its open doors when Atterman came panting up behind them, calling out their names, trailed by a younger and much thinner man.

He introduced the newcomer as Penn Warren. "He can take you out to Bollinger's."

"How much?" asked Slade.

" 'Scuse me?" Warren replied.

"In dollars, for the help."

Warren blinked at him, seeming offended. "I won't charge you, Marshal. As it happens, three, four friends of mine would like to ride along and help you find these animals, if you got no objection."

"Better late than never," Daltry said, keeping a bland expression on his face.

"Some of us woulda gone out yesterday," Warren replied and shot a glance toward Atterman. "We got talked out of it."

The constable flushed crimson from his hat brim to his stubbled chin, telling the three of them, "Well, now, you're all agreed, you won't be needing me."

"No, sir," Slade said. "We won't. But if we catch someone, I trust you've got a cell available?"

Atterman waved a hand as he retreated. Slade took it to signify assent.

"About these friends," he said to Warren.

"Yes, sir. I can round 'em up in nothin' flat."

"Have them bring guns," Hec said, "and leave their pride at home. We don't need anyone who can't take orders."

"Understood," Warren replied and left to spread the word.

"Let's see about that feed and water," Slade suggested.

"Right. I wouldn't mind some food, myself."

"Three hours out, one way," Slade said. "Then time to look around the place. Think you can wait?"

"No problem," Hec replied. "One thing, though. If you hear something growling, don't shoot. It'll be my stomach, not coyotes."

Penn Warren found them in the stable fifteen minutes later, showing up with four newcomers of the same age, more or less. Bill Farrell was the tallest of them, sporting thick sideburns and freckles. Joshua Harden had a start on a full beard, with patches that still needed filling in. Dave Jordan, shorter than the others, was their smiler, proud to show his teeth. The last in line was Mike O'Connor, quiet and reserved — either a thinker or the opposite, with nothing much in mind.

All five of them were armed with rifles, leading horses. Farrell and O'Connor each wore pistols, while the other three had knives sheathed on their belts. As posses went, it wasn't much, but Slade was used to making do with none at all.

"Before we start," he told them, "here is what we plan to do. First thing, ride out and look around the spread where this thing happened. If we find tracks leading off somewhere, and it's too late to follow them, we'll camp and get an early start tomorrow. Anyone who can't stay out until it's finished, go home now, and no hard feelings."

Warren's comrades traded looks, shuffled their feet, and stuck it out. None left.

"All right, then, Mr. Warren," Daltry said. "How 'bout you take us where we need to go."

Three hours on the trail, and Atterman was right. Dusk had begun to sneak along behind them by the time they reached their destination. The Bollinger spread — or whatever you called a place, after its people were slaughtered — lay waiting and silent, except for the clucking of hungry chickens.

Slade rode to the house first, past a bloated horse's carcass, dismounted, and tied up his roan. Whoever had come for the bodies had also forgotten to shut the front door. Slade entered, pushing the door back to let in more fading sunlight. He fought and defeated an impulse to take off his hat in respect for the dead.

He saw where Peggy Bollinger had died and edged around the rusty bloodstain, noting small animal tracks in the midst of it. The corpse-transport team hadn't lingered to clean up the house. Slade could track Sally Bollinger's ordeal through torn, scattered clothing and rumpled-up sheets on the bed she'd once shared with her husband.

He doubted that Sally would see it again — or care to, if given the chance. Her world had died here, even if she somehow managed to survive against the odds.

Hec Daltry filled the doorway, cutting off most of the light. He said, "Whoever took her must have wanted her alive, Jack. That's a good sign, right?"

"Could be," Slade said, without conviction.

Hec knew the other side of it already, without being told. Whoever raped and kidnapped Sally Bollinger, the odds that he

— or they — would carry her alive into another town, where she might be identified or slip away, were somewhere south of zero.

Daltry retreated, leaving Slade to spend another moment in the house that was no longer anybody's home. He smelled gunpowder, from the battle that was fought there, and a different smoky residue from the stone fireplace. He saw bullet scars, including one whole window shutter torn apart by buckshot.

Sally Bollinger defending Peggy, after Gene was killed? Slade knew that he might never know the full story, unless he found Sally alive. And even then . . .

He left the house to look for tracks, the smell of rotting horseflesh making him nostalgic for gun smoke. Slade found the townsmen milling aimlessly around the yard, unsettled by their close proximity to sudden death. He would have bet that none had viewed the bodies at the undertaker's parlor, but they'd all heard tales of what was done to Gene and Peggy Bollinger, enhanced by word of mouth until the homestead murders sounded more like Quantrill's Raid on Lawrence, Kansas, back in '63.

The simple truth was bad enough.

Among the townies, only Penn Warren appeared to know what he was doing. Slade observed him coming from the barn, scanning the ground in front of him, then stepping out more quickly toward the house. Reaching the porch, where Slade and Hec stood well apart, Penn glanced at each of them in turn, and then addressed the air somewhere between them.

"It appears the killers stole two horses," he declared. "I know the Bollingers *had* two, because I work part time for Mr. Sweeney at the feed store, back in Amity. I've seen 'em in the store and heard 'em talk about the animals. A dun mare and a palomino stallion."

"Missing now?" asked Slade.

"Yes, sir. And you can still see faint tracks where somebody led them out, into the yard. I'm thinking they took one to replace this one" — nodding at the carcass as he spoke — "and one . . ."

"For Mrs. Bollinger," Hec finished for him.

A jerky nod, almost embarrassed to discuss the kidnapping and what they all knew it entailed. "Yes, sir."

"All right," Slade said. "They had to go in some direction. Will you help us look for tracks?"

Another nod.

Slade stepped down from the porch and told the others, "You men come up here a minute, while we look around the yard. We're after tracks, and I don't want to wind up hunting you all by mistake."

The others did as they were told, though they were visibly reluctant to approach the house. Slade saw them shy off from the open door, as if afraid to glimpse whatever lay inside.

Hec found the tracks in nothing flat. A group of riders, headed off to the northeast.

"What does your gut say?" Slade inquired.

"They could be going anywhere," said Daltry. "Kansas, Colorado, all the way to California. Maybe someplace closer we don't know about."

Slade knew they couldn't let it go, but had to ask.

"You've got seniority," he said. "What do we do?"

Hec scowled and shook his head. "We run 'em down. What else? Too late to start today, though."

"Right."

Slade faced the townsmen on the porch and said, "Unpack your saddlebags. We're camping here tonight."

6

Jack Slade had never put much stock in ghosts. His parents had espoused a strict theology that said departed souls were either smiling down from Heaven, or else roasting in the pits of Hell. Slade swallowed that as any child might, until he had stumbled on Ecclesiastes 9:5. It informed him that "the dead know not anything, neither have they any reward."

Or words to that effect.

It had seemed simple to him, at the time. If the Bible said the dead knew nothing and had no reward, how could they be in Heaven? Soon afterward, his suspicion was confirmed by John 3:13. Jesus telling his apostles, "No man hath ascended up to heaven."

Young Jack didn't dare contradict the Almighty.

That laid any ghosts that he might've believed in, despite indoctrination from his parents. Later, when he thought he'd given up religion altogether, some of it had stuck. Whatever happened in the world around him, Slade was not afraid of spirits.

That helped, as he spread his bedroll twenty yards from where two lives had ended brutally. Slade wasn't worried about seeing either of the Bollingers traipsing around their former home by moonlight, rattling chains and wailing.

He was worried about what could happen if he failed to overtake their murderers. And how it might divert him from his search for the Frain gang.

Slade had known what Hec would say, when giving him the choice. Some others might've let the homestead killings wait and gone on after those who'd slaughtered ten fellow marshals, but Daltry had seen that they owed Sally Bollinger something. If she was alive, they might find her in time to preserve some small part of her soul and her sanity. Maybe just saving her life was enough to help balance the scales.

But Slade knew that was crap.

She would never get even on something like this, never claw her way back to the life she had known, before bad men arrived on her doorstep and turned her life into a little slice of Hell on Earth.

Slade hoped that they would find the men responsible.

He hoped they would resist arrest, go for their guns, and give him an excuse.

And he could tell that Daltry felt the same.

There was no mind reading involved. Slade knew Hec well enough to read his moods — well, some of them, at least — and took for granted that he'd leave no stone unturned while searching for a child killer. Match that with Hec's suggestion that they shoot the Frains from ambush, without warning, and he knew Daltry would have no qualms about eliminating those responsible for the Bollinger atrocity.

As for the others in their makeshift posse, who could say how they'd react if faced with life-or-death decisions, far from home? Slade pulled a trigger when he had to — to defend his life or someone else's, to cut short a crime in progress or prevent a violent felon from escaping. None of Warren's friends from town were lawmen, and Slade had no reason to believe that any of them had been called upon to take another human life.

Some men took to it naturally, almost without thinking. Others hesitated, but went on to do the job, assuming that an adversary didn't kill them first. And some could never bring themselves to fire that shot, regardless of the stakes involved.

Slade hoped the men who'd answered Warren's call to arms were capable of self-defense, at least. They didn't strike him as a pack of blood-crazed vigilantes, but he'd have to wait on judging that until they'd found the renegades that they were looking for.

Always assuming that they *could* be found.

Statues of Justice showed the lady with a blindfold, indicating that she played no favorites. The downside of it, no surprise, was that she simply came up blind sometimes and couldn't get the job done. Some bad men escaped and never faced the punishment that man-made laws decreed for them.

As for some higher court, if it existed, that brought Slade's mind back to ghosts, the afterlife, and other subjects better left alone.

He had a job to do on Earth, among the living, and with any luck he'd have a chance to do it right this time.

Hec Daltry's voice distracted him, announcing, "Beans are ready!"

"Be right there," Slade answered, turning toward the campfire's reassuring light.

Hec Daltry wasn't much of a chef, but he

couldn't botch coffee and beans. He'd brought a coffeepot and cooking pan from home, for use along the trail, and while those tools had been selected with two men in mind, not seven, he made do by rationing the vittles.

Camped a few yards from a murder scene, nobody had the heart or stomach to complain.

"Not bad," Slade said, around his first mouthful of beans. Hec knew it might have been a sop, but he was willing to accept it, all the same. The others bobbed their heads and muttered, out of basic courtesy.

None of the men from Amity had anything to say, so far, about the crimes at hand, no speculation on the men they would be hunting in the morning. They'd been whispering amongst themselves a little, earlier, before he'd built the campfire, and he wasn't sure if they would stick or start making excuses to go home.

Thinking about it, Daltry knew he wouldn't blame them if they left. *Resent* it, possibly, but none of them were deputized or getting paid, and some might argue that the victims hadn't even really been their neighbors, anyhow. The good news, if it happened, was that he and Slade would be relieved from watching over them like children on a holiday.

Just then, Penn Warren asked nobody in particular, "What do we do tomorrow?"

"Chase the tracks, long as we can," Hec answered. "See what happens."

"But suppose we lose them?" Mike O'Connor interjected, feeling chatty now.

Hec shrugged. "When tracks run out, you look around, see if they pick up anywhere close by. Consider the direction you've been traveling, and whether the men you're tracking might be up to something."

"Such as?" That from Joshua Harden.

"Running men will try most anything," Hec said. He hadn't volunteered to teach a class in man hunting, but now he had to talk with his mouth full, to keep his beans from getting cold.

"They'll double back, sometimes," Slade interjected. "Maybe head off on a tangent to confuse you, then come back to the direction they were traveling before. Drag brush behind their horses to wipe out the tracks, whatever. Sometimes, with the soil, wind, rain, you just lose tracks."

"But that means losing Sal —" Bill Farrell caught himself. "Means losing Mrs. Bollinger."

The young man's cheeks had more pink to them than the firelight could explain. Hec

110

didn't jump to any rash conclusions, but he could imagine Farrell sneaking glances at the farmer's wife in church or maybe finding an excuse to greet her on the street, some shopping day.

"You all need to prepare yourselves for that," Slade cautioned them. "We don't see many happy endings in this line of work."

"You mean . . . ?" Dave Jordan couldn't find the words he needed to go on.

Hec made it plain. "We mean she could be dead already. Likely is, in fact. Thinking of the alternative . . . well, maybe it would be a blessing in disguise."

That silenced them until their plates were all scraped clean. There was a pump nearby, for washing up, and Daltry left them to it, dawdling over coffee with Slade while the rest rinsed their mess gear.

"Was I too rough on 'em, do you think?" he asked.

"Just honest," Slade replied. "It sticks some, going down."

He sensed that Slade had something else to say and asked, "What's on your mind?"

"Just wondering," Jack told him. "How they'll do if we catch up to whoever we're looking for."

"Of if we don't?"

"That, too," Slade said.

111

"They don't strike me as fighters," Hec replied. "But who knows? If we come up empty, they can shake it off and go back home. Do whatever it is they do in Amity."

"Make visitors feel welcome," Slade suggested, smiling.

"Yeah. There's always that."

"But if it comes to killing . . ."

"Business first," Hec said. "I plan on getting back in one piece, whether we come up against the Frains or anybody else. This bunch are volunteers. They're grown-up men, or close enough. As long as they stay out of my way when it counts — and yours — I say it's each man for himself."

"It could get bloody."

Daltry finished off his coffee and replied, "It might, at that."

Mike O'Connor finished drying off his dinner plate and said, "I guess there's no way telling how long we'll be out here."

"Stay out till the job's done," Bill O'Farrell said.

"Easy for you to say," Dave Jordan told him, not quite smiling.

"What's that s'posed to mean?" asked Farrell.

"You know what he means," Penn Warren interjected. "Half the folks in town have seen you mooning over Sally Ann."

"The hell you say! I never did!"

Dave Jordan had to snort at that. "Nothing to be ashamed of, Bill," he said. "She was a pretty woman. No mistaking that."

"*Is* pretty," Farrell hissed at him. "*Is*, not *was*. Don't talk about her like she's dead!"

Josh Harden stood, plate dripping in his hand, and said, "You heard the marshal, Bill."

"So, what does he know?" Farrell challenged. "He can't say if she's alive or not. Who's *he* to say that being dead's a blessing?"

Warren began to say, "He just meant —"

Bill rounded on him. "I *know* what he meant! I'm not a goddamned infant! Do you think I didn't . . . Jesus!"

Something seemed to choke him, then, and Farrell bolted toward the barn and darkness. Seconds later, his companions heard faint retching sounds.

"Boy's got it bad," Dave Jordan said, "considering she's someone else's wife."

"Not anymore," O'Connor said.

"That's cold," said Warren.

"I'm just saying, on the off chance that we get her back —"

"For Christ's sake," Harden interrupted. "Would *you* want her? After what she's been through? What she's likely done?"

"You mean what's been done *to* her, don't you?" Warren challenged him.

"Same thing, ain't it? I mean, a widow's one thing. But this, here —"

"Sometimes I think you're full of shit, Josh," Warren told him.

"What'n hell did *I* say?"

Warren faced him, with the pump standing between them. "If some drifter robs the store you work at, and he shoots you in the arm or leg, is that your fault?"

" 'Course not."

"Suppose he steals your horse and rides it for a while," Warren continued. "Would you want it back or sit around wishing he'd kill it?"

"Penn, I don't know how to break this to you," Harden answered, "but a woman ain't a horse. There's riding, and there's *riding*. No one's saying it's her fault, but she's still . . . you know . . . damaged goods."

"*That's* why I say you're full of shit."

Josh bristled, fists clenched, but he didn't make a move to come around the pump. Bill Farrell's voice distracted both of them.

"You need to shut up now," he told Harden. "I'm serious."

Josh seemed to think about responding, then stepped back a pace and shook his head, eyes downcast. "I don't want to fight you boys," he said. "This ain't why we come out here."

"Josh is right," said Jordan. "And we need to talk about what's coming."

"Meaning?" Warren asked him.

"Well . . . hell, I don't know. You asked us, would we ride along, and here we are. But now, what? Are we gonna be out here another day or two? A week? A month?"

"Until it's done," said Farrell.

"Bill, the marshals draw a paycheck hunting men. We don't. You think we'll still have jobs in Amity, if we stay out here weeks on end?"

"Nobody's saying weeks or months but you," O'Connor said.

"Because they *can't* say. They don't *know*," Jordan replied.

"I'm covered," Warren said. "I talked to Mr. Clark before we left, told him we might be out a couple days. Beyond that . . . well, I'll have to think about it."

"Just hang out and see what happens," said O'Connor. "Go back when we have to, any one of us."

"I guess," said Jordan.

"And if we catch up to them tomorrow or the next day," O'Connor offered, "man, oh man!"

"That's something else we need to think about," said Harden. "Going up against a pack of killers."

Farrell scanned their faces in the firelight and replied, "I wouldn't mind a bit."

"They're having second thoughts," Slade said. He hadn't eavesdropped on the townies, but it figured, from the way they clustered up together, almost whispering.

"Who wouldn't?" Daltry asked.

"Yeah. I'm just saying."

"One boy's pining for the woman, and she isn't even his. The rest are skylarking. They want an adventure."

"Watch out what you wish for," Slade said.

"You got that right."

"Whoever did this, they're a full day and then some ahead of us."

"Closer to two, by the time we get started tomorrow," Hec said.

"That's a fair lead."

"Not hopeless," said Daltry. "I've done with worse."

"Granted. We'll need some luck, though."

"Cuts both ways. Good for us, bad for them. I'll take either," Hec said.

"I'd like both," Slade replied, "but it feels like that's asking too much."

"We haven't talked about who's standing

watch tonight," Daltry reminded him.

"Some of these eager volunteers," Slade said.

"Seems fair."

"As many of them as we've got, a couple hours each seems more than ample."

"Plenty," Slade agreed.

"Give us a chance to get our beauty sleep."

"It couldn't hurt," Slade answered, smiling.

"Laugh now," Hec said. "But when you get to be my age —"

Movement among the townies interrupted Daltry's thought. Slade saw them moving all together, coming toward the spot where he and Daltry sat. Penn Warren led the group but didn't look too pleased about it.

Before Warren could speak, Slade said, "We're going with two-hour watches overnight. Work out the schedule amongst yourselves. Nobody ought to lose much sleep, that way."

"Um, sure. Okay," said Warren. "First, though —"

Mike O'Connor interrupted him to ask, "You think they might be coming back? The ones who did this, here?"

"I doubt it," Slade replied, "but we've seen people do some crazy things. And, then again, we don't want someone else surprising us, do we? Word gets around, a thing like this, you could have looters dropping in to see what's left for easy pickings."

That made some of them shoot anxious glances off into the darkness, maybe wondering if there were strange eyes tracking them right now.

"I never thought about somebody else," O'Connor said. "You mean the neighbors, or —"

"It's likely nothing," Slade said, turning back to Warren. "There was something on your mind?"

"Yes, sir," Warren replied. "About these men we're hunting in the morning."

"What about them?" Hec asked.

"Well, assuming that we find them . . . I mean . . . What are we supposed to do with them?"

"Depends on them, I'd say," Daltry replied. "If they surrender, nice and peaceable, we'll take them back to Amity, and on from there to Enid, where Judge Dennison will try their case. If they resist, of course, we have to bring 'em in by any means we can."

"Like killing them?" Dave Jordan asked.

"A last resort," Slade answered. "But we couldn't rule it out."

"One thing we *won't* have," Daltry said,

"in case it's crossed your minds at all, is any kind of vigilante action. Lynching's murder, just the same as what was done here, to this family."

"No, sir. Nobody's planning anything like that," Warren replied, apparently sincere. "But some of us were wondering about how long this all might take. You know, with jobs waiting and all."

"The short answer," Slade said, "would be that it's impossible to say. We could be looking for some idjits who're camped out within a few miles of this very spot, thinking they're safe. Or, we could chase their tracks from here to Christmas and come up with nothing."

"If your jobs can't wait, or you've got family that needs you," Daltry told them, "you can go back any time and no hard feelings. That's what *volunteer* means."

"We were only looking for a guide to get us this far," Slade reminded Warren. "Now, we're here. You fellows want to ride back in the morning, we'll go on and earn our pay."

Slade couldn't say for sure if Penn Warren was blushing or if firelight put the crimson in his cheeks.

"Nobody's going back tomorrow," he said, quickly. "But if it drags on too long, well . . ."

"Understood," Slade said. "Why don't you figure out that night-watch schedule now and get it started?"

"Right. Sure."

"I rustled up some eggs for breakfast, in the barn," said Daltry, as they scattered. "We can give the beans a rest until tomorrow night."

Long ride or not, Slade found it difficult to sleep. He lay awake for half an hour, maybe longer, after he'd turned in and heard some of the others snoring in their bedrolls. Lying there and analyzing *why* he couldn't doze just made it worse.

He wasn't worried about anything, per se. The murders and kidnapping troubled him, but no more than such crimes had ever bothered him before. He hoped to find the men responsible and see them pay, but Slade was not prepared to let it haunt him if they somehow managed to escape.

He didn't think their posse was the problem. Young civilians on a manhunt often had to cope with doubts and second thoughts. Slade would've worried more if they were all happy-go-lucky, looking forward to a turkey shoot. If they were nervous, it would make them doubly careful — which, in turn, might get them home alive.

Slade's problem wasn't Faith, though she had kept him up all night on more than one occasion, and the image of her cost him sleep sometimes, when they were far apart. Tonight, though, love and all that went along with it had been the last thing on his mind.

It was the Frains, he finally decided, and their gang of cutthroat trash. Their crimes offended Slade. By killing other U.S. marshals — even though he'd never met the victims, didn't know if they were good men or sadistic brutes, like some lawmen he'd known — the Frains had threatened Slade himself and everything he'd come to stand for since he'd donned a star and gone off to avenge his brother's death.

Was *that* it? Was it nagging at his mind that he'd been called to hunt a pair of twins?

If so, it made no sense. There was a world of difference between the Frains, himself, and Jim. Slade's brother, to the best of his knowledge, had never harmed a soul, much less killed anyone or raped and robbed them. It seemed foolish even to consider that Slade might be put off tracking fugitives simply because two of them looked alike.

And yet . . .

No, it *was* foolish, he decided, rolling over

with his blanket snug around him in the campfire's glow. Ethan and Evan Frain were renegades, known murderers, and worse. If Slade could find them, he would not be influenced by their appearance or the family tie that bound them.

He would do his duty or die trying.

But he'd have to watch the twin thing, Slade decided, even if it didn't color how he viewed the Frains or dealt with them. From what he'd heard and read, some twins *did* seem to have a kind of psychic bond that gave them an advantage over other people, helping them coordinate their thoughts and actions. If the Frains enjoyed that kind of synchronism, it could make them doubly dangerous.

And, maybe, twice as hard to kill.

Slade still hoped he could bring them in alive, but with their records, and with other hardcase scum to back their plays, he knew it would be difficult. Maybe impossible. But in the last analysis, it didn't really matter if the Frains went back alive or not, as long as they were brought to book for what they'd done.

What *really* mattered was that Slade and Daltry made it home alive. In Slade's case, to spend time with Faith. In Hec's . . . well, for whatever it was that he did in his free time, to make himself happy.

There had to be more than the job and the badge.

But tomorrow, the job would come first.

7

Evan Frain lit a cheroot and drew its acrid smoke into his lungs. He'd started smoking, with his brother, at the age of nine or so and wasn't sure exactly why, beyond the fact that it had made him feel grown-up.

Whatever that meant.

In some ways, he still felt like the boy he'd been in those days: knocked around but always willing to accept a dare, dodging the sweaty "honest" work in favor of an easy buck whenever possible. Of course, today he played with real guns.

And when Frain's guns made a racket, people died.

The racket in his camp tonight was mostly rattling coffee cups and low-pitched conversation, with some whimpers coming from the bedroll where Tom Dahlquist kept the woman busy. Knowing Tom, he'd probably convinced himself that sounds of pain and loathing equaled love.

Good help was hard to find, these days.

Evan had tired of the woman already, but some of the others still wanted to keep her around for a while. He hadn't insisted they dump her yet, since she wasn't slowing them down, but he and Ethan had agreed that she would not lay eyes on Abaddon.

They'd break it to the others soon enough, and anyone who felt like arguing could rest in peace beside her.

Anyway, until the buzzards and coyotes came along.

Frain never flinched from killing when it served his purpose. Ethan had been slower with the knife and gun, at first, but now they'd more or less drawn even. Evan wasn't one to notch his guns or keep a running score in mind, but he could still remember faces of the folks he'd slain.

Well, most of them, at least.

Sometimes they kept him company.

That was a good thing, not like being haunted by a spirit bent on showing you the error of your ways or driving you insane. He'd seen *A Christmas Carol* performed on stage, and Evan's ghosts were nothing like the preachy, chain-rattling shades from the story. They never spoke at all, in fact. Just stared at him with gloomy eyes, which he interpreted to mean, *You did this to me, Evan Frain.*

It always made him smile.

Holding that power over life and death — when he'd been powerless in childhood and again more recently in prison — meant the world to Frain. He didn't live to kill, but there was no denying that he'd chosen crime as a profession for the thrill it gave him, taking cash and property from others, using force to silence their objections.

Lording over them, in ultimate control of whether they survived or not.

He'd never talked about it with his brother, wasn't sure if Ethan felt the same or not. What did it matter? They still traveled in the same direction, side by side, no matter what one or the other might be thinking at a given time. And in a world where most people would stab you in the back for half a dollar, that was something.

A sobbing squeal from Dahlquist's bedroll made Frain want to cross the camp and drop his fat ass on the cooking fire. He was considering it when his brother sidled up beside him with a coffee cup in either hand.

"That Tom," he said and handed one of the cups to Evan.

"Yeah."

"He's got the stamina. You have to give

him that."

"Uh-huh."

"What's eating you?" asked Ethan.

"You want to know the truth?"

"Sure do."

"Okay. I still feel like a part of me is on that train to Leavenworth. They had me caged for seven months. I don't feel *free* yet, even here."

"There's always Abaddon."

Their refuge from the world at large.

"There is," Evan agreed. "I'm looking forward to it, Brother."

"So am I. We can forget about all this. Rest up awhile."

"And figure out how I'll be paying off a few outstanding debts," said Evan, with a smile.

In the dark hour after midnight, Sally Ann Bollinger stirred. It wasn't waking up. She hadn't slept a wink since her abduction, and in fact she wondered whether she would ever sleep again.

Closing her eyes meant seeing Gene and little Peggy, dead and bloody. It meant seeing, smelling, tasting each one of the filthy pigs who'd used her since they tore her simple life apart.

But sleeping meant that she might dream

her loved ones back to life, then wake and lose them all over again. That might not kill her, but she reckoned it would snap whatever frail reed still connected her to sanity.

Let go of it, she thought. How could it hurt to lose her mind, when all it held was images of horror? Wouldn't she be better off without that fragile link to rationality? Perhaps she would go blind and deaf and lose all feeling in her body.

Cheat the slimy bastards that way, if she couldn't hurt them otherwise.

Or, then again . . .

The pig she knew as Tom was snoring next to her, mouth gaping. Sally wished she had a scorpion that she could drop into his gaping mouth, or possibly a hot coal from the campfire. It would sear her fingers, granted, but her satisfaction would eclipse the pain.

And maybe, then, they'd kill her.

Moving slowly, stealthily, to keep from waking Tom or any of the others, Sally asked herself, *Why wait?* Tom's gunbelt, with its holstered pistol and its great long-bladed knife, lay coiled beneath his right arm. Within her reach, if Sally rose to all fours and leaned over him.

The pig on watch — they called him Dick — might catch her at it, but so what? Stripped of all modesty, she counted on her naked body to distract him long enough for her to draw the knife and plunge its blade between Tom's ribs. They'd kill her then, beyond a shadow of a doubt.

Or, she could choose the gun.

Why not?

Gene had insisted that she learn to shoot, not that his lessons did them any good. She knew the raw mechanics, how to cock and aim a weapon, how to fire it. Not that aiming mattered, when the snoring pig was close enough for her to put the six-gun's muzzle in his ear.

But after that, how many others could she kill or wound, before a bullet finally erased her suffering? Six shots, six men, but it was foolish to expect that she could take all six of them. Granted, they were asleep, except for Dick, but Sally's first shot would alert them, and she knew they'd come awake with guns in hand.

So much the better.

Even if she only splattered Tom's pig brain and sent him off to Hell ahead of her, that had to count for something. Maybe then, the souls of Gene and Peggy could find peace.

Deciding was the hardest part, the simple act of making up her mind to do it. After she accomplished that, the simple act of rising to her hands and knees, leaning across Tom's supine form to reach the pistol, seemed like nothing. She was almost smiling with her bruised lips, as her fingers curled around the weapon's grip.

The warning shout behind her came too soon, but Sally rose and turned to face Dick with the stolen six-gun clutched in trembling hands, aimed more or less directly at his heart.

Ethan Frain bolted up from his bedroll, drawing his Colt on instinct, spinning on one knee to find the naked woman standing over Dahlquist, leveling a gun at Dick Eyler. Dick hadn't managed to clear leather, and he'd missed his chance now, worried that the farmer's wife might drop him from a range of fifteen feet.

Frain could have shot her, and she seemed to know it, dropping suddenly to one knee, so that her stance mirrored his. At the same time, she swung the pistol down, away from Dick, and jammed its muzzle against Dahlquist's chest.

"Go on and shoot," she taunted Frain, surprising him with the strength of her voice. "I'll take the fat one with me."

"No! Don't do it!" Dahlquist yelped.

"Shut up, Tom," Frain commanded.

"Make believe you're smart and shut your goddamned mouth."

The woman actually laughed at that, a sharp note of hysteria drawing its razor's edge along Frain's nerves. He felt his brother, standing somewhere to his left, and saw the others holding weapons now, still huddled in their bedrolls, trying not to give the woman any decent targets.

"Take it easy, Sally," Ethan told her. "That's your name, right? Sally?"

"What's your interest in my *name,* you bastard?" she spat back at him.

"We got off on the wrong foot," Ethan said. "I see that, now."

That wrung another rasp of laughter from her, and she leaned in on the pistol, putting weight behind it, grinding it between Tom Dahlquist's ribs.

"Do you suppose he has a heart in there?" she asked. "Or will the bullet just splash through a lot of shit?"

Tom whimpered, making Ethan wish she'd pull the trigger and be done with it.

"I'd guess he has a heart, and you can hear it pounding," Ethan answered. "When you stop it, we stop yours."

"Sounds good to me," she told him, almost sneering. "Big men. Five guns against one, and no one makes a move?"

"Jesus! Don't do it!" Dahlquist wailed.

"I said *shut up,* Tom," Ethan hissed. "Next word I hear you say will be your last, I swear to God."

"Oh, no," the woman argued back. "This pig is mine. Go get yourself another one."

"You want to kill him, go ahead," said Ethan. "Hell, the way he's disappointed me, I'll thank you for it. How you look there, I might want to thank you all night long."

"You missed your chance," she told him. "I'll be gone before you know it."

"Maybe not," he said. "I grant you, anyone could plug old Tom at that range, but smart money says I'm better than you are, from here. My shot won't kill you. That's a promise."

"Where you fail," she said, "is thinking anything you say or do can scare me now."

"She means it," Evan whispered, somewhere on his left.

Frain nodded, holding eye contact with Sally What's-her-name.

"Want me to try it?"

Ethan shook his head, just barely, trusting Evan to see it.

"How much is this piece of filth worth to you?" the woman asked.

"Not much," Frain said, "considering he's spoiled a good night's sleep."

132

She forced another laugh. "Well, then, to Hell with all of you," she said.

And raised the six-gun to her head.

Tom Dahlquist reckoned he was dead. The woman had him covered — more than covered, with the pistol pressed against his rib cage — and it made him want scream out loud that he was on the verge of being executed with his own gun, by some crazy woman, and he didn't even know her name.

As if that would've helped him.

He closed his eyes, waiting to feel the bullet slam between his ribs, rip through his lungs and heart. He wondered if the muzzle blast would set his shirt on fire and how much it would hurt before he died.

Dahlquist had been shot once before, but it was just a graze across his left thigh, suffered as he rode off from a bank job in some Colorado mountain town whose name was long forgotten, even though the little scar reminded him to thank his lucky stars from time to time.

One of his friends — Joe Something? Christ, he couldn't even think of *his* name in his present circumstance — had been less fortunate the day they'd cracked that bank for a lousy hundred and fifty dollars. He'd taken a shot in the back and spilled out of his saddle, leaving Tom Dahlquist no choice but to ride off and leave him behind.

And now, this.

He felt like weeping, but what good would that do?

He heard Ethan talking to the crazy woman, trying to calm or distract her, he couldn't tell which. All he knew was that if someone shot her, she'd fall. And her finger would clench on the pistol's hair trigger before she went down.

Lights out for Tommy Boy. But would it hurt like fury in the seconds he had left, before his heart and brain shut down?

And what came afterward? What if his old man had been right about that lake of hell-fire, all along?

He heard the woman ask, "How much is this piece of filth worth to you?"

Frain's answer chilled him. "Not much," Ethan said, "considering he's spoiled a good night's sleep."

Dahlquist *was* weeping, then. He couldn't stop the tears that spilled out of his eyes, but he was quick enough to bite his tongue and keep from sobbing like a hopeless sissy. Maybe he'd die crying, but he wouldn't wail and beg.

Above him, somewhere in the dark, the woman laughed and said, "Well, then, to hell with all of you."

Tom braced himself, went rigid where he lay, as if clenching his muscles in a panic made him bulletproof. Hard to believe, with all he'd seen and done, that he would die like this, instead of gunned down on a job or kicking at the short end of a rope.

Don't let it hurt, he thought. *Please, Jesus, don't —*

At first, he didn't miss the pressure on his abdomen, as she withdrew the gun. Another second, and he heard the others laughing, felt like calling out to ask them what in hell was so damned funny.

Then the gun went off.

Its sharp report made Dahlquist jump six inches off the ground, just as a splash of something wet and warm spattered his face. At first, he thought it was his own blood, pumping from a fatal chest wound, but the lack of any pain caused him to open sticky eyes and look around.

The woman lay beside him, staring at him glassy-eyed, with one side of her skull blown off. And yet, somehow, she looked . . . peaceful.

One of the twins stood over him, sneering.

"Get up, you tub of guts," Ethan or Evan said, "and wipe your mug."

■ ■ ■ ■

"You had a lucky break tonight," Ethan told Dahlquist, once the other man had cleaned his face. There seemed to be a little something stuck in his mustache, but Frain would let him sort that out when it began to smell, assuming Dahlquist even noticed.

"Lucky is right," Dahlquist agreed.

"We *all* got lucky," Evan said. "No thanks to you."

Dahlquist was smart enough to see where this was going, and he tried to head it off.

"Hey, now," he said. "You don't think this was *my* fault, do ya?"

"How could it be your fault, Tom?" asked Ethan. "All you did was fall asleep and let her take one of your pistols."

"If she'd had more nerve," Evan reminded him, "we might be two or three men down, by now."

"She might've grabbed both guns and killed us all while you were snoring in your own sweat," Ethan said. "But hell, it couldn't be *your* fault. I've known you going on four years now, and I've never seen you claim the fault for anything."

"Now, that ain't fair! I —"

Evan hit him with a roundhouse left, not

hard enough to fracture anything, but Dahl-quist landed on his backside, dazed. The brothers stood above him, giving him a chance to try for either of his holstered weapons, Evan aching for the opportunity to end it there and then.

Dahlquist disgusted him, for some reason. He couldn't say exactly what it was, something besides Dahlquist's preoccupation with the woman they'd abducted. All of them had had a turn with her, though Evan couldn't say that he'd enjoyed his very much.

"You want to pull those irons," Ethan advised their stunned companion, "now's the time."

Dahlquist blinked once, then shook his head.

"I reckon not."

"Then stand up like a man and take your medicine."

Dahlquist began to rise, but hadn't made it fully to his feet when Ethan whipped a fist into his ribs and dropped him to all fours.

"Get up," Evan commanded.

"Just a minute," Dahlquist wheezed.

Evan gave him ten seconds, then kicked him in the ribs. Dahlquist flipped over on his back, keening, then tried to cover up, raising knees to his chest, shielding his face and skull with beefy arms.

The brothers booted him until they tired of it, the others standing back and watching from a distance. They avoided testicles and kidneys by some kind of silent, mutual consent, but left Dahlquist with bruises that would ache for days and keep him shifting in his saddle.

When they'd finished, Ethan asked their battered comrade, "Can you hear me?"

"Yes, sir," Dahlquist whimpered, from behind crossed arms.

"You've got a mess to deal with," Ethan said. "Get up and bury it or drag it off, whatever you can manage. I don't want to smell it in the morning."

"And you're standing watch till sunrise," Evan added. "Keep the damned coyotes out of camp."

"Okay," said Dahlquist, starting to unfold his body, like an armadillo sensing that a threat has passed.

Evan felt better, somehow. Mayhem did that for him, sometimes, leaving him imbued with peace.

Maybe he wouldn't have a problem sleeping, after all.

"Brother," said Ethan, at his side, "I need a moment of your time."

138

"What's up?" asked Evan. "You decide we ought to plant him?"

"Tommy?" Frain considered it. "Not this time. Let's see if he's learned his lesson."

"Right. What's on your mind, then?"

"Abaddon."

"We'll be there in another couple days," said Evan. "Get some rest and plan our next move."

"Rest? I wonder."

"What?" Evan demanded.

"Do you think they'll just forget about what happened on the *Flier?* We're all marked, now."

"We were marked before," Evan reminded him. "They would've got around to filing murder charges on you soon enough, once you were up at Leavenworth."

"Maybe."

"And if they didn't, you'd be rotting in a cage."

"I know all that," Ethan replied. "Hell, I just thought we'd get a little breathing room."

"What do you call this, Brother? If there's someone on our trail, I haven't seen 'em."

"They'll be coming," Ethan said. "You

know it, too, as well as I do."

"Fair enough. If they can follow us to Abaddon, we'll leave 'em there, with all the other ghosts."

"I guess so."

"Guess, nothing. They haven't built a prison that can hold us, and the lawman who can stop us hasn't drawn his first breath yet."

"That's cocky talk. It sours luck."

"You going superstitious on me, Brother? Did a black cat cross your path? You walk under a jailhouse ladder, back in Texas?"

"I've just got a rotten feeling. Hell, maybe they broke me."

"Way I see it, *we* broke *them*."

"Something's coming. I can feel it."

"It's called life. Long as you're breathing, Brother, something's *always* coming."

Ethan smiled and shrugged the slump out of his shoulders, turned to see his own face smiling back at him by firelight.

"Sure. You're right," he granted. "Don't mind me. I guess this deal with Tom just threw me for a minute. Why don't you turn in and get some sleep?"

"And you?"

"I'm right behind you," Ethan said.

But it was half an hour later when he lay back down and pulled the blanket over him.

Dahlquist was back by then, from somewhere in the scrub brush, squatting by the fire to pass the remnant of the night on guard. Frain watched him on the sly, until he'd satisfied himself that Dahlquist didn't plan to seek revenge by moonlight, while they slept.

Not brave or dumb enough, he thought.

Tom had to know that one of them would kill him, even if he got the other. That was why the brothers always slept apart in camp, by silent, mutual consent. No one could take them both together, in a single stroke, before one or the other could react.

Frain closed his eyes at last and hoped he would not dream.

8

The chickens had been busy overnight, so Hec had twice the eggs he'd planned on for their breakfast, serving seconds all around. Slade thought the townies were a little quiet, but he chalked it up to circumstance and didn't bother polling them to see if any planned on turning back.

They'd made the choice last night and then had time to sleep on it. If they planned to call it quits, Slade couldn't stop them, but he wouldn't make it easy for them, either. Any man who faded in the stretch could face him like a man and say good-bye or slink off in the night, while they were sleeping.

Truth be told, Slade didn't care much, either way.

He'd never hunted with a posse in the past, although he'd welcomed help from various civilians now and then, along the way. Having a townsman or a farmer pitch in to assist him in a fight was one thing, but long riding with a bunch of amateurs who missed their jobs and women would get tiresome in a hurry. And he had to wonder how much good Penn Warren's friends would be in any kind of shooting scrape.

They carried guns, of course, and might be decent marksmen on a hunt or shooting cans and bottles on a weekend. That kind of practice honed the eye, but it did nothing for the nerves. Sport shooters could pick off a thousand jackrabbits and still freeze if they ever had to face another man.

"Quiet today," Hec said, around a bite of eggs, and nodded toward the townies seated in a cluster, several yards back from the fire.

"They're thinking," Slade replied. "Deciding whether anything that happened here is worth their time."

"Or worth them getting shot."

"That, too."

"My guess, the Warren boy will stick until we hit a rough patch, anyway. And Farrell has an eye for Sally Bollinger. He'll want to be among the heroes if we find her."

If.

"How would you rate the odds of that?" Slade asked.

"Unless we lose the tracks out there" — Hec nodded in the general direction taken by the fleeing murderers — "I'd say they're good. Now, finding her *alive . . .*"

He let it trail away.

"You sounded hopeful, yesterday," Slade said.

"I try that, sometimes," Hec replied. "It works from time to time, but nothing you could set your watch by."

"Odds?" Slade asked again, ever the gambling man.

"Smaller, each day they have her. She'll be eating up their food, drinking their water, getting on their nerves just being there. Seeing her face reminds them of their crime and what's most likely coming up behind them."

"They'll expect us, then," Slade said.

Hec shrugged.

"Unless they're all dead simple, they'll expect *somebody.*"

"I don't think the Frains are stupid," Slade replied.

"Me, neither. We should keep our eyes peeled as we go along."

They broke camp after breakfast, cleaning up as best they could and burying the embers from their fire. When all their mounts were saddled and their gear was packed, Slade walked his gelding to the spot where they'd found tracks the evening before.

There'd been no wind to speak of, overnight, and Slade quickly confirmed what he'd seen yesterday. Hoofprints of five, six horses, maybe more, leading away to the northeast.

Hec joined him, then the others, hanging back.

"How far you reckon we can follow them?" Dave Jordan asked.

"To Hell and back," Bill Farrell said, then looked embarrassed by it, not quite blushing.

"It depends on weather and terrain," said Daltry. "We could see their tracks for days or lose them two miles out. Then, if they split up anywhere along the way, we can divide our force or choose which group to follow."

"I was thinking more in terms of days," Jordan replied.

"We covered this last night," Slade told the lot of them. "Marshal Daltry and I are paid to take it all the way, no matter where we have to follow them. You gentlemen are free to leave at any time. Right now, whoever's coming with us needs to saddle up."

Slade hadn't meant to shame them, but it seemed to work — at least, for now. As they rode off to the northeast, he wondered whether he had done himself and Hec a favor, after all, or if he'd only made things worse.

The tracks weren't always plain to see, but half a dozen horses left their share of droppings on the trail, aside from flattened blades of grass and hoofprints in the soil. Between Hec Daltry and himself, Slade thought they did a decent job of following the killers, but it wasn't speedy work with swift rewards.

The came upon a stream at half past ten o'clock, stopping to let the horses drink and graze a bit on tender grass. Beside the stream, Daltry found evidence of others stopping there and judged the day-old droppings cause for optimism.

"Could be that she's slowed them down," he told Slade. "One way or another."

Which was good for them, Slade understood, but might be living Hell for Sally Bollinger. And how long could it be before the novelty wore off and her abductors came to see her as an obstacle to progress, rather than a toy?

Slade tried to conjure up a map from memory but couldn't make it work. He hadn't passed this way before and wasn't sure what lay ahead, in terms of settlements.

"You've worked this corner of the territory, Hec," he said. "Is there another town nearby, in the direction that we're headed?"

"Crossing into Kansas, there'd be Liberal," said Daltry. "That's a three-day ride, the pace we're setting. Heading east from here, there's Forgan, but it don't amount to much. There used to be another town up this way, maybe two days out. I disremember what they called it, but it doesn't matter. It dried up and blew away."

"No place that we could find a telegraph," Slade said, "and let the judge know we've been sidetracked."

"Nope. But since they sent a rider off from Amity to Enid, he's most likely heard about the raid by now. Best we can do."

Slade was used to scraping by on his assignments from Judge Dennison. The Oklahoma Territory encompassed some seventy thousand square miles, with an estimated eighty-five to ninety thousand settlers. Half of those were townsfolk, though, which left large tracts of land unoccupied. Tent cities sprouted churches, schools, saloons, and homes as people sought safety in numbers. Some towns grew and prospered. Others withered on the vine and died.

Like human beings.

They ate lunch in the saddle, jerky, hard-tack, and fresh stream water from their canteens. No one suggested stopping to make coffee, since it felt like wasting precious time. Their first full day of tracking was half gone, and Slade sensed that the others shared his feeling of frustration as the minutes turned to hours, lost like dandelion fuzz in a stiff breeze.

As they rode on, the townies talked to hear themselves. Harden declared that he had never ridden so far north from Amity, while Jordan and O'Connor both had been to Kansas. Neither one said why, and no one asked. Farrell reckoned that the restaurant in Amity would serve meatloaf that night, with gravy. Warren kept his mouth shut, staying close to Slade and Daltry, studying the killers' trail.

It was an hour past midday when Slade saw vultures wheeling in the sky, perhaps three miles ahead. They were just specks at first, but nothing else in nature looked the same, circling on high above a meal they had discovered, left for them by Providence.

Or by some human hand.

"We'll need to have a look-see," Daltry said, after Slade pointed out the scavengers.

"It could be nothing." Mike O'Connor sounded worried.

"Must be *some*thing," Hec replied. "From here, looks like it won't be far out of our way."

"Oh, Lord," said Billy Farrell. "Let it be a deer, a coyote, anything but Sally Ann."

"Don't borrow grief," Hec cautioned. "Life serves up enough, without asking for seconds."

"I hear that," Slade said and nudged his roan into a gentle trot.

One of his old man's Bible stories came to Slade from nowhere. Moses and his people, following a pillar of clouds through the desert to freedom. Now a circling pillar of carrion birds led the posse toward death.

Finding the body wasn't difficult. The hard part was examining what man and scavengers had left behind. Slade left his roan a few yards from the corpse, upwind, and walked the final distance, Hec beside him, while the townies hung back, muttering.

The naked woman had been shot at point-blank range, through the right temple, blowing out a fist-sized chunk of skull on the left side. Vultures had been at work — they scattered when the posse came too close — but Slade still thought that he could track the upward angle of the shot from right to left.

"I've got a picture in my mind," Hec told

him, "but I hate to spell it out."

"Because you think she did this to herself," Slade said.

"The head shot, anyway," Hec said. "Not all the rest."

Some of the rest was bruising, dark against the pale skin of her body, and the work of prairie scavengers. Slade knew that corpses didn't bruise, so that had happened while the lady was alive. She'd missed the feeding frenzy, Lord be praised.

The diagnosis of a self-inflicted death came down to crude geometry. If she'd been shot by someone else, while standing, then the shooter was significantly shorter than his victim. Even more so, if she had been kneeling at the time. All bets were off if she'd been lying down, but there was no way Slade could tell unless he found the spot where she'd been slain.

Not here.

A human body didn't bleed much, either, once the heart stopped pumping. Cuts would seep, veins drain if opened soon enough, before the clotting started, but you wouldn't find great spills or splash marks from the arteries.

So, she'd been shot elsewhere and dragged or carried to the spot where buzzards found her. Scrape marks on her legs and backside cast the winning vote for dragging, possibly a sloppy one-man job.

"We need a confirmation," Slade observed.

"You know it's her," said Daltry.

"More than likely, but we never met her. This is where we do it by the book. No shortcuts."

"Right. Okay."

Slade rose and turned to face the young men who were hanging back. There was no point in sugarcoating it.

"We need a confirmation of identity," he said.

The five stood silent for a moment, then Bill Farrell said, "All right. I'll do it."

Moving like a man about to mount the gallows, he approached the spot where Slade and Daltry stood over the woman's prostrate form. At fifteen feet he caught a sour whiff and hesitated, then pressed on. A moment later, he stood between Slade and Daltry, staring down at their find.

"Is that Miz Bollinger?" Hec asked.

"I can't tell," Farrell answered. "Christ! What happened to her face?"

"The shot's impact did some of it," Hec said, "and buzzards did the rest."

Farrell was softly weeping now, trailing his eyes along the pale length of her violated body while he tried to breathe.

"I've never seen her like . . . like this. I guess her hair's about the same."

"That's good enough for now," Slade said.

Farrell turned and retreated, veering off from his companions, toward a clump of sagebrush where he doubled over, sicking up the remnants of his meager lunch.

"No useful tracks around here," Daltry said. "But I expect they won't be far away."

Slade nodded. "So, we need to find the spot where she was killed and go from there."

"Sounds right."

"We can't just leave her here, though."

"No. Can't haul her back without a spare horse, either."

"No one waiting for her back there, anyway," Slade added.

"Do you reckon souls just find each other, somehow?" Daltry asked him.

Slade, who didn't think much about souls or any kind of afterlife, could only shrug. "Beats me," he said.

"Guess it don't matter, anyhow. We need to deal with this and find our spot before we lose the light."

Slade faced the townsmen, reunited now and gathered around Farrell, talking at his grief.

"We need to deal with Mrs. Bollinger right now," Slade told them, "then locate the spot where she was killed and look for tracks."

"I'll take her home," Farrell half moaned.

"You've only got one horse, son," Hec reminded him.

"I'll lead it, if I have to," Farrell said.

"Walking, it'll take you three, four days, at least."

"Don't care," said Farrell, stubbornly. "I can't leave her out here."

"You understand we'd bury her, somehow?" Slade asked, certain that none of them had brought shovel.

"No, sir!"

Hec exchanged a wary glance with Slade, one eyebrow cocked, then gave a lazy shrug.

"All right," Slade said. "You'll need to wrap her up in something and get started."

Farrell's friends were arguing about whose blankets should be sacrificed when Slade and Daltry started looking for the killers' last known camp.

They found it something like a hundred yards due east, in line with the route they'd been following when they were lured aside by the vultures. The campfire's ashes had gone cold, but they smelled fresh enough to make Hec speculate that they had shaved a few more hours off the gang's head start.

Slade found the place where Sally Bollinger had died. Her blood had soaked into the thirsty soil and dried a rusty brown, coating the grass where she had lain. Red ants were busy with it, stripping any morsel they could find.

"Still think she shot herself?" asked Slade.

"It wouldn't be the first time, in a situation similar to this."

"That's true enough," Slade said. "We had a widow there in Enid, five or six years back, took arsenic when folks found out what she was doing with her handyman. Plain old embarrassment."

"Sure, I can see it happening that way," Daltry replied. "Too bad she didn't drop a couple of the bastards first, while she was at it."

"Too bad," Slade echoed, thinking that it would've shaved the odds.

"Okay, let's find them tracks," Hec said. "I want 'em in my sights before they do the same to anybody else."

Finding the tracks was simple, and their general direction hadn't varied. They were traveling northeastward, heading who knew where.

Penn Warren found them as they stood, eyeing the trail. His face was troubled, but he tried to cover it.

"We got her swaddled up and mounted," he announced. "Billy still means to take her back alone. We couldn't talk him out of it."

"No point our trying, then," said Slade.

"A couple of the others wanted to escort him," Warren added, "but I nipped that in the bud. At least, for now."

"We've told you that you're free to go back anytime," Slade said. "Nobody's forcing you to stick."

"I need to see it through," Warren replied.

"Okay," Slade said. "Sort out the others, then. Whoever's riding with us has five minutes for good-byes."

Warren returned with Harden, Jordan, and O'Connor to find Slade and Daltry mounted, waiting for them.

"Are you all agreed, then?" Daltry asked them. "This is what you mean to do?"

"It is," said Warren, while the others nodded, more or less convincingly.

"And Farrell?" Slade inquired.

"He's got . . . determination," Warren said. "He'll be all right."

"Well, then," Slade said, "we're burning daylight. Let's be on our way."

"What's wrong?" asked Ethan Frain.

"I've got a feeling," Evan told him.

"Gas? A backache?"

"Joshing never was your strong suit, Brother."

"What, then?" Ethan pressed him.

"Trouble coming up behind us."

"Hell, you didn't need a Gypsy's help with that one, did you?"

"Coming *fast,*" said Evan.

"We're making better time without the woman."

"It's not good enough. We need to slow them down. Or, better yet, get rid of them entirely."

"I can't see us doubling back," Ethan observed.

"No need for that. They'll find us soon enough, if we just wait for them."

"That doesn't strike me as the smartest thing we've ever done."

"It's necessary. We can find a place, lay up, and hit 'em when they least expect it."

"Why not ride on through the night, to Abaddon?" asked Ethan.

"I don't want to lead them there," his twin replied.

"You'd rather waste time on a daydream."

"No. A feeling. There's a difference."

"Okay. But does your *feeling* say who's coming? Or how many?"

"No."

"Suppose you're right —"

"I am."

"*Suppose* you're right, and we're out-gunned. We sting a few of them and get surrounded for our trouble. What's the good of that?"

"They won't have sent an army."

"They don't need an army," Ethan said. "There's only six of us."

"We'll take them by surprise."

"Sounds like you're set on doing this."

"Alone, if no one else will help me."

"Don't be stupid, will you? Have I ever *not* been there to watch your back?"

"Seven months ago, in Texas."

Ethan scowled and told him, "Watch it, damn you! First, I figured you were dead. And second, I was hip-shot. Third, if I'd gone back for you, we'd both be up in Leavenworth right now."

"That's true," Evan allowed. "Sorry."

"I don't want your apology. Just tell me what you have in mind."

"I did, already. Find someplace where we can watch and wait. Give it a day to prove my feeling right or wrong. If someone comes along, we take 'em. If they don't . . . well, then, we've lost nothing by resting up."

"I still say we should push on through. But what the hell, I'm with you."

"Want to tell the others, or should I?"

"It's *your* feeling."

"Uh-huh."

The others didn't argue, though a couple of them looked askance at killing time along the trail for no good reason. Dahlquist wore a bruised and sullen face, but seemed to welcome any time out of the saddle he could get. The rest conceded in the way they greeted most ideas, aside from robbery, with thinly veiled bad grace.

Once they'd decided, it remained for them to find the ambush site. Evan demanded cover, preferably elevated ground, with clearance for retreat if it went badly. Five miles farther on, they spied a cluster of low hills bristling with trees, off to their left.

"Ride past them for a quarter mile or so," Evan instructed his companions. "Then cut over to your left and swing a wide loop doubling back. Whoever's following will pass by on our trail before they know what's happening."

"*If* anybody's following," said Jimmy Beck.

"You doubt it," Ethan challenged him, "then you won't mind if we all stake you out for bait."

"Screw that," Beck answered back. "I'm just not sure there's anybody on our trail."

"Then all you're losing is a few more

hours in the saddle," Evan said. "Your ass should thank us."

"Fine with me. I ain't complainin'."

"Good. Then follow close and do exactly as you're told."

They rode a half mile past the hills, just to be sure, then swung out to the left and rode west for about two hundred yards, before they doubled back. Any pursuers should be fooled, unless they sent a scout ahead to chart their course.

And if that was the case, too bad for him.

Concealment is the key to any ambush, as the Frains knew well enough from past experience. The wooded hills should serve, as long as no one in their party showed himself or made any unnecessary noise.

Evan decided he would see to that, himself.

If necessary, he would show them how to emulate the silence of the grave.

9

"They slowed down, coming through here," Hec advised, as afternoon was shading into early evening.

"How can you tell that?" Slade asked. He still aspired to learn the craft of tracking, but Slade doubted whether he would ever rival Hec, much less Deputy Marshal Proudfoot, who was something like one-quarter Cherokee.

"Hoof marks don't cut as deep," said Daltry, "and their stride gets shorter. They were slowing down, no question."

"Why?"

Slade recognized the foolish question too late to retrieve it.

"Couldn't tell you that," Hec said. "Most likely, resting up their animals, but who knows? Maybe one of 'em is butt sore."

"Slowing down, not stopping," Slade took pains to clarify.

"They didn't stop along in here," Hec

verified. "If we're a day behind 'em, though, they might've been considering a spot to camp."

"They'd look for decent grass and water," Slade said, almost talking to himself.

"And cover, if there's such a thing around these parts."

"There just might be," Slade told him, pointing forward, toward a group of hills that thrust up from the prairie some three-quarters of a mile ahead.

"Are those trees on the crest, there?" Daltry asked.

"Looks like it."

"Means there's water, and they would've had the high ground overnight."

"At least," Slade said.

Hec cut a sidelong glance in his direction. "Meaning what?"

Slade shrugged. "Nothing that I can prove from here," he said. "And by the time we're close enough . . . too late."

"You think they're *waiting* for us, up there?" Daltry asked.

"No reason to believe it," Slade replied. "But my gut tells me something's wrong."

"I normally don't argue with another marshal's gut," Hec said. "What do you have in mind?"

"We're still too far away for them to count

us, without spyglasses," Slade said. "I'd like to veer off here and circle up around those hills from the northwest. It'll add another twenty minutes to our ride, I'd guess, but if I'm wrong, we ought to have a decent place to spend the night."

"Okay, I'm sold," Hec said.

He reined in, signaled for the townies to do likewise, and explained in broad terms what was happening. He didn't make it Slade's idea, in case, and no one argued with him anyway.

"You think they're *up there?*" Mike O'Connor asked.

"For now, it's just a thought we're checking out," Slade said.

"We should be ready for 'em, though," said Joshua Harden.

Daltry raised a hand for silence, then said "*Ready* doesn't mean we ride in shooting. Just forget that, altogether. We don't know that anyone is in those hills — and if there is, it might not be the men we're looking for."

"But if it *is* them —" Harden interrupted.

"Then we have our rifles out, with live rounds in the chambers and the hammers *down.* Hear me? I'd better not see anybody's finger on a trigger, unless something gives you cause to shoot. Which don't mean birds

162

or rabbits or some tired old drifter sittin' by a fire with empty hands and nothing special on his mind. You hear me? All of you?"

Hec waited while the four remaining possemen nodded their heads or answered him aloud, in the affirmative. When he was satisfied, Hec said, "All right. Prepare yourselves as we've agreed."

Four rifles flourished, and their actions click-clacked as their owners chambered cartridges, then lowered hammers to prevent the weapons from discharging accidentally.

At least, in theory.

Slade readied his Winchester, braced its butt against his thigh to keep the muzzle pointed skyward, and swung his roan into line as the posse veered off to their left, riding westward.

Twenty minutes at the most, he thought, to see if he was right or wrong.

"The hell are they doing?" Creed Sampson asked.

"They're being careful," Evan Frain replied. "There's someone halfway smart in charge."

"That, or they never meant to follow us at all," Tom Dahlquist said.

"You saw the way they stopped and

changed directions, yes?"

"I can't see shit, this far away," Dahlquist replied. "Looks like a buncha bugs crawling around out there."

"You need to get your eyes checked," Evan said.

"Oh, sure. And have you call me goddamn four eyes all the time? Not likely."

"You're right, Tom," Evan replied. "Why have clear vision, when you've got a chance to peep and squint like some old man with one foot in the grave?"

"Just drop it, will you?"

"Absolutely," Evan said. Thinking: *I'll drop you, if you give me any kind of an excuse. Just one more little thing.*

"They're ridin' off, due west," said Jimmy Beck.

"Just watch and wait," Ethan instructed all of them together. "If they don't turn back, we're fine."

"And if they do?" asked Beck.

"It's why we're here, Jimmy. Give them a nice warm welcome that they won't forget."

"Or live long enough to remember," said Dahlquist.

Ethan leaned closer to his twin and said, "It struck me odd, the way they stopped and then turned off our trail."

"Same here," Evan replied. "When was

164

the last time you saw that many men riding together, if they weren't hunting or driving stock?"

"There's six of us," Ethan reminded him. "Don't we count?"

"That proves my point. We're always hunting."

"It's a long ride back from where we left the *Katy Flier,*" Ethan said. "I doubt they could've caught up with us yet, starting from there."

"Maybe they didn't have to. This could be related to the settlers, outside Amity."

"You're thinking town folk, then."

"Could be."

"That makes it easier."

Townsmen talked big, sometimes, but they were usually slow to pull a trigger, going for the bluster over brute force nine times out of ten.

"Let's hope so," Evan said.

"They're turning," Sampson called out. "Circling back in this direction, like they mean to take us from our blind side." Sampson winked and grinned at Dahlquist, adding, "No offense, Tommy."

"Screw you, half-breed."

"That's what your mama said."

"You must be robbin' graves, then," Dahlquist countered. "She was dead before you got weaned off the tit."

"Shut up, you two," Evan commanded. "Pay attention. Try to stay alive."

Hec Daltry had begun to pick up Slade's bad feeling, by the time they finished their detour and turned back toward the wooded hills. None of the three stood more than forty-odd feet high, and Daltry saw no cliffs or other obstacles that should prevent a horseman scaling any one of them.

Of course, a firing squad on top would change all that.

They were a hundred yards out from the westernmost hill when Hec saw a puff of gun smoke at the tree line. Reflex made him duck and call a warning to the others, no one in particular.

"Spread out!" he shouted, as the whiplash of the first shot reached his ears. "Stay low! Don't ride straight in!"

It the best advice that he could offer, in the circumstances, as the tree line blossomed smoke from half a dozen weapons, give or take. The bullets sang among them now, like hornets swarming to defend their threatened nest, but any sting from one of these could put a man down for good.

Hec wasn't much for shooting with a rifle at the gallop, when he needed one hand for the reins, and he was still some fifty yards from anything resembling decent pistol range. The best that he could do was hang on, keep his head down, kick his gray into a lather — and, if there was time, cuss Jack Slade up and down for his damned feelings.

Off to Daltry's left, he heard the clear slap of a bullet striking flesh, but couldn't tell if it was horse or human. There were two men on his left, Warren and Jordan, but he didn't recognize the voice that whooped in pain or startlement before its owner left his saddle.

Daltry galloped on, aware of Slade some distance to his right and the O'Connor lad beyond that. They were fanning out as he'd commanded, but with five or six guns on the hilltop facing them, would it do any good?

Almost before he realized it, Daltry crossed the hidden line that brought his would-be killers within six-gun range. He couldn't count on making any trick shots from that distance, more particularly as his gray began to lurch and strain uphill, but he could damn well make some noise.

His first shot was a waste. The second, too — but closer that time, as he glimpsed a shadow figure ducking back behind a tree and out of sight. Hec seized that opportunity to haul hard on his horse's reins, steering the gray off to his left at forty-five degrees or so. A rifle bullet whispered past him, close enough for Hec to hear it sizzle, but he still rode on.

Close to the crest, no more than four or five long strides from the tree line, he leaped out of his saddle and snagged his holstered rifle with his free hand as the gray ran on without him, seeking safety out of range. Hec landed in a crouch and didn't wait to gain his balance, sprinting for the cover that was close enough to smell and yet so far away.

A bullet whipped between his blurred feet — *Jesus, did it graze his boot heel?* — then Hec reached the trees and threw himself facedown on grass and moldy fallen leaves.

So far, so good.

But was he all alone up there, against his unknown enemies?

Hec slipped his pistol back into its holster, clutched his Winchester, and made up his mind not to die.

Not here.

Dear Jesus, not just now!

"Watch out there, on your flank!" commanded Evan Frain. He swung his Winchester around and sent a wasted slug whining down range. His target, yet another mounted stranger, disappeared into the trees.

"Damn it, get after him!" he snapped at Tom Dahlquist. "That side is your responsibility."

"Nobody said we had to run 'em down on foot," Dahlquist replied, but he was off and moving, jogging toward the point where Frain had lost his man.

Six trackers, and they'd dropped one coming up the hill — which seemed pathetic, when he thought about it. How could they *not* do better than that? A cross-eyed drunkard with a bow and arrow could've done that much, but it was still better than nothing, Frain supposed.

His own shots hadn't found their mark, so far, which was embarrassing. Frain wondered if he'd lost some of his edge while he was caged in Texas. It was worrisome, not only for the moment but beyond, imagining how others in his gang would take it if they figured he was weakening.

Another rider charged across his field of vision, firing toward the trees as he galloped from right to left. A glint of something on his shirt was probably a badge, not that the law had any great sway in the badlands. Out here, strong men took what they could and dealt harshly with those who stood in their way.

Frain pumped the lever action on his rifle, tried to lead his racing target, then squeezed off. Frain saw the man flinch, as if hit, but he wasn't unhorsed and had passed out of view by the time Frain had jacked a fresh cartridge into the weapon's chamber.

All along the skirmish line, his men were firing. But at *what?* Even the wounded posseman had disappeared. Frain couldn't find a target now to save his life — and that was what it might come down to, any minute now. With their pursuers in the trees, invisible, the only plan that he could think of was retreat, before they wound up being cut off from their horses.

"Pull back!" Evan snapped at Sampson, closest to him on the firing line. "And pass it on!"

Frain didn't want to shout the order, tip the lawmen off to what was happening. He guessed the hunters were dismounted now, making it easier to stalk his people through the trees. If he could give them one more solid jolt, then ride off hell-for-leather while their heads were down, he might just leave their enemies behind.

Watching for shooters, moving out as swiftly as the tanglefoot terrain permitted,

Evan Frain retreated toward the horses and escape. He trusted that his twin would be there, either waiting for him or arriving on his heels.

As for Tom Dahlquist and the rest . . .

Screw them, he thought. If they could slow the posse down, maybe discourage them enough to make them turn and head for home, it would be worth the price in blood.

All that he really needed was his brother, and some time to think, rest up, start planning what came next. If that meant gathering a new gang, then so be it. Frain had done that time and time again.

The only thing he cared about, right now, was getting off this goddamned hill alive.

Slade had dismounted as soon as he crossed the tree line and found cover, slapping his roan on the rump to propel it away from the focus of gunfire. He carried his Winchester cocked, tracking his quarry by the sound of firing and the acrid scent of burned gunpowder.

He was close, Slade knew that much. He thought that Hec Daltry had reached the trees but couldn't vouch for any of the townsmen. He had seen one of them, Harden, toppled from his saddle by a rifle shot but didn't know how badly he'd been hurt.

As for the rest . . .

In Slade's experience, every gunfight was personal. Someone tried to kill him, and Slade did his damnedest to return the favor. Even with a dozen men involved, the fight came down to individuals, bent on surviving if they could.

Slade heard a rustling, somewhere up ahead of him, and froze. The sounds were drawing closer, someone moving cautiously, but not adept at stalking in the woods. Slade crouched and froze, half hidden by a lacebark elm.

Waiting.

He heard the shooter stumble, cursing at whichever root or bush had snagged his foot. A moment later, Slade saw him emerging from the shadows, clutching six-guns in both fists. The portrait on his wanted poster wasn't quite as homely as its model, but Slade recognized Tom Dahlquist easily enough.

Slade framed the gunman in his rifle's sights from twenty feet, deciding whether he should fire from ambush or allow Dahlquist the option of surrender. Not that it seemed likely, but —

"That's far enough," Slade cautioned.

"Show me empty hands."

Dahlquist dropped to a crouch and fired both guns at once, in the direction of Slade's voice. Slade shot him once, between his breastbone and his belt buckle, a killing shot, but not the quickest.

Dahlquist grunted and toppled over backward, kicking at the grass and leaves in a grim pantomime of running, going nowhere. Stunned and bleeding out inside, he triggered one more shot in the direction of the treetops, then released his pistols, bringing both hands down to clasp his punctured abdomen.

Still covered by the lacebark elm, Slade gave some thought to shooting him again, before he was distracted by a sudden flurry of gunfire, bodies crashing through the undergrowth, men shouting back and forth with unfamiliar voices.

Veering wide around the clearing where Tom Dahlquist lay dying, Slade bolted toward the sounds of hasty flight, afraid that he was already too late.

Ethan Frain knew his brother was leaving before the word reached him from Jimmy Beck's lips. He was prepared to flee the wooded hilltop at a moment's notice, and the time had come.

They'd lost the fight.

That much was obvious. If they were winning, Evan would've stayed to see it through and stand tall and proud over the corpses of his fallen enemies. He wouldn't be retreating in the middle of a fight.

But had they failed in their intent to stop the posse?

He'd seen two of his enemies unsaddled, one framed in his own gun sights, but Ethan couldn't swear that either one was dead. Of course, you didn't have to massacre a posse to dissuade its members from continuing their manhunt. Fear, fatigue, and minor injuries could do the trick.

Killing them off was just a bonus.

Ethan saw a shadow moving to his left, lined up the shot, and took it. Down range, someone — friend or foe — slumped out of sight and didn't rise again. Frain grimaced, knew his time was swiftly running out, and bolted for the spot where they had left the horses tied.

He hated fleeing from a fight but was accustomed to it nonetheless. A fugitive who didn't run and hide quickly became a jailbird, and he didn't plan to go that route again.

Not even if his stay in jail was brief, just waiting for the hangman.

Ethan reached the horses just as Evan climbed aboard his piebald gelding. "There you are," his twin said. "I was worried you forgot the way."

"You know I hate to run out on a party," Ethan answered, as he swung into his bay mare's saddle. " 'Specially when I've set it up myself."

"This party's going nowhere," Evan said, as Creed Sampson and Jimmy Beck appeared, claiming their horses.

"Dick was right behind us," Sampson said.

"Still am," Eyler reported, as he reached the clearing, heading for his tethered chestnut.

"Where's Tom?" Sampson asked.

"I sent him on an errand," Evan answered. "Guess it was too much for him."

"You want to leave his horse?" asked Beck.

"Hell, no," said Evan. "We might need it."

"And he won't," Ethan confirmed.

Eyler untethered Dahlquist's tobiano mare and held its reins while he mounted his own animal. "Ready," he said.

They swept down from the hilltop, left the battlefield behind them, with the sounds of gunfire in their ears. The posse's members didn't know they'd been abandoned to waste their bullets on trees and shadows.

With any luck, before they learned the

truth, Ethan and his companions would have put a mile or more between themselves and their pursuers. Then, the hunters would need time to lick their wounds or plant their dead. Maybe debate the wisdom of proceeding with their mission, after all.

And if they turned back, Evan would have won.

At least, for now.

It took a while for Slade and Hec to make the others hold their fire. Harden and Jordan had been shooting at each other, without knowing it, each convinced he had an outlaw pinned down in the woods. Penn Warren thought he'd hit one of their adversaries, but he wasn't sure. He nursed an injured shoulder, having fallen from his horse on the approach to the tree line.

They found Mike O'Connor propped up with a tree at his back and a gun in his lap, dark blood staining his blue denim shirt on the left side, low down.

"Not as bad as it looks," he informed them, "but hurts like blue blazes."

"Let's see it," Hec ordered and knelt to examine the wound. O'Connor gasped and grimaced during the procedure, which included opening his ruined shirt, peeling it back, and probing at the wound.

"It's through and through," Hec said, at last. "Looks fairly clean. I'd rinse it with some whiskey, if we had some, 'fore I bandaged it."

"I've got a bottle in my saddle bag," Dave Jordan said. "You know, for celebrating when we caught them."

"Now we have another use for it," Hec said, "if you can find your horse."

"No problem," Jordan said, turning away.

"Jesus! I can't believe we missed them all," said Warren, bitterly.

"Not all," Slade answered, speaking more to Hec than anybody else. "I dropped one, coming in." He turned and pointed. "Thirty yards or so, that way."

"Anyone we know?" asked Daltry.

"Tom Dahlquist."

"So, it *is* the Frains."

"Looks like it."

"And we missed them."

"If at first you don't succeed —"

"Try, try again," Hec finished for him.

"There you go."

"Who are the Frains?" Josh Harden asked.

"The people we were tracking when we got to Amity," Slade said.

"Wish I could help you out with that," O'Connor told them, from his tree trunk. "But I think I'm done."

177

"He can't go back alone, like Billy did," Harden said.

"No, that's a fact," Daltry agreed.

"You take him home," Warren told Harden. "That leaves four of us."

Jordan returned just then, trailing his horse, and said, "Just three."

Warren turned on his friend, wincing from shoulder pain. "You're quitting on us, too?" he challenged.

"Looks that way," Jordan replied. "Say anything you want to, Penn. I'm not cut out for this. *We* aren't cut out for it."

"Speak for yourself, damn it!"

"And how's your shoulder feeling?" Slade asked Warren.

"Good enough to ride and shoot," Warren replied.

"Or slow you down and get you killed," Hec said.

"Hey, what is this?" Warren demanded. "I'm the only one who wants to stick, and now you're trying to get rid of me?"

"Your heart's in the right place," Slade granted, "but you're no good to us injured."

"I tell you, I can ride!"

"Maybe," Hec said. "But if the hurting slows you down, you're just a ball and chain.

"Plus, in a fight," Slade said, "we'd be distracted, looking after you."

"So, that's it, then?" asked Warren.

"End of story," Hec responded. "You can spend the night here, or head back once you've patched up your buddy. Find someplace to camp on the way."

"And what about you two?"

Slade met Daltry's gaze, saw him nod, and replied, "We'll be moving on while we've still got some daylight."

"What about the dead one?" Jordan asked.

"There's a reward on him," said Slade. "Five hundred dollars, down in Texas, if you want it. Cash and carry."

"By the time we got him there, who'd recognize him? Anyway, we need to get Mike home."

"It's all the same to me," Slade said. "Next time your people send a runner off to Enid, have him tell Judge Dennison we're on the trail. Tracking the twins."

10

With nightfall coming on, the twins slowed down their pace, to let the horses rest. Creed Sampson lagged a few yards back with Jimmy Beck, nerves finally unwinding from the shoot-out and their desperate escape.

"So, that's one down," Beck said, keeping his voice low-pitched, just short of whispering.

"You never liked Tom, anyway," Sampson reminded him.

"So what? Who did? That ain't the point."

"What *is* your point?"

"We busted Evan out of jail —"

"It was a train," said Sampson.

"Same damn thing. We shot up all those guards. Seemed like a good idea, okay? But now —"

"Too late for second thoughts, Jimmy. It's been too late for quite a while, in case you hadn't noticed."

"Okay, sure. I ain't exac'ly stupid, I know if they catch us, it's the rope for everybody. I'm talkin' about somethin' else."

"Well, get to it, then," Sampson suggested.

"I'm gettin'. It seems to me like the brothers are differ'nt these days. All for each other, and don't give a shit about nobody else."

"Meaning Tom?"

"Meaning *any* of us," Beck insisted.

"Tom was an idjit, or kissing close to it. Last night, he damn near let the farmer's woman shoot us in our sleep. He took a licking for it, but you want to know the truth, I doubt he learned a goddamned thing."

"And now he's dead."

"Sure is. People get killed sometimes, in gunfights. I recall you've done some killing of your own."

"So, you think it was just an accident?"

"Hell, no. I think whoever killed him knew what they were doing. They *were* hunting us, remember?"

"Still are, I suspect."

"Maybe. And maybe not. Recall that posse out of Fort Smith, early last year? We spanked them a little, and they all ran straight back home."

"Didn't kill any of us, neither," Beck replied.

"You miss old Tom so much, why don't you ride on back and volunteer to join him? Personally, I don't care. Him getting killed ain't gonna cost me one wink of my sleep tonight."

"That's if we *do* sleep."

"We'll get to it, later. Cold camp and an early morning. Now's the time for putting ground between us and that posse, if they've still got sand enough to follow us."

"And that's another thing," said Beck.

"What is?"

"We're puttin' miles behind us, sure. But goin' *where*, exactly?"

"Someplace where the twins hid out, before."

"Uh-huh."

"You don't believe 'em?"

"I ain't sure, no more," Beck said.

"So, what's your notion? Are they leading all of us out to the middle of nowhere, to kill us and clean out our pokes? I've got about two dollars left in mine."

"I don't know where they're leadin' us," Beck answered. "That's my point. It could be Hell, for all I know."

"You gone and got religion on me, Jimmy? Guess I must've slept through that revival meeting."

"Hey! I never said I don't believe in God

or Lucifer," Beck fairly hissed at Sampson. "I expect to burn for what I've done in this life, when the time comes. But I ain't inclined to rush it, neither."

"Listen to yourself, will you?"

"I know exac'ly what I'm sayin'."

"Then you know it doesn't make a lick of sense."

"It does, to me," said Beck. "Listen! We always used to talk about the jobs we done, beforehand. Big jobs, anyway. Not somethin' like the farmhouse, but the banks we stuck up. Things like that."

"So, what? You see a bank around here, somewhere?"

"I see *nothin'*. That's my point, Creed. After all that killin' on the *Katy Flier,* we're supposed to hole up somewhere, but they won't say where we're goin'. That ain't natural."

Just then, one of the twins — Sampson believed it might be Evan — called back to them, "Don't fret, Jimmy. It's a place called Abaddon. We'll tell you all about it, when we camp tonight."

"We're losing light," Hec Daltry said.

"I see that," Slade replied, still focused on the trail in front of them.

"Maybe another hour, if we're lucky."

"Let's not waste it, then."

"You know," Hec said, "it's not your fault the boy got shot."

"The idea never crossed my mind."

"So, what's the problem, then?"

"We had them, Hec. We *had* them, and we *lost* them."

"The way I saw it, for a while there, they had us."

"We should've taken them."

"You took one, Jack. Under the circumstances, that's not bad."

"One out of six. Not damn near good enough."

"You're mad about the woman, right? The woman, and the little girl, and all the rest they've done."

"Aren't you?" Slade asked.

"No, sir. One thing I learned the hard way, comin' up. You wear a star and want to stay alive, you can't make any of it personal."

"Easy to say."

"Not easy. Necessary. Once you start to grieve for every person you see killed or damaged, there's no time for anything *but* grieving. Start to hate the men you're hunting and it gives them power over you. They own you, then."

"How's that?" Slade asked.

"They get inside your head. You start to

think about 'em all the time and put yourself in their place, thinkin' like they do."

"It helps to find a man," Slade said.

"O' course it does," Hec granted. "But the trick is lettin' go of it and comin' back to who you really are. True hate won't let you do that. It gets wrapped around you, till there's nothin' you won't say or do to get the job done. And you can't get back to normal when it *is* done. Like as not, you can't be sure what normal is."

"That hasn't troubled me, so far," Slade said. "But since we're chasing men who murdered thirteen people in the past three days, I'll risk it, to be rid of them."

"Your call," Hec said. "The second most important thing I ever learned is that I can't live anybody else's life."

Night's wings swept toward them from the east, as daylight dwindled in the west. Reluctantly, Slade had begun to watch for likely campsites, even as he tried to focus on his quarry's trail.

"You think they'll ride on through the night?" he asked.

"No way to tell," said Daltry, "but we can't afford to. If we lose their tracks, we could be thirty miles off plumb by morning, one direction or another. Take a week to find their trail again, assuming that we

185

ever do."

"You're right, damn it."

"Look on the sunny side. If they camp out, we won't fall any farther back."

"And if they don't?"

"No sign of rain, that I can see. There tracks'll still be there, come morning."

Hec's optimism chafed at Slade. "You're pretty chipper," he observed, "considering the way we got our asses kicked back there."

"I'd say we fought 'em to a draw, at worst."

"You may have noticed that we started out with seven, and we're down to two."

Hec shrugged and said, "I never thought the rest would stick this long. They're late for supper and their cozy beds."

"You like the odds at five to two?"

"Better than three to one, the way we started out."

Slade let it go and squinted through the dusk.

"Looks like more trees," he said. "Likely a stream."

"I doubt they'd stop so soon," Hec said. "But we should scout it, anyway."

Slade drew his Winchester and urged his gelding forward, as the shadows closed around them, smothering daylight.

■ ■ ■ ■

Without a fire, supper came down to pemmican and corn dodgers. In place of coffee, there was water and a half bottle of cheap red-eye to make the rounds.

No one proposed a toast to Tommy Dahlquist's memory.

When everyone had shared the whiskey, Evan Frain said, "It occurs that some of you are wondering about our destination."

He scanned the faces ranged before him, barely visible by faint starlight, and spent no extra time on Jimmy Beck's.

"It crossed my mind," Creed Sampson said.

"Mine, too," from Dick Eyler.

"Well, then, allow me to enlighten you," Frain said. "We're headed for a town called Abaddon."

"What kinda name is that?" Beck asked.

"It's from the Bible," Ethan Frain replied. "Specifically, from Revelation, chapter nine. You want to look it up?"

"Musta forgot my copy when I runned away from home," Beck said, drawing a chuckle from the others.

"Nothing to fret about," Evan replied. "It's just a name."

Ethan picked up the story, then. "We first discovered Abaddon about nine years ago," he said.

"What do you mean, *discovered* it?" Dick Eyler asked.

"Just that. It was a stroke of luck," Ethan replied, with something of a faraway expression on his face. "Or maybe Fate."

"Say what?" Beck piped up, from his left.

"We had some other lawmen after us, that time, and couldn't seem to shake them," Ethan said. "Four days and counting, out from Medicine Lodge, in Kansas. Four of them, as I recall it."

"Four," his twin confirmed.

"Then, on the fourth day, just as night was falling, out of nowhere, there's a town. The sign reads 'Abaddon.' It rang a bell, but I still had to research it. That came later."

"We were of a mind to pass it by," said Evan. "But the place was so damned quiet — *deathly* quiet — that we took a chance and rode in. Pretty soon, it's obvious that no one lived there anymore, but we still went around and hailed them, just in case."

"No answer," Ethan said. "Some rats and lizards. Thought I saw a coyote running off, one time. Nobody home."

"A ghost town," Sampson said.

"So it appeared. We settled in to spend the night at the saloon," Ethan went on. "And then, it came to us."

Evan took over, asking them, "What better place to wait and meet the lawmen who were tracking us? We figured it could go any one of three ways. They might lose our trail farther back and miss the town entirely, or get spooked by Abaddon and pass it by. But if they rode in —"

"Where better to dispose of somebody, than in a ghost town?" Ethan asked his silent comrades.

"Jesus," Eyler muttered.

"So, what happened?" Jimmy Beck inquired.

"Yeah," Sampson prodded. "Did they find you?"

Evan smiled and answered, "It was more like *we* found *them.*"

Sitting hunched over a small campfire, Slade said, "I wish we knew where they were going."

"That would be a treat," Hec answered back. "At least we know it's them, for sure. Two jobs rolled up in one. I was afraid we'd lose 'em altogether, getting sidetracked on the other thing."

"Maybe it's in the cards for us to find

them," Slade suggested.

"And what cards would those be? Poker? Pinochle?"

"Figure of speech," Slade said.

"Maybe it's in the stars," said Daltry, casting eyes up toward the sky above. "Or we could get some tea leaves, like the Gypsies use."

"What's eating you?" Slade asked.

"Nothin', I guess. Just out of sorts. But, Jack, you oughta know that there's no magic in the badge. The only kind of outside help you'll ever get, policing, is the kind we got from those town boys. It's hit or miss, and sure as hell ain't got no Fate behind it."

"Okay."

"Don't get it in your mind that I'm some kind of heathen, now," Hec said. "My mama raised me right, the best she could, goin' to church and all. I *do* believe in God — most days, at least — but all I've seen convinces me that He's got other, more important things to think about than what happens to us. We're bugs to Him. Maybe he watches us, sometimes, or maybe He's forgotten we exist. One thing I *know* is that He doesn't punish bad folk here on Earth, the way some preachers claim. Often as not, the bad folk win."

"I've seen it happen," Slade agreed. "But

we still have a job to do."

"Hell, yes, we do. By any means we can. But son, I'd hate to see you let your guard down, thinking there was some almighty power standin' by to help you when you're in a pickle."

"You don't need to worry on that score," Slade promised him.

Hec sat in silence for a moment, then began to speak again, his tone somber.

"Long time ago, when I was fresh behind a shiny badge, younger than you, I worked a spell in Abilene. That summer, we had someone sneakin' up on hookers, takin' 'em by force. Sometimes he'd show a knife, or other times just slug 'em from behind and go to work. They kept it quiet for a while, then someone tipped the marshal I was workin' for. He didn't pay it any mind — said it's the price of doin' business on your back — but I was . . . curious."

"You thought the law should treat all folks the same."

Hec smiled. "I told you I was young. So, anyway, after a couple months I found a girl who'd talk to me, on the condition that she wouldn't have to testify. As it turned out, that never was a problem."

"Oh?"

"She'd seen the fella's face and reco'nized

him. No point namin' him today, you wouldn't know him anyhow. I gave the marshal what I had, and he advised me to forget about it."

"Why is that?" asked Slade.

"The piece a shit in question was a favored boy. His daddy was a member of the town council and owned one of the biggest stores in town, with plenty land besides. The marshal wouldn't touch him on a hooker's word. He couldn't, I expect, and keep his job."

"I'm guessing that wasn't the end of it," Slade said.

"Not quite. I went around to see the lad, off-duty. Told him what I'd heard, without namin' the girl. He laughed at me. I didn't break his nose until he offered me a chance to come along and join the fun, next time."

"And you got fired."

Hec nodded. "I was dumb enough to stick around awhile, looking for other work, but Daddy made it clear I wasn't wanted in his town. The night before I was supposed to leave, Junior came at me with his knife, outside the Rose saloon."

"He must've missed," Slade said. "I notice you're still sitting here."

"He'd have been wise to keep on beatin' women," Daltry said. "That night, he had . . . a little accident. Fell on his blade, somehow. It happens."

"Small loss to the world," said Slade.

"I didn't wait around to watch them mourn him," Hec said. "It was time to go."

"No Fate involved, then," Slade observed.

"Nary a bit. Just plain, dumb luck."

"Well, then, I hope we catch some," Slade replied. "I'm turning in."

"They didn't miss our tracks," said Evan Frain. "And once they got a look at Abaddon, they had to check it out. So, in they came."

"And you were waitin' for 'em," Sampson said, not making it a question.

"None of them were ever seen at home again," Ethan confirmed. "I don't know whether anyone came looking for them, later. If they did, we didn't see them."

"You just shot 'em?" Eyler asked.

"Now, where's the fun in that?" Evan replied. "Besides, the noise of dropping one would spook the rest."

"I caught the first one sniffing around the hotel," Ethan told them. "Came up behind him with my pigsticker and let the air out of him, nice and quiet."

"The second one was mine," said Evan. "Something made him check inside the church, first, then what used to be the barber's shop. I didn't have a razor handy, but my bowie shaved him close enough."

Ethan picked up the tale, saying, "By then, the other two were getting nervous, calling for their pals. No answer coming back. It looked to me like they were weighing whether they should just ride out and leave the others, or go looking for them."

"Thinking it was ghosts," said Eyler.

"Maybe," Evan granted. "Anyhow, they took the bait. Decided they should stick together for the rest of it, to keep from losing track of one another. There was no point being quiet, after that."

"It wasn't much of a showdown," Ethan went on. "They poked around the hotel for a bit, then stepped out into rifle sights. We planted them together at the livery. More fertilizer where the horses used to crap."

"So, it's a real ghost town," said Eyler, sounding twitchy.

"Maybe so," Ethan allowed, "if you believe in stuff like that. I never gave it too much thought, but Abaddon's been good to us. It's nice and peaceful. No one else has ever tracked us there. We stop in, every now and then. Rest up and have a think."

"I never heard you talk about it," Jimmy Beck observed.

"No need to," Evan answered. "It's just . . . there."

"Suppose somebody else moves in?" asked Sampson.

"All depends," Ethan replied. "Handful of squatters, we'd find some way to discourage them. If we come back sometimes and find a settlement in place . . . well, then, I guess we just move on and tell them adios."

"What happens when we get there?" Beck inquired.

"We take it easy," Evan told him. "And decide what happens next."

"New jobs?" Dick Eyler asked.

"What else?" asked Ethan, in reply. "Man's got to work, you know."

"Best get some sleep, now," Evan said. "Work out the watch schedule among yourselves. We ride at dawn."

Slade got four hours' sleep before Hec woke him to complete the night watch. He'd been plagued by troubling dreams before the gruff voice roused him, but they vanished like wind-tattered smoke when his eyes opened.

Just as well.

Slade didn't put much stock in dreams, particularly as a means of scrying the future. As far as Slade recalled, he'd never dreamed

195

any event before it happened, nor had he received any apparent warnings against future hardships from Queen Mab. On balance, though he welcomed rest after a long day in the saddle, Slade preferred to be awake.

The quiet predawn hours gave him ample time to think — which didn't mean that he reached any meaningful conclusions. He'd learned nothing new about the Frain brothers or their companions, other than confirming their complete and utter disregard for human life. Slade briefly wondered how they'd come to be that way, divorced from any civilizing influence, but quickly gave it up as wasted effort.

What he *didn't* know about the gang was all that mattered now.

Slade didn't know where they were going, or who might be waiting to join them.

He didn't know if they were planning new jobs, or were hoping to rest up awhile.

He didn't understand why they were heading northward, when his own instinct, in their place, would've been a hard ride south to Mexico.

He didn't know what they were thinking.

And why should he?

Just because Judge Dennison had set a twin to track and capture twins, that didn't mean he had some special insight into how their minds worked, what they felt and shared. The spate of bloody crimes aside, Slade's personal experience was worlds apart from that of the Frains.

He knew nothing about their childhood, but Slade understood that they had spent their lives together, barring jail time, whereas he and Jim had separated when Slade ran away from home. He'd never had the extra decade-plus of shared events, emotions, wins and losses, trials and tribulations.

None of which, Slade calculated, would've helped him anyway.

Because, when all was said and done, Slade and his brother were not criminals. Some might have judged him harshly for his gambler's life, but Jim had been square from the start to his last living day. He'd been putting down roots, bent on building a life for himself.

And for Faith.

They even differed, there. Slade loved her to the best of his ability — and, yes, as often as he could — but he still hadn't given up a kind of drifter's life to tend a herd or plow the soil on her behalf. Today, in place of cards and easy money, it was a "duty" and a badge that kept him moving, never safe of settled long enough to know if he had truly found a home.

Was he supposed to learn some lesson from the Frains?

Was anyone truly *supposed to* learn anything, during their transit through life?

That belief took some "higher power" for granted, a leap of faith Slade couldn't make. Not with all that he'd seen, done, endured, and survived in his time.

So far, his status as a severed twin had not contributed a damned thing to his manhunt for the Frains and those who rode with them. He hoped it wouldn't prove to be a hindrance, if and when they finally stood face-to-face.

Maybe tomorrow.

Wishful thinking, Slade supposed, but it was all he had to get him through the prairie night.

11

If there was one thing Hollis Deacon hated, it was being late. The Hubbard, Fly, and Downing Coach Line paid him to be punctual, not only with the U.S. mail he carried but with the dwindling list of passengers who rode with him each week across the Oklahoma Territory.

Stagecoach lines were on their way out, Deacon realized. Had been since '69, when the golden spike was hammered home at Promontory Summit, Utah, linking up the Central Pacific and Union Pacific railroads. Deacon had been a shotgun rider for Wells Fargo at the time, then graduated to the driver's seat and never got the knack of any other job.

Too bad, since he had nothing to fall back on when — not *if* — HF&D shut down. The day was coming when his next paycheck would be the last. But in the meantime, Deacon treasured every minute on the open road, regardless of the aches and pains that had begun to plague him as his hair turned gray, his shoulders stooped, his eyesight dimmed.

Today, a broken wheel had slowed them down and made him late. He hadn't seen the jagged rock in time to miss it, and the coach's left-front wheel had lost three spokes as a result. That meant unloading his four passengers and getting the two men to help him find a log, then drag it over, hoist the left side of the coach while Deacon arduously wedged the log beneath the axle and removed the broken wheel.

The passengers were grumbling by that time, but they were lucky that he had a spare wheel in the rear boot. After hauling out their luggage, Deacon had installed the new wheel, put the old one in the boot, and then repacked their precious bags while his four charges stood around and gave advice on where the bags should go.

Deacon had met some interesting people driving coaches, Wyatt Earp and Judge Roy Bean among them, but today's quartet weren't in that class. Two married couples — so they said, although he'd noted that the semi-fancy redhead wore no wedding ring — heading from Sublette, Kansas, down to Oklahoma City. Why they hadn't caught the train in Wichita eluded Deacon, and he frankly didn't give a damn.

They were his people now, until he dropped them off at last and washed his hands of them.

And who would be his next lot, if there *was* one?

In his day, Deacon had ferried bankers, gamblers and loose women, lawmen and their prisoners, a few who'd later turned up famous or notorious. In thirty-five years, he'd been robbed six times — not bad, considering — and he had killed a pair of clumsy would-be bandits who, beneath their masks, were barely old enough to shave.

That incident had bothered Deacon for a little while, but he had gotten over it, remembering that pistols had no age and didn't care who aimed them at your heart. A callow youth or damned old geezer leaning on a cane, it made no difference. Deacon was paid to take care of his passengers and cargo.

No one had to pay him extra to protect himself.

Bearing in mind the rigors of the road, he wore a Colt Model 1878 Frontier double-action revolver on his belt, positioned for a cross-hand draw that Deacon found most comfortable and effective. At his feet, concealed from prying eyes inside the front boot, lay a Greener double-barreled twelve-gauge shotgun, hand-loaded with silver dimes.

Not that he planned on shooting anyone, this trip.

But you could never tell.

"That what I think it is?" asked Evan Frain.

His brother squinted and replied, "If what you're thinking is a cloud of dust, I'd say you're right."

"Nobody likes a smart aleck."

"All right, you're thinking . . . what? Another posse?"

"How'd they wire ahead to meet us?"

"Right," Ethan acknowledged. "Scratch that. So, then . . . a stage, you think?"

"Why not?"

Ethan considered it. Why not, indeed? Stagecoaches still ran here and there, throughout the West, to towns not served by railroads. They still carried passengers and mail, with the occasional strongbox that might hold cash or who knew what.

The stage, if stage it was, was running on a north-south track, a mile or so due east of where the Frains and their companions sat, resting their horses on a grassy ridge. It wasn't dawdling, but there was no doubt in

Ethan's mind that they could head it off, if they were so inclined.

"You want to?" he asked Evan.

"Why the hell not?"

"Then, we'd best see to it."

Without asking their companions, seeming not to care if any of the others followed them or not, the twins both spurred their horses, charging down the ridge's gentle slope and off across the flatland in a race to intercept the stage.

Creed Sampson was the first to follow, whooping at the prospect of some action. Beck and Eyler shared a frown between them, then pursued the half-breed at a headlong gallop, bent over their pommels, Eyler reaching up with one hand to secure his hat.

A quarter mile ahead of them, Evan called out to Ethan, "You know, this could mean more trouble."

Ethan flashed a grin and answered, "Hell, what doesn't?"

It took them just over two minutes to cover the mile, angling off to make sure that they came in ahead of the stage, not trailing behind it and eating its dust while they chased it. The twins planted themselves directly in its path, trusting the others to catch up and join them in completing the blockade.

Suppose the stage driver refused to stop or even slow his team? Then, what?

First, shoot the horses. Try to pile them up and wreck the coach that way, if there was time. Of course, an instant kill might not be possible. They'd all seen animals run on and on after a lethal shot, before they dropped. The coach and team could plow right through them — mangle, maybe even kill them — with a dead horse in the lead, a dead man on the driver's seat.

Still, Ethan and his brother drew their pistols, cocked them, and sat, waiting calmly, wearing identical smiles, as if this were something they did every day.

The others joined them when the stage was still a hundred yards or so away from impact. All looked winded, nervous, but they saw the brothers sitting ramrod straight and knew it would be worse than folly to retreat.

It could be suicide.

The three latecomers drew their six-guns, thumbed back hammers with a chorus of metallic clicking sounds — and waited.

"Any second now," said Evan, as the hoofbeats thundered closer.

"Christ, I hope so!" Sampson muttered to himself.

"Have faith," Ethan replied, still smiling.

"Hell, in his place," Beck replied, "*I'd* try to run us down."

"But he's not you," Evan observed.

"This won't be pretty," Eyler told whomever might be listening.

But even as he spoke, the stagecoach driver hauled back on his reins and started calling, "Whoa! Whoa!" to his team. The horses slowed, passed from a gallop to a trot, and then a walk, before they halted altogether, fifteen feet from contact with the smiling twins.

"They're goin' somewhere," Daltry said. "We haven't worked it out, is all. Hell, *every*body's goin' *somewhere*."

"I suppose," Slade said.

But was it true?

Drifters, by definition, *drifted* aimlessly across the landscape. Some outlaws, within his personal if limited experience, were similar. They might select specific targets, but between jobs, being rootless and cut off from civilized society, they roamed at will, looking for easy pickings on their lazy way to nowhere. Some he'd heard of didn't even plan their robberies, just rode in one direction of the compass or another until they crossed paths with some unlucky soul.

Much like the Frains and Bollingers.

And what if Hec was right? Suppose the bandit twins had some hideout in mind? What good did that do Slade and Daltry? With no means of knowing what went on inside those dark and twisted minds, the best that they could do was follow, closing up the gap whenever possible, and hope they overtook the gang before the Frains added more victims to their ever-growing list.

Detachment, Slade recalled. *Don't make it personal.*

Too late.

Slade couldn't say whether or not Judge Dennison had chosen him for this job in the hope that he would make it personal, but anyone of average intelligence could guess that tracking twins would spark something inside him, even if Slade couldn't pin it down, himself. He didn't liken the feeling to his love for Jim; that was ridiculous.

But there was something . . .

"Since we're winging it," he said to Daltry, "is there any chance you know a Gypsy out this way, or someone else who's good at reading minds?"

"I wish," Hec answered. "All I've got is tracks to follow, same as you."

"I'm getting better at it," Slade acknowledged. "But there's been a time or three I would've lost them, if you weren't along."

"That's why they keep the old dogs in the kennel," Daltry said, "instead of shootin' us behind the barn. Some of us still have tricks to show the pups."

"It's been a while since anyone mistook me for a pup," Slade said.

"Depends on where you stand, I guess. Or sit, in my case, when I get the chance."

"We're sitting now," said Slade.

"But making progress."

"God, I hope so."

"Half a day, with any luck," said Daltry. "If the Frains feel safe enough to light a fire tonight, we just might get a fix on them."

"Sneak up and catch them sleeping," Slade suggested.

"Wouldn't mind a bit," said Daltry. "Wake 'em up with gunsmoke, if a call won't do it."

"Makes that five to two sound better, anyway."

"Whenever possible, I try to stack the deck."

"I won't forget that, next time we play cards," Slade said.

"Oh, I don't mean in friendly games," Hec answered, showing him a grin.

"Uh-huh."

The banter helped a little, calming Slade, easing his sense that those they hunted had already slipped beyond his grasp. Slade knew that wasn't literally true, but after missing them — well, *most* of them — when they were almost literally in his rifle sights, it felt as if the whole damned hunt had soured.

Get over it, he thought.

The Frains could not avoid mistakes forever. No one could.

And sometime, somewhere, when they made one, Slade would be on hand to take advantage of it.

If it took forever, he would bring them down.

"This is your lucky day, friend," Evan told the stagecoach driver.

"How you figure lucky?" asked the grizzled older man.

"Play your cards right, you get to be a Good Samaritan and live to tell about it."

"I ain't haulin' gold, or anything like that," the driver said.

"No strongbox?"

"Not this trip."

"We'll need to see that for ourselves," Ethan advised him. "There'll be mail, though?"

"Mail, there is. Take that, and you'll have U.S. marshals after you."

"We'll risk it," Evan answered, beaming. "What about your passengers?"

"Ain't asked 'em what they're carrying," the driver said. "None of my business, anyhow."

"We'll make it ours," said Ethan, as he steered his bay mare toward the coach's right-hand side and peered in through the windows at four frightened faces.

"Everybody out, now," he instructed, with a flourish of his pistol.

And behind him, Evan told the driver, "Toss that Colt away, old man. Left hand, two fingers. You'll live longer."

"Sure as hell hope so," the driver grumbled, as he threw the gun away.

The passengers were slow at disembarking. For a moment, Ethan thought he'd have to fire a shot over their heads to get them moving, but they finally lined up beside the coach, huddled in pairs.

"Ladies and gentlemen," he said, "my friends and I are presently in need of funds. Our circumstances force us to rely on strangers for assistance."

"So, you're robbing us," one of the passengers — a stocky man, sporting a black mustache — replied.

"You have a keen eye," Ethan said. "We'll take your cash and any jewelry you might be carrying, before we have a look inside your luggage."

The pistol shot behind Frain made him flinch. Half turning from the passengers, just as one of the women screamed, he saw the stagecoach driver toppling from his high seat with a shotgun spilling from his hands. The old man fell atop his gun and set it off, somehow, the double blast shredding his booted feet.

That set the other woman screaming. Ethan let her wind down on her own, with no attempt to soothe her. When the noise died down, he told the four survivors, "That's unfortunate, but he was warned. Now, back to business."

"Never mind their money," Eyler said, goading his chestnut forward. "How about these ladies?"

"Back off, Dick," Ethan warned.

Eyler ignored him, leering at the curvy redhead as he said, "I'll have me some of that."

"Like hell, you will!" her man replied.

"Don't worry, mister. You can watch."

Ethan was fuming. "Dick, goddamn it!"

But the husband or whatever beat him to

it, spitting out, "You'll have to kill me, first."

"Okay," Eyler replied and shot him in the chest.

Evan swiveled, firing from the hip, almost before the redhead had a chance to scream. His bullet took Dick Eyler underneath the chin and launched him from his saddle, vaulting over backward in a lifeless sprawl. The chestnut wheeled away and bolted.

"Any other stupid bastard think he calls the shots?" Ethan demanded, staring hard at Beck and Sampson. Covered by both twins, the startled gunmen didn't even risk shaking their heads.

"Not me," Sampson replied.

"No, sir," said Jimmy Beck.

"You know what this means," Evan said. He sounded weary.

"Right," Ethan replied. "No witnesses."

The sounds of gunfire, warped and muffled over distance, lifted Slade out of his saddle slump and set his eyes locked on the skyline. Two shots fired by different weapons, one maybe a shotgun, then two more from pistols, and a flurry at the end, too quick and numerous for him to count.

"Well, now," said Hec. Just that, and nothing more.

"That can't be good," Slade said.

"Unless our boys ran into trouble and it finished them."

"You think so?"

"Nope," Hec said. "Just wishful thinking."

"Might have nothing to do with them at all," said Slade.

"Coincidence? Some other shooting match out here, just now? It's possible, I guess."

"But you don't buy it."

"Sorry."

"Still northeast, I think," Slade said.

"As near as I can tell."

"And distance?"

Daltry shook his head. "Your guess on that would be as good as mine."

Slade urged his gelding to a trot and held it there. He saw no point in pushing it beyond endurance, when the shooting site could be ten miles away. Unless they heard more shots, Slade knew they'd have to wait and hope the gang's tracks led them to the shooting scene. If he and Daltry lost the trail somewhere along the way, it would be hell to find the right spot.

If they ever did.

"You think they'd make noise just to wear us out or throw us off the scent?" he asked Daltry.

"It's possible. But no, I don't. I'm thinking they found someone they could pick on, without running much of any risk theirselves. I think what we just heard was people dyin'."

"Yeah."

Slade focused on the fact that they'd be strangers. Innocent of any wrongdoing, most probably, but no one that he knew or cared about, beyond a general sense that most people deserved to live in peace. There was no reason, if he found them, why he ought to take their ghosts on board as passengers, to shadow him and haunt his dreams.

"They seem bent on running up a score," Slade said.

"What have they got to lose?" Hec asked him, in reply. "The judge can only hang them once apiece."

"That's if we get them back to Enid."

"Oh, they're going back. It may be tied across a saddle, but they're going back. I promise you."

Slade hoped Hec's confidence would not rebound to jinx them, but he'd never been a superstitious sort. No more than any other gambler, anyway. He knew that luck existed, good *and* bad, but Slade had never been convinced that simple words influenced it.

Slade didn't want to think about the

Frains claiming new victims when he'd missed a chance to stop them cold, but it was unavoidable. He had to face that chilling prospect every hour, every day, until the gang had been corralled and caged.

Or killed.

The hilltop ambush had confirmed what Slade already knew: the Frains would not surrender. They had tasted prison, didn't like it, and would almost certainly prefer a bullet to a hanging rope, if they could not escape.

And could they pull it off?

Remaining in the Oklahoma Territory or environs smacked of suicide, but what would happen if the twins managed to gain some distance from their latest crimes? What would happen if they split up, even for a little while, and traveled separately?

Farther north or west. Back east. Even if those around them had some vague familiarity with what the Frains had done in Oklahoma, who was likely to identify one of them, on his own?

But could they do it? Could they function separately, on the same level they did when teamed? Or would their birth bond now compel them to ride, stand, fight, and die together, come what may?

Slade couldn't answer any of those questions from his own experience.

The best that he could do was find and stop them now.

By any means available.

"What's wrong with you two?" Evan Frain inquired.

A few yards distant, Creed Sampson and Jimmy Beck were picking through the luggage they had taken from the rear boot of the stagecoach. Women's clothes and men's things they would never wear lay scattered all around them, with a few books, shaving gear, and such.

"Nothin'," said Beck.

"Same here," Sampson replied.

Frain watched them for another moment, let his eyes drift briefly to the bodies sprawled beside the coach, and frowned.

"You know we had to kill them, right?" he asked.

"Sure," Sampson said.

"O' course," Beck answered.

"Otherwise," Evan pressed on, "the law might call them up to testify about the driver. One more strike against us. You can see that."

Beck and Sampson traded glances, frowned at one another, then Creed straightened up from pawing over clothes and faced

Evan directly.

"Okay, that's the thing," he said.

"What is?"

"If we were gonna kill 'em anyhow, then why'd your brother shoot Dick over nothin'?"

"Ah," Frain said. "You call that nothing? Breaking ranks and interrupting Ethan? Killing when he wasn't ordered to? Risking some kind of panic with the passengers, before we even knew if they were armed?"

"Turns out they weren't," Sampson reminded him.

"Well, sure. We know that *now.*"

"All due respect, Evan," the half-breed said. "This ain't the army. None of us joined up to wear a uniform and march in line. We're tired of takin' orders."

"Are you, now?"

The words came from behind them, Ethan Frain appearing from wherever he had gone off to relieve himself.

Sampson and Beck half turned to him then, attention split between the twins. It clearly made them nervous, being flanked. And with good reason.

"Ethan," Creed began, "I was just sayin' —"

"I heard what you said," Frain interrupted him. "You think I dealt too harshly with poor Dick. Maybe I should've laughed it off and clapped him on the back."

"Well —"

"You know why gangs like ours don't last?" Ethan inquired. "Any idea?"

"I never thought about it," Sampson said. Beck kept his mouth shut.

"That's one problem," Evan interjected. "Men not thinking."

"Or," Ethan replied, "sometimes they think too much, when it's beyond them."

"True," said Evan.

"But the problem that I had in mind," Ethan continued, "is a lack of discipline. Okay, we're *criminals.* I see your point. Nobody's asking you to be a soldier, marching up and down a field all day for no good reason. But we have to *plan* our moves, the best we can. It isn't always possible, I grant you, like this business here. But even when you act on impulse, it demands a sense of order. Understand?"

Beck wore a blank expression. Sampson looked confused.

"All right," said Evan. "Put it this way: are you with us, or against us?"

"Make your choice," Ethan advised. "Right now."

"Hey!" Beck said, sounding panicky. "Nobody said nothin' about bein' *against*

217

you. That ain't what Creed meant, at all."

"It wasn't?" Evan asked.

Ethan chimed in, "Is Jimmy right about that, Creed?"

Sampson delayed his answer for a beat, then gave a jerky nod and told the twins, "Sure is. I didn't mean no disrespect at all."

"Well, damn! That's a relief," said Evan Frain.

"I hope to shout," his brother said, beaming.

"So, if we're finished here," said Evan, "we can just forget about old Dick. Bygones."

"Bygones," Creed Sampson echoed, almost whispering, as he moved quickly toward his sorrel.

12

They found the stage a little after noon. Its team was restless, hungry, and Slade freed them from their traces after he and Hec had finished scouting the immediate vicinity. The horses wandered off some distance, seemed confused at first, then started grazing peacefully.

Six corpses sprawled around the empty coach. Slade recognized Dick Eyler from his poster, head-shot, but the rest were strange to him. Three men, two women, all gunned down.

"This one'll be the driver," Hec observed. "Looks like they shot him off his seat. The shotgun underneath him went off when he landed on it. Left him footless."

"So, he tried to stop them," Slade suggested.

"Sounds right."

"And when he went down . . . what? It touched off the rest of this?"

"No sign that any of the passengers was armed," Hec said. "And I'm guessing that Colt Frontier will fit the driver's holster, if we try it. Since it wasn't fired, all of the six-gun work came from the other side."

"Why would they shoot one of their own?" asked Slade.

"I couldn't tell you that. Some kind of falling out among the jackals. Doing us a favor, maybe."

"Not on purpose," Slade replied.

"I'll grant you that. Still, now they're down to four. I'll take what I can get."

"A lot of spadework here," Slade said.

"That's something else. We bury them, even the five deserving it, and we'll have lost the best part of a day. That only helps the Frains."

"You mean to leave them as they are?" asked Slade.

"Damned if we do, damned if we don't," Hec said. "Will it be worse to leave them and prevent more people getting killed, or spend a day doing the so-called Christian thing?"

"The worst is leaving them and *still* not running down the Frains," Slade said.

"Agreed. But we can only catch 'em if we saddle up and try. We're just a few hours behind them, now."

Daltry was right. Slade couldn't argue with his logic.

"Right, then. Let's stop wasting time."

Once the decision had been made, Slade shied away from looking at the bodies. There was nothing to be gained by studying their faces. Glazed eyes, mouths agape as if to gulp a final breath.

"At least, it seems they didn't tamper with the women," Daltry said.

"Small favors," Slade replied.

"They're all we get, sometimes."

The trail was plain before them. After deviating from their northeast course to intercept the stage, Slade's quarry had resumed their interrupted line of travel.

"That's not drifting," he told Daltry. "They're intent on going somewhere."

"I believe you're right," Hec said. "Too bad we don't know where that is."

It could be worse, Slade thought.

They'd shaved the gap between themselves and those they hunted from days down to hours. Barring some kind of disaster or crucial mistake, he believed they could catch up and finish the job they'd been sent out to do.

It had been three to one when they started, now cut by one-third in the course of twelve hours. It was too much to hope that the gang would go on in that manner, consuming itself, but like Hec, Slade would take what was offered.

Small favors.

The only kind going around.

"We can do this," Hec said. "We can stop them."

"I hope so," Slade answered.

"Hell, son, you're the one stopped the Benders, for God's sake."

"Dumb luck, like you said a while back."

"I'll take that, too, if it's all we get."

"One thing about you, Hec. You're right easy to please."

"That comes with age, Jack. Stick around a while, you'll feel the same."

I'm working on it, Slade thought to himself.

All that he had to do was stay alive.

The stagecoach, after all, had offered only slim pickings. Less than two hundred dollars shared among its passengers, together with a bloodstained thousand-dollar check made out to Roger Thomas Clark, uncashable. The strongbox had contained some legal documents, worthless to Evan Frain, but he had taken them just for the hell of it and started shredding them a few miles past the slaughter site, letting the pieces blow away.

"Expecting company?" his brother asked.

A frown pulled Evan's mouth down at the corners.

"What?"

Ethan nodded toward Evan's hands, the tattered papers that they held. "The trail you're leaving," he replied, "I wondered if you're helping someone track us."

Evan half turned in his saddle, saw the paper scraps trailing away behind him, agitated by a soft breeze.

"Shit! I didn't think," he said and crumpled the remaining papers, thrusting them into a pocket where their lumpy shape would make him mindful of his addlepated foolishness.

"You're mad about the stagecoach," Ethan said. "A lot of fuss for next to nothing."

"I could've done better with Dick."

"Looked like a nice, clean shot to me," Evan replied.

"I mean, without the shot."

"He had it coming, stepping out in front that way."

"We'll have to watch the others closer, now."

"When haven't we?" Ethan inquired, smiling.

And Evan nodded. Said, "You're right."

They'd never *really* trusted anybody else

since starting out together in the outlaw way. Even as children it had been the two of them, against a world that took delight in punishing and holding back rewards.

Evan glanced over to his left, where Beck and Sampson rode together, silent. He believed he'd spoken quietly enough with Ethan that they couldn't hear him, but it hardly mattered. They were allies of a sort, or what the law would call *confederates,* but Evan never thought of them as friends.

Ethan aside, he wasn't sure he'd ever had one.

Beck and Sampson would be spooked over Dick Eyler, but he figured it would pass, given sufficient time. If Frain was wrong, and one or both of them decided that he had to leave the gang, Evan knew he could live with that.

But what of Abaddon?

This was the first time Evan and his brother had invited anyone to share their ghost town, ride along its dusty street and prowl its empty buildings. Frain thought Beck and Sampson should feel honored, in a way, though maybe that was stretching it.

Still, if they chose to split the gang, could he allow them to ride off with his most precious secret tucked under their hats?

The thought disturbed him.

"We can send them packing now, if you'd prefer," his twin said, as if reading Evan's mind.

"Not yet," Evan replied. "Give it a chance."

"Okay. Suits me."

As always, they were in accord. Of course, they'd had their rows like any pair of brothers, but the arguments had never driven any kind of wedge between them. Money, women, or the next stop in their long, strange travels. None of it meant more than blood.

Meaning the blood they *shared,* and not the blood they'd *spilled.*

Evan had every confidence there would be more of that. The law was after them and meant to make it stick, this time, regardless of the cost. The brothers needed to consider their alternatives, maybe start looking for a place where they could start over. Someplace where everything was new, but they'd fit in all right, with their white skins and native tongue.

Out of the blue, he asked Ethan, "What do you think about Australia?"

The women bothered Slade. He pictured buzzards circling over them and dropping lower, lower, until they were squatting on the ground beside the coach, and he nearly turned around. Almost rode back to do the burying.

Almost.

Slade *almost* wished the Frains were on their way to Mexico, where he was barred from following, instead of heading north for no good reason he could think of. With an ironclad boundary between them, Slade could double back and ease his conscience with a bit of spadework.

Maybe later, he consoled himself.

When he and Hec had settled with the Frains and their companions, Slade could double back and do the decent thing. It would be ugly work, but he could stand it.

Or, he might return and find it done by someone following the stage route.

That is, if he managed to return at all.

Stop that, he thought, stern-faced.

"Something the matter, other than this whole damn thing?" Hec asked.

"Just thinking," Slade replied.

"That's how you get in trouble out here, underneath an empty sky."

"How's that?"

"Well, first you start in worrying about some problem. Take your pick. Gnaw at it long enough, it starts to make you think you've got *more* problems, and it goes from there. First thing you know, your whole life looks like someone played a nasty trick on you the minute after you were born."

"It's not that bad," said Slade.

"Just give it time. Your brain's a cannibal, I tell you. Give it half a chance and it'll eat you up alive."

Slade had to smile at that, which made him wonder when he'd smiled last.

On the farmhouse porch, with Faith.

And instantly, his mind skipped to another image of her, home alone, surprised to see the Frains and their leering companions in her dooryard.

"See?" Hec interrupted him. "It's gnawing at you. I can see it."

"Maybe."

"Uh-huh. Well, maybe I can cheer you up a bit."

"How's that?" asked Slade.

Hec pointed north, in the direction they were headed. "Take a look," he said.

Slade saw the scrap of paper, then, caught on a small, dead-looking bush. And some yards farther on, another, breeze-tossed. If he squinted . . .

"What in hell?"

"Somebody's careless," Daltry said. "Or maybe *they* got started thinking and the brain took over. Sprucing up the trail a bit."

"There's writing on it," Slade observed.

He reined his gelding to a halt, dismounted, and retrieved the bit of paper.

"Make that printing. Parts of words, torn through. A page number. Looks like some kind of legal paper."

Hec received the clue, examined it, and passed it back to Slade. "No point collectin' all of 'em," he said. "Let's just be thankful for the help."

Slade let the paper fly and remounted his roan.

"I'm grateful," he told Daltry. "Fact is, I can't wait to deliver my thank-you in person."

"Australia?" Ethan echoed. "Where's that coming from?"

"I read about it. Some old magazine they had at Huntsville."

"Well, I'd have to say I've never given it one bit of thought," Ethan replied.

"We ought to think about it," Evan said.

"Why's that?"

"For one thing, its about the same size as the U.S.A., but with a lot less people. Ranchers, mostly, and some miners, putting all their money into nice, fat banks, in towns scattered along the coast. Inland, it's like another world. Wide-open spaces, no damn law to speak of, and the strangest animals you ever saw."

"You plan on *working* there," said Ethan.

"And they all speak English," Evan added. "Well, except their version of the Indians, I guess. Who, in Australia, happen to be black."

"Just pack it up and . . . what? Sail over there?"

"A ship would be required, it's true," said Evan.

"What if I get seasick?"

"Then, you puke and shrug it off, same as a hangover."

"Australia."

"It's a thought."

"Who's in charge?"

"The queen of England, since you ask. Of course, she's sitting back in London, so we likely wouldn't meet her."

"I expect not. What's so strange about their animals?"

"They've got one like a giant rabbit with a gator's tail, that hops all over. Some live up in trees. Some kind of beaver with a duck's bill."

"Now you're lying."

"Nope. I swear to God. And it lays eggs."

"My ass!"

"See for yourself, when we get over there."

"You have it all planned out, do you?"

"Food for thought, is all."

"How far away is it?" asked Ethan.

"From the dock in California, right around eight thousand miles."

"And water all the way."

"Sailing, not swimming. I imagine there'd be other stops, for food and such."

"Sea monsters."

"Well . . ."

"You never know, right?"

"None were mentioned in the bit I read," Evan replied.

"They wouldn't be, I guess. Not if they're wanting people to sail over there. You need some kind of paperwork to settle in another country?"

"Not from this end," Evan said. "Get to the other side, hell, you can be most anyone you want to."

"How about myself?"

"Until the posters catch up with you, anyway."

"You understand we're heading the wrong way for California."

"It occurred to me."

"So, should we turn around?"

"Not yet," Evan replied. "I want another look at Abaddon before we go. Tie up loose ends."

"Find out if anyone's still tracking us?"

"That, too," Evan agreed.

"Nobody's trailed us back to Abaddon since that first time," Ethan observed. "You don't think that'll ruin it?"

"Won't matter, if we're leaving anyway."

Ethan considered that and nodded. "Still," he said, "give up all this?"

Evan laughed first, then both of them together, spooking Beck and Sampson with the sound of it. After the moment passed, they settled back again to ride in silence, Evan picking out a red-tailed hawk that soared above them, riding updrafts in its endless search for prey.

"Wish I could fly, sometimes," he said.

"Off to Australia?" asked his brother.

"Somewhere. Anywhere. This shit gets old."

"It does," Ethan agreed. "But what else are we fit to do? You want to be a doctor, now? Maybe a banker or a preacher? Go on back to school and learn a trade?"

"I've got a trade," Evan replied. "But one day soon, it's gonna be the death of me. Of us."

"You should've poked that redhead from the stagecoach when you had the chance," Ethan opined. "It might've cheered you up."

"Next one we run across," said Evan, "I

might take you up on that. Meanwhile, we need to plan the party."

"Party?"

"For whoever follows us to Abaddon."

Creed Sampson wasn't normally a worrier. He'd hold a grudge, damn straight, but looking down the road and fretting over what might happen next had never been his style. He lived from day to day and generally got along all right.

But he was worried now.

The twins were acting strange, to say the least. Their huddled talk about some stupid ghost town put him off, without even considering Dick Eyler. Ethan Frain had shot him from the saddle without warning, and for what? Gunning a man the brothers planned to kill, regardless?

Now, Sampson and Jimmy Beck were walking on eggshells, thinking that some idle gesture or word could set the brothers off again. The gang was being whittled down, and Sampson knew damn well the twins would look out for each other first.

Why not?

He understood the pull of blood and family. Sampson had lost two brothers of his own, riding the outlaw trail. They'd been a miserable pair of bastards, but he missed them every now and then, when there was nothing else to do or think about.

Not now, when he was focused squarely on survival.

For a start, he didn't like the whole ghost town idea. Creed Sampson wasn't superstitious, but he figured, why tempt Fate? If such a thing as ghosts existed, anyone with brains would let them rest in peace, not poke around their graves or places where they used to live when they were flesh and blood.

He wanted out, but that was problematical. The Frains pretended anyone was free to come and go at any time, but did they *mean* it? Or would Sampson wind up like Dick Eyler, if he tried?

One thing Sampson promised himself. If he went out that way, it wouldn't be without a fight. Maybe take one or both twins with him in a cloud of gun smoke.

What he *wouldn't* do was be a sucker, let his guard down, so the twins could take him by surprise. It might mean losing sleep, until he saw a chance to slip away, but Sampson didn't mind that. Sleepless nights were nothing new to him.

But now he wondered what to do with Jimmy Beck. They weren't the best of friends, but Beck had never ragged him with any of the half-breed crap Tom Dahlquist liked to toss around for personal amusement. Sampson couldn't rightly say that he and Beck were friends, but it could make things easier if he and Jimmy left the gang together.

One more gun against the Frains, if anything went wrong.

They'd have to talk about that soon. And cautiously. The sharp-eared twins had overheard the last time he and Beck were speaking privately. Before they started shooting their own men.

Sampson would have to take it nice and easy, watch his back and every other side until he knew if Beck was with him, or preferred to hang around and take his chances with the Frains.

Sampson had made his choice.

Facing the law was one thing. It was normal, part of doing business. But he hated never knowing if the shot that killed him would be fired by someone he was riding with, someone who was supposed to do his thinking for him.

It was giving him a headache, so he focused on the trail, letting his eyes drift over toward the twins from time to time. Watching their hands and faces.

Looking out for number one.

■ ■ ■ ■

"I still can't fathom why they're heading north," Hec Daltry said. "Nothing but trouble for them, up in Kansas. It was me, I woulda turned back toward New Mexico. Ride long and hard to make the Rio Grande."

"Makes sense," Slade said. "They're after something."

"Hey, you don't suppose they've stashed something away, to see them through hard times?"

"You mean, like buried treasure?"

"Stranger things have happened," Daltry said.

"There's nothing on their posters about any missing fortune," Slade replied.

"So, what? They wouldn't have to steal it all at once, would they? Lay by a little here, a little there. It adds up, over time."

Slade shrugged. "I can't say that you're wrong. From what I've heard about the Frains, though, they don't strike me as the kind who'd start a pension fund."

"Swipe it and spend it. More that kind of thing?"

"That's my guess," Slade agreed.

"Which brings us back to why they're

heading north."

"North*east*," Slade said, gently correcting him. "Could be as simple as a fear of being caught or shot on sight, if they went back through Texas."

"That's a thought," Hec said. "Them Texans do love to nurse a grievance. Rangers down there like to shoot first and forget about the questions, afterward."

"Maybe they'll go ahead and kill each other off before we find them," Slade suggested.

"Wouldn't that be nice?"

"Just wishful thinking," Slade replied.

"No harm in that. I heard about a gang once, in Missouri, got to fighting over money and they wound up killing one another. Four or five of 'em, I think it was. Somewhere around Aurora. Come to think of it, there were some brothers in on that deal, too."

"Blood's supposed to be thicker than water."

"I've heard that. But you know what's often thicker?"

"Money," Slade suggested.

"That's the ticket. Once some people get a whiff of the almighty dollar, ever'thing else goes out with the bathwater."

"It's a weakness we could use against

them," Slade suggested, "if we had something they want."

"Big *if*," Hec said. "They don't have any kinfolk on the record. No place they call home. No friends outside the gang, as far as I can tell."

"And now, they're killing those."

"Maybe there's justice, after all. You ever read the Bible, Jack?"

"It's been a while," Slade answered, understating it.

"There's something in the first part — up around Leviticus or Deuteronomy, I want to say — about a curse that made some parents eat their young'uns. Like some kind of punishment for sin."

"Sounds odd," Slade said, remembering why he had given up on holy writ.

"Or maybe it was Lamentations. Anyhow, my point is, something like that could've happened to the Frains."

"You think they're turning cannibal?"

"I think they're turning on their own," Hec said. "Some men, they get that rot inside 'em, and they're barely human by the time they finish. Like the Harpes."

"That name's familiar," Slade acknowledged.

"Long before our time, it was. Brothers or cousins, I'm not sure. They started robbing travelers and killing them, gutting the bodies, weighting them with stones, and hiding them in rivers."

"Wonderful."

"Before too long, they got a taste for it, you see? Killed their own women and their children. Some of 'em, at least."

"Too bad we can't sit back and let the twins do our work for us," Slade said.

"Too bad, is right. I'm getting saddle sore."

"Don't give up yet, old-timer."

"Oh, we'll see who goes the distance, youngster," Hec replied. "Five dollars says I bag the next one."

"You're on," Slade said, as afternoon's long shadows sprawled across their trail. "Five it is."

13

They passed another homestead in late afternoon, smoke curling from the chimney and a cool breeze carrying the scent of roasting meat. Evan considered stopping in to share the grub and any women they might find around the place, but when they got a little closer, he saw three men in the yard, watching some horses trot around inside of their corral.

Frain couldn't hear what they were saying from two hundred yards away, but he could tell when they *stopped* talking, three heads swiveling around in unison to watch the unfamiliar riders pass. He saw no guns, but guessed there would be some inside the house, an easy jog of thirty feet or so from where the farmers stood.

"I wouldn't bother," Ethan said, riding along beside him.

"No."

It wouldn't be the same as last time. They

were two men short, almost an even match, assuming there were no more men inside the house or barn. Most likely, they'd be riding into gun sights all the way, as likely to be blasted from their saddles as to be invited for a sit-down meal.

"It's being smart, not being scared," Ethan reminded him.

"I know."

"Might be a waste of time we can't afford."

"I hear you," Evan said.

He glanced at Beck and Sampson, found them studying the farm in silence, neither looking keen for an adventure at the moment.

"Passing by," he told them, without asking their opinions.

"Just as well," Sampson replied.

"Screw 'em," said Beck.

A short time later, when the farm had dwindled at their backs, the occupants presumably returning to their normal chores, Evan said, "I think we're losing them."

"Who, Creed and Jimmy?" Ethan asked.

"The very same."

"They haven't gotten over Dick, yet. Give them time."

"We don't have much to spare."

"Is this about Australia?"

"It's about our getting out and going *anywhere*," said Evan. "We can't hide the fact we're brothers, but we should consider separating from our known associates. Too many poster faces in one place."

"When did you want to break the news?"

"No rush," Evan replied. "May as well wait until we get to Abaddon."

A sudden whirring in the grass made both their horses shy. Behind them, Sampson's sorrel nearly bolted. Jimmy Beck's tobiano reared, squealing, and pitched him over backward to the ground.

"Rattler!" Creed warned, unnecessarily. He fired his Colt at something in the grass, then once again before the angry whirring stopped.

Beck scrambled to his feet, putting more space between himself and the dead snake. His face was blanched, as if he'd seen a ghost — or glimpsed his own mortality. He dusted off as best he could, then whistled for his horse.

The tobiano came back limping, favoring its right foreleg. Beck grabbed the reins, then crouched beside the animal, examining its leg.

"Goddamned thing bit him," he announced. "The leg's already swelling."

"That's unfortunate," Evan remarked.

"God*damn* it!"

Striding over to the lifeless rattlesnake, Beck stamped it with a boot until the grass was muddy crimson.

"Better save some of that energy for walking," Ethan told him.

Jimmy gaped at him. "Walking?"

"Your horse is snakebit," Evan said. "It's finished. Even if we had a vet out here, he'd only put it down."

"Uh-huh. Well, would you tell me where in hell I's s'posed to walk from here?" Beck asked.

"You're free to tag along with us, as long as you don't slow us down."

"That's funny," Beck replied, without a smile.

"Come one and double up with me," said Sampson. "You can bring your rifle and canteen, but leave the rest."

"Jesus! No saddle, even if we find another horse?"

"I'm stretching it to carry you," Sampson replied.

"We're wasting time," Evan observed.

"All right, for Christ's sake! Wait a minute, will you?"

Beck retrieved his canteen and his Winchester, then paused to stroke the tobiano's neck. The horse wheezed at him, not quite whickering.

"He feels the poison," Ethan said. "You need to finish it."

"I'm gettin' to it," Beck replied and drew his Colt.

"Just three, this time," said Daltry, as the echo of a gunshot reached their ears.

"How many does it take?" Slade asked.

"You think they're still thinning the herd?"

"I won't complain about it, if they are."

Three shots, and from the sound of it, Slade guessed they had been fired four miles or so ahead of them. Sounds carried over flat land, but he found it difficult to gauge the distance.

"Maybe we can find it while it's still warm," Hec suggested.

"It?"

"Or him. Whichever."

Maybe *them.* Three well-placed shots would leave the twins alone.

Slade urged his roan back to a trotting pace. "I guess they could be hunting."

"Maybe. Split a jackrabbit four ways, it ain't much of a feast."

"We don't know how they're fixed for grub."

"That's true. Maybe they bagged an appetizer," Hec suggested.

"Which reminds me that we've had nothing since breakfast," Slade replied.

"Tell you the truth, that whole thing with the stagecoach put me off my jerky."

"Yeah."

But Slade's stomach was growling now, reminding him that life went on and needed feeding. He considered reining in to rummage through his saddlebag, then shrugged it off.

Priorities.

Their first and most important job was running down the Frains, Sampson, and Beck — if all of them were still alive. Reduction of the gang made the survivors no less dangerous. If anything, they might be more inclined to bloodshed now, if dwindling numbers threatened their security.

Slade didn't think the Frains were hunting. Not for rabbits, anyway. He was embarrassed by his private thoughts, but . . .

If the gang had found more victims — stopped off at another lonely farm to sate their appetites, for instance — then the lone shot could have been a person dying. And if there was looting to be done, or some other diversion from the weary trail, it might give Slade and Daltry time to overtake the gang.

Catch them red-handed, as it were, and finish it.

Or try to.

Slade knew that the odds were still against them, two to one. But with surprise on their side, and a willingness to strike the first blow, he believed those odds were beatable.

In fact, Slade was prepared to bet his life on it.

"Smell something on the wind?" Hec asked, urging his gray to match the pace Slade set.

"I hope to," Slade replied.

"There's nothin' wrong with that, you know. Wanting to catch them any way you can."

"It feels wrong."

"Feelings pass," Hec said.

"I hope so."

"Trust me on it."

"If we find them —"

"*When,* not *if,*" Daltry corrected him.

"Okay, then. *When* we find them, no mistakes. No holding back."

"No quarter?" Hec inquired.

"That's up to them," Slade said.

"Sounds fair to me."

Fair's got nothing to do with it, Slade thought.

The killing had to stop, even if killing was

the only way to get it done.

Slade put the moral question out of mind and focused on his roan, riding the echo of a gunshot down the wind.

Creed Sampson's sorrel couldn't move as quickly with two riders, slowing even though it didn't show the strain. Afraid of being stranded if he pushed the horse too hard, too quickly, Sampson held it to a pace somewhere between a walk and trot, letting the twins increase their lead to fifty yards or so.

"Think they can hear us now?" Beck asked him, barely whispering at Sampson's shoulder.

"Don't see how they could," Sampson replied.

"I think they mean to dump us."

"Why would they do that?"

"Hell, why do they do *anything?*" Beck asked. "It's them against the world. Peas in a pod."

"What's their percentage, getting rid of us?" asked Sampson. "It's not like we have any loot to share."

"Maybe they'd rather travel light."

"What's that supposed to mean?"

"I overheard them talkin'," Beck explained. "Just bits and snatches."

"So?"

"They're thinkin' about goin' to some other country. Austria, I think they said."

"Where's that?"

"The hell should I know? Far enough they need a sailin' ship."

"That's all you heard?"

"Some crap about a beaver layin' eggs," Beck said.

"Hell, now I *know* you're crazy."

"Think so? Why not ask them, then?"

"And say what? That you eavesdropped on 'em, and it made me curious?"

"No, Jesus! Don't say that!"

"Well, then."

"Look, it doesn't matter *where* they're goin'," Beck said. "What I care about is bein' left behind."

"I thought you'd want to get away from them, by now."

"I mean left in a hole, to rot."

"No reason they should do that." Sampson didn't sound convinced.

"What reason do they need?" Beck asked. "Because they feel like doin' it? Or 'cause they think we might tell someone where they went?"

"How would we know, unless they told us?"

"Crazy people are afraid of ever'thing."

"You think so?" Sampson asked him.

"*I* ain't crazy, damn it! You saw how they dealt with Dick."

"So, what's your plan, then?" Sampson asked. "We can't outrun 'em, riding double."

"No. But we can sure as hell be ready for 'em, if they try somethin'. Watch every move they make and get them first, if it comes down to killin'."

"You're so afraid, why don't you shoot 'em in their sleep?"

"I would, before I let 'em do the same to me — or you."

"You're lookin' out for *me* now, are you?"

"And why not?" Beck challenged, fighting nerves to keep his voice down. "Ain't that how it's s'posed to be? We ride together, helpin' one another. Hell, we took the *Katy Flier* down for Evan, Dick included. Does he give a damn?"

"I don't know what he cares about," Sampson replied. "But what I *do* know is, he's fast. Both of 'em are. We ever try to get the jump on 'em, we damn sure better do it right the first time. There won't be no second chance."

"That's all I'm sayin'. Keep our eyes peeled. If they try to play false with us, then we do it right the first time."

"And if they're straight with us?"

"No problem, then. Why would there be?"

"They might still want to dump us, only not the way you think."

"It's a free country, right? Man wants to split off from his friends, who's gonna tell him he can't go? I just don't want a bullet in the back for a good-bye."

"Can't fault you there," Sampson replied.

"We're good then? If there's trouble?"

"If there's trouble," Sampson echoed. "Good as gold."

They found the tobiano — brown and white, a nice one — lying on its left side, leaking from a bullet hole between its eyes. The right foreleg was swollen up three times its normal size below the knee, deeply discolored around two puncture wounds.

"Snakebite," Hec said.

"It's over here," Slade told him, pointing out a mangled twist of flesh whose blood had stained the grass.

"I'm guessing no spare horse, since they went off and left the tack and saddle.

"Took the rifle, though," Slade noted, nodding toward the empty scabbard on the saddle's off side.

"So, either one of them's afoot or riding double," Daltry said.

"Making him walk would slow them down too much," Slade said.

"Unless the other three rode off and left him."

"In which case," Slade replied, "he could be anywhere."

"Pick a direction. Wander off. We'd never know the difference."

Hec scouted the perimeter, using the horse and snake as starting points. At last, he said, "No walking tracks lead off from here, that I can see. O' course, that doesn't mean he *didn't* walk. Just means that I can't spot the trail."

"If he's walking," Slade said, "then it's Beck or Sampson. Neither Frain would leave his brother."

"And we've lost him. If he's walking."

"So, we focus on the twins. They've been the bull's-eye on the target all along."

"Them, and whoever's left," Hec said.

"That's it."

"Just go on, hoping that we haven't missed one. Or that if we have, he stumbles off a cliff before he kills somebody else."

"Maybe he'll meet another rattler," Slade suggested.

"You're just saying that to cheer me up."

"Our other option is to split up," Slade replied. "One of us chase the brothers and their sidekick, while the other tries to find the one who got away."

"Without a trail, that could be tricky."

"Just what I was thinking."

"If we catch up to them —"

"When," Slade said.

"Right. *When* we catch up to 'em, if they're one short, we can ask 'em where he went."

If anyone can talk, Slade thought but kept it to himself.

"Nothing you want to check about the horse, before we go?" Hec asked.

"Like what?"

A shrug. "Maybe go through the saddle-bags for evidence."

"Of what? I wouldn't know what I was looking for."

"Me, neither. Anyway, if all the murder charges ain't enough to hold 'em, I don't want to bother with somebody's stolen watch and chain."

"Speaking of which . . ."

Slade checked his own watch. Fifty minutes had elapsed since the last gunshots reached their ears, the time it took to cover four miles at a combination walk and trot, to spare the horses.

"How we doing?" Daltry asked.

"If they were riding hard, they could've

covered fifteen, maybe twenty miles."

"Shave five off that, if they've got one horse doubled up."

"So, ten to fifteen, then," Slade said.

"We're close, damn it!"

"So's nightfall. What, another hour?"

"More or less. Let's use the light we have, and see what happens."

"Right."

A moment later, they were riding north, pushing their horses for the extra speed required to overtake their quarry. At the same time, Slade kept one eye on the setting sun and tried to stay alert for likely ambush sites ahead. He didn't trust the Frains as far as he could throw them both, together, and he hadn't even glimpsed them yet.

But soon, perhaps.

Please make it soon.

"We gonna camp sometime tonight, or what?" asked Jimmy Beck.

"We are," said Evan Frain.

"Maybe before my ass gives out," Beck muttered, hearing Sampson give a huffing little laugh.

"Your ass is wearin' out my horse," the half-breed answered, not quite whispering.

"Well, 'scuse me all to hell."

"We've got some scrub brush coming up," said Ethan Frain. "Could mean a spring."

"Looks good," his brother granted. "Even lets us have a bit of cover."

"Reckon we could light a fire?" Beck asked. "You want us standin' watch, some coffee wouldn't go amiss."

"Coffee for Mr. Beck," one of the twins replied. "Why not?"

"You think we're clear, then?" Sampson asked. "Nobody trailin' us?"

"Clear as we'll be, at least, until we get to Abaddon," one or the other said, not turning so that Sampson could tell which one spoke.

Even their voices were the same. Sampson could close his eyes while they were talking, and it sounded like a crazy person asking questions of himself, then answering.

They reached the scrub a moment later, Ethan craning from his saddle, off to one side, pointing as he said, "There's water, like I thought."

The horses smelled it; Sampson's sorrel turned toward the little spring that burbled from a cleft between two mossy stones, until he pulled back on the reins.

"We'll camp here," Evan Frain confirmed. "Jimmy, you want to stretch your legs, go on and scout around for firewood."

"Hallelujah!" Beck replied, under his breath, as he dismounted with grunt of pain.

"To play it safe, we ought to leave the horses saddled," Ethan said. "Go on and wipe them down, if you've a mind to, but be sure to saddle up again before you hit the hay."

"So much for bein' clear," Beck hissed at Sampson, then moved off to search for kindling.

Sampson took Ethan's advice, unsaddling his mount and wiping off its sweaty back before he led it to the spring and let it drink. He'd graze the roan awhile before re-saddling it and keep his fingers crossed that there'd be no need to skedaddle in the middle of the night.

"Why risk a fire," he asked the brothers, "if you think there's someone tailing us?"

The twins exchanged a glance before Evan replied. "We won't be vexed," he said, "or let them see us running scared. If they control your actions, then you might as well be sitting in a cell."

"I guess," said Sampson, not convinced.

"Look at it this way," Ethan told him. "Your demeanor is what most folk judge you by. If we're running and hiding, then it tells the lawmen we're afraid."

"We *are* running," Sampson reminded him.

"No, sir!" Evan cut in. "We're on the same course we've been following since you all got me off the *Katy Flier*. But for stopping to refresh ourselves, we haven't deviated by a mile."

"If someone's after us," Ethan went on, "remember that we're *leading,* and they're *following.* If they catch up to us, they're going to regret it."

"Seems to me that didn't work so well, the first time," Sampson said.

"We scorched their fingers," Evan answered. "Never doubt it. And we cut some deadwood, in the bargain."

Meaning Dahlquist. Sampson frowned and bit his tongue.

"You're worried they might take us, next time," Ethan said.

"It crossed me mind, sure."

"Well, what of it?"

Sampson must have looked confused, for Ethan jumped in, asking him, "Would you prefer to die fighting, under a clear blue sky, or do the air dance on some judge's rope?"

"My preference is not to die at all," Sampson replied.

"Good luck with that," Evan replied, and both twins laughed.

"I mean to say, I'd rather put it off as long as possible."

"Us, too," said Ethan. "Now, let's see if we can stay alive *and* hang on to our pride. How's that?"

"How's what?" asked Jimmy Beck, returning with a load of sticks and smaller kindling.

"Jimmy, boy," said Evan, with a smile. "You're just in time."

"Is that a fire I see?" Hec asked.

In truth, it looked more like a spark than any kind of steady flame. It flickered, seemed to disappear, but then came back again. A speck of light, no bigger than a firefly and as insubstantial in the vast darkness.

"You think they'd be that stupid?" Slade replied.

"Stupid, or clever? Maybe hoping it'll draw us in."

"Another setup."

"That'd be my guess," Hec said. "Unless it's someone else entirely."

That was also possible, Slade knew. Across the Oklahoma Territory, he supposed there must be people camped out every night, trusting a fire to keep them warm and hold the terrors of the dark at bay. They might succeed in warding off four-legged predators, but firelight only beckoned the two-legged kind.

An open fire hinted at hot food, maybe coffee. More important, an individual or group with no walls to protect them from attack. Bad men could charm their way into a camp or lie back in the dark and snipe at targets cast in silhouette.

"We have to go and see," Slade said.

"No doubt."

"You reckon it's a mile off?"

"Hard to say, without knowing how big the fire is. Could be more," Hec said.

"So, nice and easy, then."

Aside from rattlesnakes and burrows that could snap a horse's fetlock, gullies that could force them miles off course, they had to worry about noise and maybe even scent. A camper with a keen nose, if it wasn't spoiled by wood smoke, might smell sweaty men and horses coming, if the wind was right. A whinny at the wrong time might draw gunfire from the camp, even if those huddled around the fire were not the Frains.

"Before we get too close and have to hush," Hec said, "how do you want to play it?"

"Go in nice and quiet," Slade replied. "If we can make out faces, we'll know whether it's the men we want. No point disturbing anyone, unless it's them."

"And if it is?"

That was the crux of it. If they had found the gang they sought, should Slade and Daltry sacrifice the slim advantage of surprise by calling for the outlaws to surrender?

Why not simply gun them down?

"See how it feels, when we get in there," Slade replied. "I like a plan that's flexible."

"Suits me," Hec said. "But if we call 'em and they come up shooting, we could wind up losing 'em again."

"Hold steady on a target while you make the call out," Slade suggested.

"Starting with the twins?"

"Seems right. Cut off the head, the snake dies."

"Two-headed snake," Hec said.

"Two bullets," Slade replied.

"Still leaves two shooters."

"Long as they don't make it to their horses," Slade told Daltry, "we should be all right."

14

When they were still a hundred yards out from the fire, Slade and Daltry split up. Hec rode off to the east, circling slowly around to come in on the camp's northeast side, while Slade took his time closing the gap from due south.

Hec had the longer trip to make, by half, while Slade was forced to drag his heels, creeping along to give his partner extra time. It grated on his nerves, but he took deep breaths to relax himself and ease the nervous flutter in his stomach.

It was almost killing time.

For all his talk with Daltry, Slade didn't believe the Frains or their companions would surrender. And why should they? They had all served jail time and presumably disliked it, but a noose was waiting for them this time, guaranteed. Surrender was equivalent to suicide.

On top of that, they'd rescued Evan Frain

from custody while he was on his way to Leavenworth, then shot up Slade's posse from Amity. The gang was on a winning streak.

Which ends tonight, Slade told himself. *Right here.*

At least, he hoped so.

Splitting up with Daltry made the job more difficult. Without some kind of signal, Slade would never know if Hec had reached his post, ready to pin the outlaws in a crossfire. So they *had* to give the gang a warning call, which fell to Hec. His shout would be a double message, telling Slade that he was in position, even as he gave the hunted men one final chance to live a little longer.

Or, would he just cut loose from ambush? Maybe let his Winchester speak for him?

Slade planned to be ready, either way.

That meant leaving his roan behind, when he was still some fifty yards out from the ring of firelight. Slade trusted the gelding to stay put and graze, without any unnecessary noise, but anything could happen if a rattler or coyote came along. Even a swooping owl could spook the horse and warn his enemies of Slade's approach.

All he could do, from that point on, was watch his step, try to avoid making unwanted sounds himself. Identify his targets if he could, and back off if they'd stumbled on somebody else's camp. The worst outcome that Slade could think of would be Hec surprising total strangers, spooking them to reach for guns and open fire without waiting to find out who the prowler was.

Just take it easy, Slade thought. *One step at a time.*

At thirty yards, Slade heard male voices, but he couldn't recognize them, since he'd never heard the Frains or any of their side pals speak. Faces were something else, and when he'd cleared another twenty feet or so, Slade saw one of the twins in profile, talking to a blond who must be Jimmy Beck.

All right, then. No mistake.

Slade thumbed back his Winchester's hammer and crept toward the fire, counting heads.

Three men visible.

Where was the fourth?

Creed Sampson had first watch. The others weren't asleep yet, but he didn't mind leaving their circle to patrol the night alone. He needed a break from watching the twins and wondering if they were plotting his death in the night, or tomorrow.

It wouldn't be hard to surprise them, he thought. Even now, with the pair of them

261

still wide awake, he could drop one before they suspected a thing, duck and roll in the dark, likely pick off the second without getting hit by return fire.

Or not.

As they'd found out the day before yesterday, planning an ambush was one thing, but pulling it off was another. With two-to-one odds and Beck in his way, Sampson wasn't convinced he could do it.

Besides, it might all be for nothing.

Sure, Ethan had blasted Dick Eyler for shooting that guy from the stage against orders, but that didn't mean he was planning to drill Beck or Sampson. It proved that the twins had bad tempers, but what else was new?

Hell, who didn't, in Creed Sampson's world?

So, he'd wait. Not be hasty about starting something the brothers might finish. Pretend he was sleeping tonight, if his nerves were on edge, and be ready for trouble without causing any.

And watch Jimmy Beck.

Beck was edgy, and then some, convinced that the twins meant to plug him the first chance they got. But they'd had plenty of chances, already, and Beck was still breathing.

So far.

If Beck went off his chump and drew down on the brothers, what then? They could probably take him, between them, but would they be watching for Sampson's reaction?

Hell, yes.

So, he had to decide how he'd play it, in that case. Jump in on one side or the other? Or sit back and watch it play out?

If he sided with Beck, they could both die together.

Just watching the play would raise doubts with whichever side won.

No, backing the Frains was the smart way to go.

Sorry, Jimmy, he thought. *Just be smart, for a change.*

Sampson craned his head back for a look at the stars — and then froze.

What's that noise?

Maybe nothing. A scuttling field mouse or a breeze in the grass. Their own horses beyond the firelight, cropping grass, breaking wind.

Check it anyway. Just to be sure.

Taking care to make no sound himself, Sampson turned and retraced his slow steps through the darkness.

■ ■ ■ ■

Hec Daltry took a while to make his circuit of the camp, walking his horse over the final hundred yards or so to keep it nice and quiet. Even so, he scuffed his boots against a stone or two and had to stop himself from cursing his own clumsiness.

I'm getting too damned old for this, he thought. Not for the first time, either, but he'd spent the best part of his life behind a badge. What was a man supposed to do when he was getting on in years, and all he'd ever mastered was the art of hunting other men?

Hec knew a few lawmen who gave it up, but none of them seemed happy in retirement. They were either crotchety and mean or drank to take the edge off. One he knew had tried to peddle his life story, or a puffed up version of it, but he'd found no takers.

After all, he wasn't Wyatt Earp.

Hec sniffed the breeze to find out what the campers had prepared for supper. Beans and coffee, by the smell of it, perhaps with just enough salt pork to add a hint of flavor.

Living on the run discouraged any gourmet tendencies.

Hec made a mental note to stay upwind

from this bunch, riding back to Enid, but he guessed that wouldn't be a problem. If they didn't try to fight and force the issue, he would be amazed.

When he could pick out voices from the camp, Hec left his gray with a soft word and moved on by himself. The Winchester felt heavy in his hands, a little thing he'd noticed more than once when he expected to be using it on men who hoped to see him dead.

Hec had been lucky, so far, killing only half a dozen men who really needed it and suffering no major wounds himself. Each time he faced a gunman, though, he knew it could go either way.

And this time there were four.

But not around the fire.

His first glimpse of the little camp showed three men seated in a semicircle. Two of them were obviously twins, which told him that he'd found the right bunch, after all. The third had sandy hair and wore his pistol on the left, which made him Beck.

Which left —

The bullet struck Hec Daltry like a mule's kick, in the back, and sent him sprawling. As he hit the ground, a gunshot echoed in his ears.

You never hear the shot that kills you.

Who in hell said that?

Despite the pain that savaged him, Hec's ears were working fine. Which meant that he was still alive.

But could he move, to help himself?

To help Jack Slade?

The shot caused Slade to flinch involuntarily. Down range, the Frains and Jimmy Beck leaped to their feet, reaching for guns.

Where's Hec? Slade asked himself. *Where's Sampson?*

At the moment, Slade had no spare time for mysteries.

Down range, one of the twins had kicked the coffeepot, which spilled and doused most of the fire, plunging the campsite into darkness. Horses neighed and whinnied on the far side of the camp, away from Slade, as shadows in the form of men ran helter-skelter, snatching at their gear.

Slade chose a target, fired, and saw the figure lurch, then drop to hands and knees. He pumped the rifle's lever-action without lifting off its sights and was about to put the crouching figure down when pistols opened up on him.

Diving for cover, Slade couldn't be sure if there were two or three guns rapid-firing from the camp. He glimpsed their muzzle flashes but had no spare time for counting. Bullets sliced the air around him, as he flattened to provide the smallest target possible.

Good news: his adversaries had been staring at their campfire when the shooting started, which would hamper their night vision.

Bad news: Slade was outnumbered, had no clear-cut targets, didn't know where Daltry was — or even if he was alive.

The first shot, he was sure, had come from somewhere off beyond the camp, roughly where he'd expected Daltry to appear. Not fired *into* the camp, as if Hec had decided to attack without warning, but somewhere in the night *behind* it.

Daltry? Sampson?

From where he lay, Slade couldn't even see the man he'd wounded — if, in fact, his target hadn't simply tripped and fallen in the rush to get away. The gunfire aimed his way had ended, for the moment, and he took advantage of the lull to scrabble belly down to seek a better vantage point.

Another moment, and the ground beneath him changed from grass to gravel, gouging at his knees and elbows, grating on his belt buckle. Slade paused, fearing the noise would give him up, but no one seemed to notice.

More noise from the horses, but he couldn't venture to interpret it. The only thing Slade knew for sure was that his enemies had gained a lead after they pinned him down.

But he was not prepared to let them ride away.

Evan Frain emptied one Colt, then jammed it back into its holster while he drew another from his belt. Firing while he retreated, he could see no movement in the dark beyond their campsite, but his eyes hadn't recovered yet from sitting near the fire.

Stupid!

If he had thought that they were being closely followed, he'd have built a decoy fire and let the others gripe about another cold camp to their hearts' content. Sit waiting through the night, with dummies in their bedrolls, until hunters loomed out of the darkness and were slain.

He'd put a man on watch before they even tried to sleep, but clearly, that had not been good enough.

The first shot, Frain supposed, could have been Sampson dealing with another rattler, but there'd been no time for calling back and forth with questions when it happened. They'd been up and moving, pure reflex, and then a *second* shot had sounded, that one from a different direction.

There was no way to mistake the ambush, then.

No time for anything but up and out of there, as fast as possible, before a bullet from the shadows brought him down.

Frain didn't know how many hunters might be hiding in the dark. He'd seen one muzzle flash and fired back at it, but there had to be at least two guns outside the camp — one south, and one roughly northwest.

That left the horses clear, unless they were surrounded. If their adversaries had a man or men watching the horses, this could be the end of everything.

In which case, Evan meant to go down fighting, give the bastards something to remember.

They would get it wrong, of course, and tout themselves as heroes when the booze was flowing, but it wouldn't matter. Frain would not be there to call them liars, slap their faces, call them out into the street.

He would be worm bait, gone but not forgotten.

Evan reached the horses, grabbed his dun mare's reins, and felt his brother jostle past him, lunging toward his bay.

"Where's Jimmy?" Ethan asked.

"Gut-shot, I'm pretty sure."

"And Creed?"

"Don't know. We can't wait for him."

"Shit!"

Jamming the spare Colt underneath his belt, in back, Evan untied his mare and sprang into the saddle. Seconds later, Ethan was aboard his mount, cursing the stirrup he had missed on his first try.

A rifle shot rang out behind them, from the camp, and Evan heard the bullet hum past, somewhere to his left.

"Come on!" he snapped. "Ride while we can, goddamn it!"

Hec Daltry wasn't crippled. Not exactly.

He could feel his legs, beyond the pain that radiated from his back wound, but when Hec tried standing up, they only twitched and pawed the turf.

He'd fallen facedown, landing with his right arm bent beneath him and his left outflung, like he was waving his farewell to a departing friend. The left hand couldn't find his rifle, and he couldn't see it, with his head turned in the opposite direction, left cheek pressed into short grass.

Hec tried to free his right arm and reach

his holstered Colt, but now his torso seemed to weigh a ton. The arm itself seemed fine — at least, its fingers flexed, within their limits — but he'd have to push up with his left to haul it clear.

And at the moment, such exertion seemed to be beyond him.

More than half expecting to be shot again, Hec willed himself to lie immobile, listening for any sounds of movement, while another portion of his brain tried to assess his wound. The deep heart of his pain lay somewhere south of his left shoulder blade, and Daltry's rasping breath told him he had a punctured lung. Beyond that, it was guesswork and a waste of any time that still remained to him.

Dying, he thought.

Or, maybe not.

The fingers of his trapped right hand half-clenched around a lump in Hec's vest pocket. Disoriented as he was, he recognized the shape of his Apache pocket pistol, with its bayonet blade and its knuckle-duster grip folded against the frame.

Maybe.

Slowly, still trying not to tip his shooter that he was alive, Hec wormed his fingers down into the pocket, clasped the little gun, and drew it out, painstaking inch by inch.

He couldn't reach its trigger with the handle folded, but with any luck —

Footsteps.

The man who'd shot him was approaching, finally, to finish it or see how well he'd done with his first bullet. Hec lay still as death, only the fingers of his right hand moving as they fumbled over the Apache pistol, lowered its folded butt, released the trigger, eased the hinged blade free until its sharp point pricked his chest.

And none of that would help him, if the bastard fired again while standing over him. But if he felt an urge to see Hec's face . . .

The footsteps paused beside him, to his right. Hec heard a creak of leather as the gunman crouched, before a large hand gripped his left shoulder and tugged. Rolling him over, so that he could see the stars.

Gritting his teeth against the pain, Hec timed his move, knowing there'd be no second chance. He recognized Creed Sampson from his wanted poster, more or less, but didn't linger on the scowling face.

With all the strength remaining to him, Daltry drove the blade of his Apache pistol into Sampson's abdomen and squeezed the double-action pistol once, twice, three times. He smelled burning cloth and hair before the dying outlaw toppled forward, sprawled across Hec's chest.

Jimmy Beck guessed he was dying. Almost *hoped* he was, in fact, if that was what it took to ease his pain. Gut-shot and leaking in the dirt, beside the remnants of a cooling campfire, he lay weeping, wondering what had become of his six-gun.

And if he found it, would he try to kill the man who'd shot him? Or just use it on himself?

The twins had left him, naturally. Damn them both to Hell, where Beck was likely going, any minute now. He hoped there was some kind of hierarchy in the fiery pit his folks had always warned about. Maybe, if he got there ahead of them, there'd be a way for him to claim seniority and help the devil's imps torment them.

Six or seven thousand years of torture ought to do it.

Jimmy wasn't greedy.

Not much of a planner, either, as it happened.

He had taken off his gunbelt while they sat around the fire and left it with his bedroll, ten or fifteen feet away. They'd had a long day on the trail, and half of it with Jimmy riding double behind Sampson. It felt good to stretch his legs and shed a little weight around his middle.

He could always reach the weapon if he needed it.

Unless somebody shot him, first.

His memory of the event was hazy, drifting in and out on tides of agony, but he recalled a first shot from the darkness somewhere, thinking that it must be Sampson. Then, the twins were up and slapping leather, putting out the fire, while Jimmy bolted for his gun instinctively.

And never made it.

It was almost funny, how a bullet — such a little thing; he'd never really thought about it — could destroy a man completely without even killing him. Beck would've thought that, even gut-shot, he could rise and stagger to the bedroll where he'd left his gun. Bend down or *fall* down to retrieve it, and be ready when his enemies hove into view.

And he could take them, then. If only he could find his gun.

Which way?

Without the fire, he couldn't see a god-damned thing.

Sobbing with pain, leaving a crimson trail behind him, Jimmy Beck began to crawl.

Slade heard the horses galloping away from

him, northbound, and rapid-fired three shots into the darkness, where he thought he'd glimpsed their racing shadows. If he came within a yard of them with any single bullet, Slade supposed that it would be a miracle.

He mouthed a curse and turned back toward the camp, moving as quietly as possible after the thunder of his gunfire. Slade had no idea how many riders had escaped, but there was one he'd find in camp or somewhere near at hand.

The man he'd shot when it all started wasn't going far.

Slade thought about the shot that started everything. A rifle, by the sound of it — but Hec's, or someone else's?

He could call for Hec, of course, but that made him an easy mark for any shooter waiting in the darkness. Better to explore the camp's perimeter, Slade thought, than attract fire from a sniper who might score a lucky hit and put him down.

Slade started circling counterclockwise, seeking the spot where Hec should have been poised for a call to the camp. Every step was nerve-racking, a risk to be taken because he had no other choice.

Slade had to find Daltry and deal with the fourth man in camp, before he went back to find out if the man whom he'd shot was alive. Help a partner and run down an enemy.

All else could wait.

Moments later, Slade found them together. At first, the sight of them confused him. If both men were down, who had stopped off to stack one on top of the other? It made no sense, until Slade realized that he was viewing the result of combat to the death.

He closed the gap with cautious strides, keeping his rifle pointed at the silent heap of flesh before him. One man sprawled across the other, and the one on top could only be Creed Sampson. Long dark hair spilled over Daltry's face beneath him.

Slade prodded the outlaw with his Winchester, got no response, and realized that he'd need both hands to remove the body. Stepping back, he laid the rifle well beyond the reach of either fallen man, then went back to the pile and wrestled Sampson's hulk away from Daltry.

What he saw then, by the faint starlight, caused Slade to mutter, "Jesus, Hec!"

"Not quite," Daltry replied. "I doubt I'm gonna rise again."

15

"God's sake! You're breathing?"

"Now you rolled that side of beef away, I am," Daltry replied.

But there was liquid in his voice, a sucking, rattling sound that set Slade's teeth on edge. The whole left side of Daltry's shirt was stained with blood and dirt.

"Where are you hit?" Slade asked.

"He got me in the back," Hec said, half gasping. "But I think it's through and through."

"I see that. Can you move at all?"

"Don't rightly want to try. Where did you put the heavy bastard?"

"He's right here. Don't worry, Hec. You got him."

Daltry smiled with crimson teeth and said, "You mean to say I took him with me."

"Not a bit of it. You're doing fine."

"My ass. Can't hardly breathe," he gargled. "Hardly move, in fact. That damn

Apache pistol did it for me, though."

Slade glanced again at Sampson's corpse. The little hybrid gun protruded from his abdomen, surrounded by a bloodstain the size of a skillet.

"Yeah, I'd say it did. You want something to raise your head a bit? Might ease your breathing."

Daltry turned his head, spat blood, and forced another vampire's smile.

"Forget it. I was only hangin' on until you got here, anyway. Started to think they plugged you, too."

"I missed the twins," Slade said. "They're off and running."

"Guess it'll be a while before you see the judge again."

"Guess so."

"You *will* keep after them." Not asking Slade.

"I will. Yes, sir."

"Don't 'sir' me, son. I'm just another deputy, like you."

"Sorry. I can't agree to that."

"Man you call 'sir' should go the distance, don't you think?"

"You've done that," Slade assured him.

"Nope. I'm ending here. The job's not done."

"It will be," Slade replied. "And that

reminds me. You've got five bucks coming."

"On our bet," Hec wheezed.

"That's right." Slade dug into one of his pockets, retrieving a five-dollar half eagle coin. "You bagged one before me."

"Save your money," said Daltry. "Buy Faith somethin' nice when you get back to town."

"That's not how a bet works," Slade replied, as he slipped the coin into Hec's pocket.

"Okay, then. We're square."

Slade's eyes stung, vision blurring. He blinked twice to clear them, without much success.

"I suppose there's no shovel," Hec said.

"Haven't looked yet. Don't worry about it."

"Remember the stagecoach."

"What's that, now?"

Slade knew what Hec meant. He was stalling for time, hoping something might change and knowing it wouldn't.

"The chase is what matters," said Daltry. "Don't wait on the dead, son. They'll just slow you down."

"I can't leave before morning. No trail in the dark."

"Then, you make it *first thing,* hear me? Get on that roan and go finish the job."

"I intend to."

"Good man. But remember, intention means nothin' without follow-through."

"I hear you."

"You're a good one. The judge likely won't tell you that."

"We get on well enough," Slade replied.

"But he's not one for praise, even when it's deserved."

"Don't go soft on me now, Hec."

"Too late, Jack. I'm already gone."

"You're right here. I can see you and hear you."

"It's cold. I suppose there's no fire?"

"I can light one."

"Forget it. They'll have one lit, where I'm goin'."

"Nice fella like you? I don't think so."

"Don't matter what you think, or what the preachers say. Some things, you do 'em, they can't be undone."

Slade tried to change the subject. "Do you want some water, Hec?"

"I'm wet enough. On second thought, now, if you have some whiskey . . ."

"Not right on me. I can check the camp," Slade told him, dreading separation when he guessed that Hec would pass before he made it back.

"No need. I oughta cut back on it, any-how."

"Sounds sensible."

"You need to take my weapons, Jack. Don't want 'em fallin' into the wrong hands, do we?"

"I'll do it."

"And my tin. The judge'll want to pin it on some other sucker."

"No one fit to shine your boots," Slade said.

"At least I got 'em on. That's something, ain't it? Always worried that I might end up an old'un, dyin' in a bed somewhere."

"You fooled them."

"Fooled me, too." He coughed more blood, then called out, "Jack? Are you still there?"

"Right here, Hec."

"I can't see you. My, it's gettin' dark."

"I'm here," Slade said again, but Daltry was beyond all hearing.

Slade removed his badge and pistol, found the Winchester he'd dropped when he was shot, and turned back toward the camp.

Evan Frain reined in his sweaty mare and sat with head cocked, as if listening for signals from the night. His brother galloped on a bit, before his missed Evan and

281

doubled back.

"What's going on?" asked Ethan.

"I don't hear them trailing us."

"You wouldn't, unless they were right on top of you."

"The wind's right," Evan said. "It could be possible."

"So, maybe Creed and Jimmy slowed them down. It's also dark, you know?"

"They found us in the dark."

"Because we lit a fire, remember?"

"I was wrong about that. I admit it."

"Never mind. I could've argued, but I went along with you."

"It cost us, though."

Ethan reached down to soothe his bay. "Maybe it works out for the best," he said. "We talked about unloading them."

"In our own time," Evan replied.

"What difference does it make?"

"Suppose the law takes them alive."

"And?"

"What's to stop them turning stool pigeon?"

"And say what, that would hurt us?" Ethan grinned by starlight. "We're already being hunted for a dozen murders, just in case you missed it. They can only hang us once."

"They have to find us, first," Evan replied.

"That's right."

"And who knows where we're going?"

Ethan thought about it for a second. Lost his smile.

"Well, shit!"

"Exactly."

"So, the good news is, they've never been to Abaddon. They can't tell anybody where to go, even if they give up the name."

"It crossed my mind that lawmen might have maps."

"Of ghost towns?"

"How in hell should I know? Can you say for sure they don't?"

"I can't say anything for sure, about what lawmen know."

"Well, then."

"But I *can* say, beyond a shadow of a doubt, they damn sure won't find Abaddon *tonight*."

"Neither will we," said Evan.

"More than likely, we won't see the law for days," Ethan pressed on. "If Creed and Jimmy are alive, the posse won't like dragging them around. They'll want to lock 'em up. Which means finding the nearest town that has a jail, before they start in trailing us again."

"Maybe you're right."

"Besides, why would we hang around in

Abaddon that long? Rest up tomorrow night, and we'll be on our way."

"It's spoiled, now," Evan said.

"You know it wasn't really ours, to start with. Just some place we found."

"It had a peaceful air about it, though."

"And will tomorrow morning, when we get there."

"Morning means we ride on through the night," Evan observed.

"Why not?"

"No point in wearing out the horses."

"So, we'll take it easy. Listen to the wind, if that'll make you feel better."

"And if they find us?"

"Then, we'll do what we do best," Ethan replied.

Evan supposed that was the most he could expect. They'd always known their chosen way of life would end in violence. Somewhere, somehow, if they weren't caged and hanged, the brothers understood that they'd be slain eventually by the law, by bounty hunters, maybe even by disgruntled fellow thieves.

What outlaw worth his salt retired and lived on to a ripe old age?

All right, Frank James. But honestly, who else?

It wasn't just a risk they took, by turning

to the lawless side of life. It was an ironclad guarantee of how their lives would end, with only the specifics of a time and place waiting to be resolved.

How many other people knew that much about themselves?

Those working chumps the brothers robbed and pillaged spent their whole lives worrying about the end, dreading some accident or slow-wasting disease. Some of them worried so much that they wound up rushing it.

Not Evan. Not his twin.

They'd play the hand that they had drawn and raise the limit. God help anyone who tried to stop them now.

Slade half expected Jimmy Beck to be a goner by the time he walked back to the campsite, but he found the younger man still living. Beck was crawling somewhere, but the aimless track he'd left behind him indicated that he didn't know exactly where or why.

Slade stepped in front of him and said, "That's far enough."

Beck halted, heaved a weary sigh, and let his limbs go slack. "Reckon you got me, then," he muttered, lips against the dirt.

"Looks like it," Slade replied.

"I'm hurt bad, mister."

"I expect so."

Beck was empty-handed and he wore no gunbelt. No knife hilt or pistol butt protruded from his boot tops. Still, remembering what Hec had done to Sampson, Slade was cautious about rolling Jimmy over on his back.

It cost the wounded man more pain.

Slade didn't mind.

"The others get away?" Beck asked.

"Some of them."

"That'll be the brothers. So damn slick. Where's Creed?"

"He's done."

"Creed was supposed to be on lookout. Figures that he'd screw it up."

"Don't be too hard on him. He did his best."

"Awright, then. Guess I'm done for, too."

"I'd say so."

"Won't be goin' to the lockup, anyway."

"Not this time," Slade agreed.

"Just wish I'd kept my pistol handy. Might've done some good."

"It's hard to say."

"You wouldn't have some whiskey, would ya, mister?"

Sounds like Hec, Slade thought, then smothered that idea.

"No whiskey."

"Water?"

Slade scanned the dark, abandoned camp. "I can't see where they left you a canteen," he answered.

"Chintzy bastards."

"You might say they left you high and dry."

Beck suffered through a coughing spasm, nearly doubling over as he clutched his ventilated stomach. When it passed, he grimaced and said, "Every man for himself, right?"

"Except when they're brothers."

"Blood tells, right?"

Slade eyed Jimmy's shirt. Said, "I see that."

"You think they shoulda took me with 'em?"

"Not my call," Slade said. "But when I hear about a gang, I think of men who hang together."

"Hang around to hang," said Beck, risking a liquid laugh that stained his lips crimson.

"I guess you're right," said Slade. "It's not like you and Sampson ever helped them out. You didn't stop a prison train and loose one of the twins. Nothing like that."

"The hell you gettin' at?"

"Just thinking out loud," Slade replied.

"Don't mind me."

"We help each other out, okay? A lotta times."

"What have they done for you?" Slade asked.

"Tryin' to twist my head around."

"No point to that. You'll be dead pretty soon."

"Think so?"

"You're bleeding like a stuck pig, two days from the nearest doctor. Yeah, I think so."

"Nothing to gain from squealing, then."

"Just getting even."

"Shit, you'd never find 'em, anyhow."

"I'll find them," Slade assured him. "All it takes is time, and I've got plenty."

Jimmy's cackling laugh surprised Slade, trailing off into a soupy giggle.

"That's what you think, law dog. Wait'll they get in amongst the ghosts."

"How's that?"

"You don't know nothin'."

"So, enlighten me."

"You can't fight ghosts," Beck said, staring past Slade into the speckled void of sky. "Can't kill 'em. How you ever gonna hang 'em?"

"They were breathing when they left here," Slade replied, trying to get Beck back on track.

"Whole town of ghosts could eat you up."

"How's that?"

"Ghost town. Good luck findin' the twins in there, law dog."

"I don't mind trying. Which ghost town is that?"

"You'd never find it. Creed thought they was gonna dump us there, but what's the diff? Don't matter now."

"Can't hurt to tell me, if I'll never find it."

"Joke's on you. Chase them to Abaddon, you'll be one of the ghosts."

"Did you say Abaddon?"

"No, sir. You won't hear it from me."

"I'll see if I can find some water for you, Jimmy."

"Sure thing, Creed. Appreciate it."

Slade rose and was turning from the wounded outlaw when Beck gave another racking cough, shuddered, and died. His eyes, locked open, would be glazing soon.

Slade left him there and went to fetch his roan.

"You asleep?"

The question, uttered in a voice so like his own, made Ethan Frain jerk upright in his saddle, clutching at the pommel to preserve his balance.

"Sure am," he replied, before yawning.

"I thought you might be napping over there. About to take a header, may snap your damn fool neck."

"I'm fine," Ethan insisted.

" 'Cause I almost dozed myself, a couple miles back there. Didn't want you to make the same mistake."

"That's thoughtful of you."

"I've been thinking."

"Always helpful."

"When we're done in Abaddon, we ought to burn it," Evan said.

"Burn it? How come?"

"Because it's *ours,* Brother. I'd say it's served us well. Nobody else should share in that."

"For all we know, they have been," Ethan said. "We're only there . . . what? Once or twice a year, if that. Could be a hundred drifters passing through in that time."

"All the more reason to raze it," said Evan. "We can't share the magic with just any-body."

Ethan offered no response to that. He'd heard his brother rambling in that vein before and tried to humor him. For Ethan's part, he'd never noticed any magic in their ghost town — or any ghosts, either. They had outwitted one posse there, and it was a convenient place to hide out sometimes, when they were in the vicinity.

Beyond that . . . well, why argue with his brother over nothing?

"It's a tinderbox, you know," said Evan. "One match at the right spot, we can send the whole place up. What's funny?"

Ethan hadn't been aware that he was smiling, as his brother spoke.

"Oh, nothing," he replied.

"Tell me."

"When you were saying that, I wondered how'd it be if we rode into Abaddon and found somebody else already lit that match."

Evan snorted and replied, "Don't worry about that. If Abaddon was gone, I'd know it."

"How's that?" Ethan asked.

" 'Cause we're *connected*," Evan said, like talking to a simple child, as if it should be obvious. "It's *ours*."

"You take the place so seriously, I'm surprised you never thought of moving there to live."

"That wouldn't work," Evan assured him.

"Oh? Why not?"

"The magic only works in little doses, see? It's like one of those batteries we saw running the lights in Houston. You can only charge them up so much before they blow or all the power drains away."

"What are you saying, now?"

"The town gives us new energy, but we can only take so much. You notice that the longest time we ever stayed in Abaddon was ten, eleven days?"

"After you shot that judge's son."

"Well, staying any longer would've weakened us."

"By resting up? That makes no sense."

"Just think about it. Every time we're there a while, we get the itch to leave after a few days. Right?"

"Because it's boring."

"Wrong. Because the town knows when we've had enough."

Jesus! thought Ethan. *Where's this bullshit coming from?*

"You're telling me you think the town decides when we should leave? It boots us out?"

"And draws us back, when we're in need of energy."

"Like now, I guess."

"Well, don't you think so? I've been seven months in jail, for Christ's sake. That can take it out of you, I promise. We've been running ever since you got me out, and now we're heading for Australia. If we ever needed energy, it's right damn now."

Ethan had always recognized his brother's little quirks, the traits that made him special. This was the first time he had considered that his twin might be stark raving crazy.

"Just one thing," he said. Hoping that it was not too late for logic to prevail. "What happens once we're over in Australia, if we need more energy? Burn Abaddon, then we can never come back and recharge."

"Won't matter," Evan answered, confidently. "They've got places like it, over there."

"Ghost towns?"

"Places of power," Evan said. "I read about them —"

"In that magazine."

"Correct."

"Well, now I've learned something," said Ethan.

Thinking, *Like, for instance, that my brother's lost his goddamned mind.*

Slade didn't want to sleep with corpses, so he put himself to work. First, he dragged Sampson into camp and laid him out with Beck, to wait for the coyotes overnight or buzzards in the morning.

Next, he made a torch from firewood and a twist of Sampson's shirttail, lit it, and went back to bury Hec. Without a shovel, Slade could only dig a shallow grave, using Hec's sheath knife as a tool, to spare his fingernails.

It was laborious, backbreaking work, but Slade couldn't abide the thought of riding off at sunrise, leaving Daltry to the prairie scavengers. Part of his mind insisted that it made no difference — coyotes dig, like any other dogs — but Slade was bound to make the effort.

When the grave was eighteen inches deep or so, he eased Hec into it and put Hec's hat over his face. When he had covered Daltry up with dirt, the best he could, Slade took his torch in search of stones to build a cairn. That used the best part of an hour, to produce meager results, but it was all that Slade could do.

He had no words to mutter over Hec, at least none that would be of any use to either one of them. Slade left the shallow grave and walked back to the horses Beck and Sampson wouldn't need, wherever they had gone. He offered a one-sided conversation to the skittish animals, while he removed their tack and saddles, leaving them to roam and graze as they saw fit.

Back in the outlaws' camp, Slade sorted through the gear they'd left behind. First thing, he took time to unload four guns collected from the dead, kept all the ammunition he could use, and pitched the rest into the night. The empty guns, he left to rust.

There wasn't much else to be found. A half bottle of whiskey dropped after the first shot sent its owner scrambling from his seat. An empty coffeepot, upended in the campfire's ashes. Bedrolls and the kind of litter he'd expect to find in any hastily deserted camp.

Nothing to help him find a ghost town known as Abaddon.

The name stirred something in Slade's memory, but he couldn't retrieve it. He would ask Judge Dennison about it, later, when he turned in his report about the manhunt and Hec Daltry's murder.

If he lived that long.

Slade thought about his chances, totaling up the score of deaths since Evan Frain had fled the *Katy Flier* on his way to Leavenworth. He made it twenty-three, so far, and guessed there might be some that he'd forgotten.

All that blood, and still, the odds were only two to one. He'd beaten worse odds, when the stakes were life or death. No game was ever won or lost until the last card had been played.

And win or lose, he had to play.

There was no way for Slade to fold and still live with himself.

When he began to doze beside the dead campfire, Slade led his roan some distance off and spread his bedroll on the ground. He still had time to rest a bit, before sunrise revealed his quarry's tracks.

Slade had no doubt that he could find and follow them. He'd learned enough from Hec, and on his own, to feel that confidence. And if he lost their trail somewhere along the way, he would be patient, backtrack to recover it, and carry on from there.

To Abaddon. Wherever and whatever that might be.

A ghost town? Maybe.

And a trap? Most certainly, if he rode in and found the Frain twins waiting for him there.

The trick, if he could manage it, would be to turn the tables on them. Make their trap a cage from which there could be no escape.

He'd missed them twice, and didn't plan to make it three times in a row.

"This time," Slade told the stars, before he fell asleep, "I'll get it right."

16

"I see it."

This time, it was Evan Frain who jerked back from the hazy border of a dream, turning in the direction of his brother's voice.

"Say what?"

"Wake up, Brother. We're almost there."

Evan faced forward, felt a surge of energy at his first glimpse of Abaddon. It wasn't much to see, yet — just a smudge on the horizon — but he fancied that he could already smell the dust accumulated in its shadowed rooms. The wood sun-baked as dry as ancient paper.

And it felt like something he had never truly known.

A home, perhaps.

No, better, since the place where he'd been raised with Ethan hardly qualified as home, in Evan's mind. There'd been no shelter there from drunken rages, screaming, flailing fists and belts. Nothing to keep the brothers there a minute longer than they had to be, fleeing as soon as they were old enough and strong enough to care for one another on their own.

They'd seen — and done — some things a child should never have to witness, but he thought that it had turned out for the best. If anything had changed about their early lives, Evan supposed they might be store clerks or accountants now, toiling for weekly paychecks, drinking up their meager salary and wishing they were dead.

And Abaddon was different.

No people meant no rules, beyond whatever they decided should apply. Careful with open flames. A basic sanitary code that needed no discussion. Generally keeping quiet about Abaddon, where strangers were concerned.

They'd broken that rule, recently, and Evan took a lesson from the way it had turned out. The men they'd briefed on Abaddon were all dead, now. Cut down before their time, and who was Frain to call it a coincidence?

"I feel it," he told Ethan. And he caught the flicker of a strange expression on his brother's face.

Most likely thinks I'm crazy.

There were some things, he supposed, that

298

never should be shared with anyone, regardless of the bond between them. Some things were too *personal* for sharing. When exposed to open air and light of day, they withered and became distorted, sounded loony even to his own ears.

But he'd truly thought Ethan would understand.

"Another couple hours," Ethan said. "When we get in, I'll stash the horses. Get them settled. We can do some hunting, if you want, or eat up what we're carrying for supper."

"Sounds good," Evan replied. "You know, before . . . that stuff I said —"

"I thought about it," Ethan interrupted him. "I won't pretend to understand it, but I can't find fault. If you feel something here, beyond what I do, that just means you're . . . sensitive."

"Not crazy?"

Ethan laughed at that. It sounded forced.

"Most people look at us," he said, "they think we're *both* crazy. The things we've done. In fact, we ought to try that angle out, next time we're up before a judge."

"I never will be," Evan said.

"Nor me, I guess," his twin agreed.

"But getting back to what I said —"

"Forget it, Brother. Everybody goes a little

nuts, from time to time."

Evan knew he could take that as an insult — Ethan saying that he *was* nuts — but to what effect? His brother was the last person alive who gave a damn whether he lived or died. It *would* be crazy, if he sacrificed that for a ghost town he would never see again.

But there *was* power in the streets of Abaddon.

Evan intended to absorb as much of it as possible this time, his last time, and consign the rest to flames before they left. That way, he'd rest assured that no one else could come along behind him, steal his thunder and corrupt it.

And when they were in Australia, riding free and easy as you please, Evan would find another source of power to sustain him. He remembered reading about mountains where the natives worshipped. If they didn't want to share, Evan could always illustrate the error of their ways.

No problem, there.

In fact, he thought it might be fun.

A whole new continent to conquer — or, at least, to loot within the time remaining to him. There'd be lawmen in Australia, too, of course. And somehow, sometime, he supposed they'd hunt him down.

But what a life he would've had, in the

meantime.

The new day was beginning now.

Slade heard coyotes in the night, raiding the outlaw camp, but hadn't tried to interrupt them. Why should he? Beck and Sampson were beyond the reach of any earthly law, now. As raw meat, at least they served a beneficial function.

He was up and on the trail at dawn, as soon as there was light enough to find the tracks left by two horses speeding northward. Slade carried a map of Oklahoma Territory in his saddlebags, and he'd consulted it before he went to sleep, in what had been a fruitless search for Abaddon.

Nothing.

The map was relatively new and naturally might exclude ghost towns. Of course, there was an equal chance the Frains had lied to Jimmy Beck about their destination, either teasing him with spooky tales or simply keeping Beck and his companions in the dark.

Still . . .

Slade thought there was something in the way the Frains held to their course, northeastward since they'd left the *Katy Flier,* never deviating much except to claim a prize. Instead of veering off to shake pursuers, they were steady as they went.

Which told Slade they were *going somewhere,* not just running. Why not an abandoned town? The notion didn't trouble him. Slade meant to follow them wherever they might go.

Even if that meant riding all the way to Hell.

He thought of Faith, as always, when his day began, and some glimpse of her crossed Slade's mind repeatedly throughout the morning, as he tracked the twins relentlessly. He wasn't doing this for her, specifically, but with a thought in mind that every human scavenger removed from circulation made the world safer for one he . . . what?

Cherished? Most definitely.

Loved? Perhaps.

Slade took his time that morning, more concerned about losing the trail than giving the Frains a longer head start. He had expected difficulty tracking them, but soon discovered that no great skill was required. The tracks faded from time to time, but Slade held steady on his course and always picked them up again.

Most definitely going somewhere.

But how far ahead? How long before they stopped?

And if they chose to murder someone else along the way, would Slade be close enough to intervene?

It shamed him that he hoped the brothers *would* stop, try to raid another homestead or some drifter's camp, to let him catch up. Take them by surprise.

Again.

It hadn't worked so well last night, but even with the painful loss he'd suffered, Slade acknowledged that the gang was being whittled down. Four of the six they'd started with were dead, leaving the twins alone.

Would they prefer it that way? Or would the incessant losses work against them, wearing on their nerves?

When facing two accomplished killers, Slade couldn't afford to miss a trick. Whatever weakness he could single out and use to his advantage, Slade knew he would be a fool to pass it up.

He wished there was a way for him to play the brothers off against each other, but Slade didn't know enough about their background to attempt it. Any jealousy, resentment, anger, or whatever might divide them was concealed from him. Mind reading might have helped him, but he lacked the talent and had no idea where he could find a Gypsy on short notice.

Something ahead of Slade distracted him from idle thoughts of hocus-pocus. Riders coming toward him?

No. A wagon.

And, on second thought, it wasn't moving.

Slade's unconscious scowl mirrored the dread he felt inside. Was this the chance he'd secretly been hoping for, to catch the Frains red-handed in commission of another brutal crime?

Or was he already too late?

Cursing himself, his quarry, and the run of rotten luck in general, Slade urged his roan into a gallop, eating up the ground that lay between him and whatever fresh atrocity was waiting.

As far as Ethan Frain could tell, little had changed in Abaddon. Time marches on, of course. The whole place seemed a little more run-down, weathered and faded by exposure to the elements when there was no one to maintain it. He would likely find more spiderwebs, rat nests, and snake dens in the aged buildings than were evident last time they had visited.

But from the outside, as they moved along Main Street, there was no sign that any other human being had discovered Abaddon or tried to make himself at home there. It was off the beaten track, these days, forgotten by the outside world.

How many years had passed since any stagecoach had delivered mail or passengers to Abaddon? How long since a traveling salesman or circuit-riding pastor had come to call?

Evan had tried to look it up, once, at the library in Liberal, across the Kansas line, but nothing had revealed itself. From there, they'd made a silly game of fabricating history and occupants for Abaddon, concocting stories of their trials and tribulations, leading to the town's abandonment.

A silly way to pass the time.

But Evan, he saw now, had taken it to heart.

He'd humored Evan, going in, but Ethan kept a close eye on his brother as they entered town, passing the same familiar storefronts they had seen so often in the past. If Evan had, indeed, begun to lose his grip on sanity, Ethan would have to stay alert. Take measures to protect his brother — and himself.

It might be best, he thought, to go along with Evan's plan for burning Abaddon, before they left.

And where, exactly, would they go from there?

Ethan had been prepared to try Australia, the way Evan described it, but the rigors of a trip halfway around the world were multiplied by fears that Evan might disintegrate and lapse into a state beyond Ethan's control.

In which case, what was he to do?

Hard choices.

If a horse went lame, a dog turned rabid, or a woman cheated on him, Ethan carried the solution in a holster, on his hip. But if his only brother and the mirror image of himself became a crazy, drooling thing, would he have strength enough to end it?

And would there be any other choice?

He couldn't trust Evan to so-called doctors at a state asylum. If they recognized him, it would mean a rope. And even if they didn't, caging Evan with a bunch of other lunatics was worse than sending him to prison. He'd have met a better class of animals at Leavenworth than in the bedlam of a warehouse for the mentally deranged.

No. If it came to that, he'd pull the trigger. End his brother's suffering, the same as if he had a cancer gnawing at his bowels.

And afterward? Where would he go? What would he do?

Ethan had never seriously planned a life without his twin. Oh, they'd discussed it, certainly. Bold talk of bloody vengeance, if it came to pass that one of them was gunned down in a holdup or cornered and killed by a posse. All laughing and backslapping, sketching the details of how they would make vigilantes or lawmen regret the foul day they were born.

But there had been no talk of afterward, when one was planted and the other had avenged him, riding off into the sunset with a sack full of fresh scalps. A stranger, eavesdropping, would have surmised that neither twin believed he would outlive the other. They'd go down together, somehow, likely in a haze of gun smoke on the main street of some frontier burg whose citizens were better shots than average.

Live by the gun, die by the gun.

No problem, there.

Unless one twin was forced to wield the gun, himself.

And live with it . . . exactly how?

"Looks like we're clear," said Evan, drawing Ethan from his morbid thoughts.

"Okay," he said. "You want to check out the hotel, before I get the horses settled in?"

"Sounds good. Then we can scout the other buildings. Make sure nobody's been trespassing."

"Not much to recommend it," Ethan said.

"Unless they felt the power."

Here we go.

"Well, sure," he said, playing along.

"Tonight, I'll tell you more about Australia."

"Looking forward to it," Ethan said, as they veered off toward what had once been Abaddon's hotel.

The Prairie Rose, according to the sign out front, now barely legible. Now withered on the vine.

"Remember last time, and the snakes," Evan advised.

"I've got my eyes wide open," Ethan said.

As Slade drew closer to the wagon, he could smell a fire. He saw small figures moving, counted four of them, and reined his gelding from a gallop to an easy trot, while he released the hammer thong that kept his Colt Peacemaker holstered.

Slowing further when he'd closed the gap to fifty yards, Slade saw a man armed with a rifle, standing by a small campfire. Behind him, using the wagon for cover, he spotted a woman about the man's age, a willowy girl in her teens, and a boy likely somewhere between ten and twelve.

No twins. No danger visible.

"That's far enough, mister," the rifleman announced.

Slade stopped, identified himself, and waited while the others whispered to the man in charge.

"All right," the man in charge said. "Come ahead and let me see the badge, if you don't mind."

Slade took it easy, ready with his Colt if this turned out to be some kind of subtle trap. Up close, he saw no harm in any of the faces, but he'd been fooled once before, by members of a family that killed for profit and for pleasure. It had nearly cost his life, and Slade would not be tricked a second time.

When he was satisfied with Slade's demeanor and his star, the rifleman laid gun aside and said, "Marshal, I'm Aloysius Beane. My wife, Sarah. Our daughter, Francis. And our son, Josiah."

Dismounting for the roan's sake, Slade replied, "I'm pleased to meet you folks. More pleased to find you all alive and well."

"Some reason why we shouldn't be?" asked Beane.

"I'm tracking two men who'd have passed this way, heading northwest, within the past few hours. They're no one you'd want to meet."

"I'm glad we missed them, then," Beane said. "We're heading southwest, as it happens, on our way to Enid. This looked like a fair place for our midday meal."

"Should do as well as any other," Slade agreed. "Sorry I interrupted you."

"We haven't started yet," Beane told him, nodding toward a stewpot on the fire. "If you would care to join us . . ."

"Thanks, but no," Slade said. "I'd gladly pay you for some water, though. My animal's worked up a thirst this morning."

"No pay necessary, Marshal," Beane replied. "We're all God's creatures here."

Beane's daughter fetched a bowl, filled it with water from a barrel strapped to one side of the wagon, and the roan received it gratefully. Passing the time, Slade said, "You're bound for Enid, I believe you said."

"Yes, sir. Bearing the gospel of our Lord and Savior."

"Ah. I didn't take you for a preacher, with the rifle and your clothes."

Beane smiled. "I only wear my undertaker's suit on Sundays, Marshal. And the Lord helps those who help themselves."

Slade had to smile at that himself.

"I'm normally in Enid, too," he said.

"Maybe I'll come and lend an ear, when I get back."

Wondering when that would be, if ever.

"You'll be welcome, Marshal. As for these two desperados, should they change course by some chance, how can we recognize them?"

"They're twins," Slade said. "Identical. But if they're close enough for you to see that much, it's probably too late. The precious cargo that you're carrying, I'd keep that rifle handy all the way to Enid, just in case."

"I'll follow that advice, Marshal. Thank you."

Slade mounted, tipped his hat to Beane's women, and said, "With any luck, Parson, we'll meet again."

They waved him on his way, four travelers alone in what they chose to call God's country. Slade had covered much of it while working for Judge Dennison, and while he'd seen some wonders, he had yet to catch a glimpse of God.

The Devil, now, was something else.

His mark was everywhere Slade looked.

Or maybe it was just humanity, driven by greed and lust, anger and jealousy, duplicity and prejudice, to feed upon itself and turn what should've been God's country into

Hell on Earth.

Still, he couldn't fault it. If it weren't for crime — or "sin," as Pastor Beane would have it — Slade would need to find another job. Maybe go back to playing poker for a living, if his luck held out.

Or try his hand at ranching, if —

He brusquely pushed the thought of Faith away. She had no business sharing space inside his head with killers like the Frains. It sullied her, somehow.

He'd think of her again when it was over.

If he could.

The Prairie Rose hotel had witnessed better days. In idle moments, Evan Frain had spun a history of sorts together for it, and while he recognized the gap between reality and outright fantasy, it pleased him to imagine life in Abaddon before the town dried up and blew away.

The Prairie Rose, Frain told himself, had once been the preserve of wealthy men with elegant companions, dressed in finery befitting lucky bastards who have cash to burn. They would have dined in splendor, in the hotel's gourmet restaurant, and then retired to rutting in their grand four-poster feather beds. Between times, while the men were plotting ways to make more money, Frain imagined all the women taking baths and having people in to style their hair.

In truth, he guessed, the place had never seen a full-dress gentleman or lady cross its threshold. Stockmen, perhaps. Peddlers. Surveyors. Prospectors. Maybe a railroad scout who'd gone back home and recommended that the tracks run somewhere else. No women in their finery, unless some fancy whore had struck a bargain with the management.

Today, the Prairie Rose's rooms were occupied by scuttling, creeping things that shunned the light of day. Not ghosts, as far as Frain could tell, but little predators and scavengers who hunted one another through the dust and shadows. Some, he guessed, might dine on the hotel itself.

That's why he had to watch his step, climbing the stairs to check the upper floors. As in the street, he found no sign that anyone had passed through Abaddon since Frain's last visit with his brother.

It belonged to them, and they were back to share it.

One last time.

Frain heard his brother calling from the hotel lobby, backtracked to the stairs, and hollered down, "All clear, up here."

"I checked the shops along this side,"

Ethan replied. "We've got some rattlers nesting in the dry-goods store. Aside from that, not much."

"Ready to sweep the other side?"

"Whenever you are, Brother."

"May as well get to it, then."

Outside, the sun was just a bit off plumb, say half past noon. They'd made good time, considering the fact that more than half the last leg of their journey had been covered in the dark. Evan was more convinced than ever that the town had drawn them to it, but he didn't want to press his luck.

Crossing the street to start their exploration at the northern end of town, Ethan inquired, "Where would we sail from, to Australia?"

"Galveston would do, if we could take a chance on Texas," Evan answered. "But I wouldn't like to risk it."

"No."

"Same problem with New Orleans, going back the way we came."

"Okay."

"So, I'm thinking California. San Diego or Los Angeles. Nobody knows us there, ships leaving all the time. We'd have a chance to pick some cash up, on the way."

"They know us in New Mexico."

"Some do," said Evan. "We can take our

time, steer wide of Roswell and Portales, then we're clear in Arizona. No great rush. Australia isn't going anywhere."

"It's still a long time, being cooped up on a boat."

"They call them ships."

"Same thing," Ethan replied. "Suppose somebody spots us when we're sailing."

"Let them," Evan said. "What can they do, strap on a set of wings and chase the ship? They want to send a poster out to the Australian law, we'll land before it gets there. Home and dry."

"Not home," Ethan corrected him.

"Better. We're starting fresh."

"But in the same line."

"What else are we suited for?"

Ethan considered it, then shrugged. "You're right."

"Six months from now, it'll be like none of this ever happened."

"What kind of money do they have there, in Australia?"

Evan grinned and said, "The spending kind."

Slade found what he was looking for at 3:05 p.m. He checked his pocket watch, and then the map he carried, looking for a town located in the spot where huddled structures had appeared before him, crouched against the skyline like a set of children's building blocks.

No Abaddon, or any other name.

If he'd been riding through a desert, days from water, Slade would have suspected a mirage. This time, however, he supposed he'd found one of those settlements established with high hopes, later abandoned when the optimism turned into regret.

The West was rife with towns, camps, trading posts, and way stations deserted by their founders, left to rot when ore ran out, or wells ran dry, or politicians cancelled plans to build a railroad. Dreams died hard, but people made of flesh and blood could only wait so long, before they had to pull up stakes and seek their fortunes elsewhere.

Once life moved on, when shops and dwellings had been stripped of all that anybody valued, only shattered hopes remained. Even their echoes faded, over time, leaving the hollow shell of what had once been a community. Depending on the climate, buildings might survive for years or decades. Finally, when they had crumbled into dust, nothing remained but headstones in the local cemetery.

Slade wasn't worried about meeting ghosts in Abaddon.

He was concerned about the living, and the snares they might have laid to trap him.

The Frains were slick. He knew that much, from personal experience. They had eluded Slade, not once but twice. He meant to end it here but didn't want to sacrifice himself in the process, if he could help it.

And for starters, riding in by daylight would be a mistake. The Frains would see him coming, could lie back and snipe him from a distance with their rifles, or sit tight and take him in a cross fire, once he'd entered Abaddon. They knew the town's layout, and they'd had time to pick their vantage points for optimum defense.

He'd have to wait for nightfall, then. Let darkness cover his approach and, if his luck held, catch the Frains displaying lights to guide him. Even one poor candle would be helpful, or a cooking fire to scent the air. If he could catch them eating supper, maybe even swilling whiskey, all the better.

And what sort of warning should he give the brothers, when he found them? After they had killed eleven lawmen in a week, along with eight civilians that he knew of, was Slade bound by any legal niceties at all? Would it incense Judge Dennison if he just gunned them down on sight?

And who would ever know?

Slade had his conscience to consider, but its voice was muted by the things he'd witnessed since he left Enid with Hec Daltry, to track the Frains. There was no question of them seeing New Year's Day, if he delivered them alive for trial.

And they would know that, going into any confrontation. Slade had no illusion that the Frains would make it easy for him, crumble and surrender from fatigue or having seen the error of their ways.

They were fighters and would likely die that way.

In which case, Slade decided, *Better them than me.*

With time to kill, he scanned the countryside and found a copse of trees a half mile distant that would offer shade, and likely water for his gelding. Slade could wait there, watch the afternoon fade into night, and calculate his best approach to Abaddon. If his intended quarry offered him no guiding light, Slade would proceed to hunt them in the shadows.

Gun work in the dark seemed fitting, somehow.

Bringing down the curtain on a tragedy that had already played too long.

17

"What's that you're cooking?" Evan Frain inquired.

"Rabbit," his brother said.

"I didn't hear you shoot it."

"No, you wouldn't have. I made a snare."

"The kind we used to make when we were kids?"

"The very same."

"Well, I'll be damned. Smells good."

"There's not much to it," Ethan granted. "But a little meat can't hurt the beans."

"Too bad we didn't pass another farm on our way in. We could've had more eggs for breakfast."

"Let's eat supper first, shall we?"

"I'm just saying."

"Yeah."

Most of the Prairie Rose's furnishings had been removed when it was closed, before the owners left for good, but there remained a large stone fireplace with a flue that still worked well enough. Ethan had built a fire, using the dried-out wood from baseboards, windowsills, and doorjambs as fuel.

Abaddon was consuming itself.

In Evan's mind, it was a small but decent start.

"Feels good to be here, one last time," he said. Then, cautiously, he added, "To me, at least."

"Me, too. I have to say I'll miss the old place."

Not that anything of any great importance ever happened there, after the first time, when they'd bushwhacked the posse. Their other visits to the ghost town — nine or ten, in all — had simply been vacations from their hectic, often violent daily lives. Short periods of rest, rejuvenation.

Sanctuary.

"We'll find someplace that's better in Australia," Evan said.

"You think so?"

"Sure. Their whole damn country's like the West. Ranches and mines, prospectors, drovers. Little towns scattered to hell and gone."

"That magazine you read was full of information," Ethan said.

"It was," Evan agreed. "But some of it, I read between the lines."

"How's that?"

"You know, it's like the writer's saying something, but he doesn't want to come right out and *say* it. Or the folks printing the magazine won't give him space enough to say it all. He hints around at things and lets you use your own imagination."

"Ah."

"You doubt me, Brother?"

"Not a bit of it."

"Because you know I'd never lie to you."

"Nobody mentioned lying."

"Sometimes, you just *know* things, don't you? Like, you're looking at some picture on the wall."

"Whose wall? What picture?"

"Doesn't matter. Say a painting of a horse. It's standing in a meadow, not a muscle moving —"

" 'Cause it's just a picture," Ethan interjected.

"But you know this horse the artist painted had a whole life of its own, see? When it isn't posing for a picture, it'll graze a bit, go off and find a spring to drink from, run around the meadow doing anything it wants to."

"Or, the painter could've made it up from *his* imagination, without seeing any special horse at all. Then you come by, imagining the horse out running through some meadow no one's ever seen."

"I've seen it."

"In a *picture.* Not real life."

"So, what's your goddamned point?"

"My goddamned point is that sometimes you need to be real goddamned careful when you start reading between the lines. You might imagine things the writer never saw or even heard of. Things you make up on your own."

"I take it that you'd rather pass on going to Australia, then?"

"See, that's *exactly* what I mean. I never mentioned passing on it, never *thought* of passing on it. Did I?"

"How in hell do I know what you're thinking?"

"Right!" Ethan replied, almost triumphantly. "That's just my point. We start out talking magazines, you jump to paintings, and next thing I know, you're telling me I want to pass on going to Australia. Yank the reins on your imagination, every now and then. Okay?"

"I'm not a simpleton, you know."

"Far from it."

"I just *feel* things, sometimes."

"Could be gas. Just don't break wind in here."

"I know, sometimes, when trouble's coming."

"Yes, you do."

"Like what I'm feeling now."

Ethan stopped chewing, met his brother's eyes, and held his gaze.

"What kind of trouble?" he inquired.

"Same as usual. Somebody hunting for us."

"Close?" asked Ethan.

"Close enough."

"Damn it!"

"Finish your supper."

"Is there time?"

"Should be," Evan replied. "I'll go and have a look around. No need for you to join me."

"Hell, I've lost my appetite."

"Well, clean up, then. We don't want any damned coyotes in here raising hell tonight, in case I'm wrong."

"And if you're not?"

"Then we'll surprise them."

"Lawmen or coyotes?"

"Both," Evan replied, smiling. "Bullets for one, a hot meal for the other."

"I'd have liked to get some sleep tonight."

"You may yet, Brother. Bear in mind that this is *our* place. We're the hunters, here."

■ ■ ■ ■

Slade allowed full dark to settle on the land before he left the copse of trees that sheltered him. He'd spent the afternoon checking his weapons, seeing to his horse, eating a bit, and dozing for a while, to keep himself clearheaded through the night. There'd been no sign of life from Abaddon in all that time — no sound, no wisp of smoke — but Slade was confident that he had found his prey.

Somewhere inside that ruined town, the Frains were waiting. Resting, killing time, planning their next outrage. Unless, of course, they'd kept on riding north, through Abaddon and out the other side, then off to anyplace their hearts desired.

The joke would be on Slade, in that case. He could search the town all night, and start again at sunrise, while the Frains picked up a full day's lead. They could defeat him by the simple stratagem of moving on, perhaps without a thought that anyone was even trailing them.

Not this time.

Slade refused to contemplate another failure. He would either bag the Frains tonight or die trying.

He rode his gelding to within a mile of Abaddon, then left it free to graze at will and walked the final distance, taking care with every step. Slade didn't want a twisted ankle that would send him hobbling through the ghost town with a limp, distracted from his lethal mission by the pain.

Tonight, he needed every ounce of strength and cunning he possessed.

It seemed a long walk into town by faint starlight, no moon to help him, thinking all the way about the rattler that had dropped one of the gang's horses, the day before. The last thing that he needed — other than a snakebite — was a gunshot to alert the Frains and mark the course of his approach.

Slade wasn't one for stalking animals, had never seen the so-called sport in it, but hunting men was pretty much the same. Humans were more intelligent, according to the scientists who wrote about such things, but Slade had never heard of deer or any other "dumb" beast that would cloud its brain with alcohol or opium when it was being hunted, or distract itself with some fatal amusement at the crucial hour.

There would be no women, dice, or roulette wheels in Abaddon. No cards, unless the Frains had brought their own, to while away the time. Slade hoped they would be boozing, but he couldn't count on it.

Whatever dulled their edge was fine with him.

Crossing the dark ground toward his final destination, he reviewed what he had learned about the twins over the past few days. Slade was approximately five years older than the Frains, a seasoned thirty to their twenty-five and change. The twins were killers, stamped and certified, but so was Slade. Since pinning on a badge, he'd shot more men than both of them together. The twins were used to running, while Slade hunted other men to earn his keep.

Which all meant . . . what, again?

Maybe nothing.

The odds remained at two to one against him, and he would be hunting — likely fighting for his life — on unfamiliar ground, where his opponents felt at home. They would know every nook and cranny in the crumbling town, while Slade, the newcomer, was forced to grope his way along in darkness.

If all else failed, Slade had a way in mind to light his path and flush the twins from cover, in a single stroke. A box of matches rattled softly in his shirt pocket. A last resort, but one he wouldn't hesitate to use if all else failed.

Or if he needed a distraction to prevent himself from winding up as one of Abaddon's resident ghosts.

The downside of that plan was chaos. If he set the town on fire without knowing exactly where the Frains were located, they stood a good chance of escaping through some back door while Slade watched the street.

Which told him that he had to find their horses, first, before he sought the men.

No matter where the twins might hide in Abaddon, their animals would be the final fallback option. There was no escape for them on foot, across the open plains, from mounted trackers. They would've stashed the horses somewhere safe, with feed and water handy, ready for a hasty exit if required.

With that in mind, and no lights showing to betray his quarry, Slade changed course to flank the ghost town on his left, its western side. He guessed the horses wouldn't be tied up on Main Street, in plain sight, although the Frains — if they had laid a trap — would probably expect him there.

When he had closed to forty yards, Slade smelled the first hint of wood smoke and roasting meat. He couldn't place it, but the odors told him Abaddon was occupied.

His long ride hadn't been in vain.

Unless he lost it now.

Slade pushed on through the darkness, being doubly careful not to make a sound.

Evan Frain stood on a sagging wooden sidewalk, breathing in the night. Eyes closed, it seemed to him that he could pick out varied scents of animals and plants, the living things that made their home in Abaddon where people once had dwelled, replacing humankind with forms at once more primitive and durable.

He inhaled the night.

According to the magazine he'd read in jail — the same one with the article about Australia — every time somebody drew a breath, they took in tiny particles of everything around them. When he smelled something, it wasn't just aroma entering his nose, but microscopic pieces of the *thing* he smelled.

A steak, for instance. Or a cup of coffee.

Dog shit.

Evan didn't like to think about it too much, but his mood was right this evening. Perhaps his final night in Abaddon, forever. It seemed proper to him that he should inhale the town itself: its dry wood, dust and mold, mesquite and tumbleweeds, the creatures lurking under floorboards and in walls.

Why not?

Wasn't all life connected, in its way?

And what about the danger that he felt, approaching in the darkness? Evan couldn't smell it, yet, but he could feel the short hairs bristling on his nape, the way they did when he was just about to draw against a man who might be faster with a gun.

Excitement, mixed with just a hint of fear.

It thrilled and troubled him at the same time.

Ethan was troubled, too, but for his twin's sake. Evan saw it in the mirror image of his face, lurking behind his brother's eyes. They were identical in many ways, but when it came to temperament Ethan had always been the cooler head. Not slow to lash out, if insulted, but more likely to consider risks before he made a move that couldn't be undone.

They balanced one another, that way, and agreed on damn near everything, when there was time to talk it out. Australia was a case in point. Evan could tell his brother wasn't leaping up and down with joy over the thought of sailing halfway round the world, but he had seen the wisdom of it and agreed.

Now, Evan wondered if they'd ever get the chance.

The trouble with his feelings was that he could seldom measure them. A sense of danger in the offing might mean they'd be threatened instantly, weeks later, sometimes not at all. He wasn't always right, of course. But 80, 85 percent made Ethan a believer.

What about tonight?

Frain felt a certain urgency, but nothing he could put his finger on. It wasn't like the premonition of disaster he'd experienced two days before the lawmen captured him in Texas. He'd kept that one quiet, gone on with the job, and look what it had cost them in the long run.

He moved along the sidewalk, felt it give beneath his weight in places, weighing each step with concern for stealth and the potential risk of plunging hip-deep into darkness filled with scorpions and rattlers. If there was a prowler stalking them in Abaddon, or on his way, Frain didn't want to spook the hunter.

All he needed was a clean shot with the Winchester he carried. Just one shot.

He felt a solemn sense of circles closing. When they first discovered Abaddon, the Frains had offered up a human sacrifice. The possemen who'd followed them baptized the ghost town with their blood. Now, when they planned to leave forever, it seemed only proper that they leave a farewell gift in parting.

More blood for the thirsty ghosts.

Evan could almost feel them trailing him along Main Street. As if he could turn swiftly, catch them at it, and they'd all share one great laugh. Sadly, it didn't work that way, but Evan couldn't spend a night in Abaddon without imagining their shades around him, watching, sometimes whispering to him in confidence.

With Ethan, he had spent a long night naming them and spinning tales about the vanished citizens of Abaddon. He knew which ones were faithful to their spouses, and which ones enjoyed a little hanky-panky on the side. Some of the ghosts were drunkards — had been, anyway — while others struck a pose of public piety. Behind closed doors, beneath their clothes, all of them harbored secret sins.

Like everybody Frain had ever met.

His mind snapped back to here and now. Was that a new sound that had reached his ears? A shutter creaking in the breeze . . . or something else? Perhaps a footstep on old floorboards?

Evan frowned, turned back in the direction of the sound, and stepped down off the sidewalk, onto solid ground. Less noise that way, while he was hunting.

Smiling to himself, Frain crossed the street and vanished into shadow on the other side.

It wasn't difficult to find the horses, after all.

Slade entered Abaddon from the northwest, avoiding Main Street, easing down an alleyway between two weathered buildings near the town's north end. Because the alleyway was darker than the open ground behind him and beyond, Slade crept along, planting each foot in front of him with grim deliberation, waiting for a hiss or crunch or any other noise that might betray him.

When he reached the alley's mouth, he lingered in its shadows, sweeping the street with eyes alert to any hint of movement. All the shops that Slade could see were dark and silent. When he risked a glance along his own side of the street, its sidewalk stretched away from him, unoccupied.

And still he waited, listening, sniffing the breeze that wafted past him. Ghost towns smelled of dust and dry rot, but he picked up something else in Abaddon.

Manure.

The breeze was coming from his left, blowing the scent toward Slade from that direction. He considered taking to the street, in search of what he sought, but then decided it would be impractical. First, it increased the likelihood of being spotted. Second, Slade deemed it unlikely that the Frains would situate their animals for an escape into the open street, which might become a shooting gallery.

In their place, he'd have looked for something with a back door large enough to let a mounted rider pass. Easy to enter or to flee, at either end. A livery would be ideal. And failing that, perhaps some kind of warehouse.

Slade retraced his steps along the alley, accelerating slightly on the second pass. He knew its obstacles by now, unless some living thing had wandered in behind him while he scanned Main Street.

But nothing had.

Slade left the alley, turning right — or north — and moved along the back side of successive buildings he could not identify. They had been vacant for so long, weathered inside and out by now, that no distinctive odor clung to any of the structures.

Just the smell of fresh horse shit, still some distance ahead of him.

Slade found the horses tethered in the next-to-last building on Main Street's west side. More of a shed, in fact, with a flat roof, two solid walls running from west to east, and gaping doors at either end. Beams kept the roof from sagging too much, though some gaps admitted starlight. Grass sprouted from a dirt floor underfoot.

There were no stalls in the building, so it hadn't been an ordinary stable. Possibly some kind of storage shed or open market-place. Slade couldn't tell and didn't care.

He cared about the horses, standing saddled but at ease, cropping the grass around them. Stopping now and then to nuzzle at a washtub filled with water.

Drawn from where?

Slade guessed that Abaddon must have a pump and well, still operating after all those years. It would be something else to look for, when he'd finished with the Frains.

Slade could have put the horses down — shot them, or used his knife to keep it quiet — but he couldn't bring himself to do it. Rather, he approached them, speaking softly, and removed their tack and saddles when they'd calmed enough to let him work. He saw nowhere to hide the gear, so hauled it to the far end of the shed and dumped it all together in a dark corner, then doubled back and freed the horses from their tethers.

They seemed disciplined enough to stay exactly where they were, but Slade had done his best for them, in case the whole thing went to hell. And in the process — hopefully, at least — he'd spoiled the twins' escape plan.

That accomplished, Slade moved back toward Main Street. Standing in the front door of the open shed, he had a new perspective on the town. He still saw nothing in the way of lights, but he could smell wood smoke again, competing with horse dung for his attention.

Slade was late for supper, but he hoped the party hadn't broken up.

Finding the smoke's source would require more effort, since a fire could have been kindled anywhere in town. It needed only fuel, a flame-resistant surface to prevent it from consuming everything in sight, and something like a chimney or a stove pipe to disperse the smoke.

So, find it, sneered a small voice in his head.

Where were the Frains most likely to retire in Abaddon? They'd want both shelter and mobility, no place where they'd be cramped or cornered. Still, most of the shops would qualify, but Slade yielded to logic and convention.

He would start at the hotel.

Ethan Frain cleared off their supper scraps and left the cook fire burning as he left the Prairie Rose hotel. Leaving the meager light behind, he moved along a hallway leading past the former kitchen's swinging doors, beyond the absent manager's small office, to an exit at the rear.

The night outside was almost fragrant, by comparison with the hotel's musty interior. The only flowers found in Abaddon were those that bloomed from wretched weeds, but they imparted something to the air.

Or maybe it was simply wishful thinking.

Never mind the flowers, Ethan thought. *You're looking for a posse.*

Either that or something Evan had dreamed up, out of thin air.

Granted, his brother had a fair record for sensing trouble. His instincts had saved them half a dozen times that Ethan could recall without taxing his memory. It was an eerie kind of thing, but if it kept Ethan alive, he wouldn't bitch about it.

And it wouldn't hurt to have another look around the town. A little exercise to help the beans and rabbit settle.

Knowing that Evan was patrolling Main Street, Ethan chose to scout the burg's perimeter. Between them, they could cover Abaddon within an hour, give or take, including look-ins at the empty shops. If they found nothing, Ethan would relax and try to get some sleep.

If they found prowlers, there'd be hell to pay.

Ethan thought it wise to check the horses first. Aside from guns, they were the one essential thing the brothers owned. Without them, cast afoot, he knew their future would be virtually nonexistent.

Moments after leaving the hotel, he reached the shed where they had left the animals. He entered from the rear, taking his time to sweep the shadows there, and noticed nothing out of place at first. Then, as his eyes adjusted, Ethan noted that the horses had somehow contrived to slip their tethers, drifting to the wrong side of the shed.

And there was something else . . .

It took a minute, staring at them, then he realized that neither animal was saddled. All their riding gear had been removed somehow, nor could he see it lying on the earthen floor before him.

What in hell?

Ethan thumbed back the hammer on his Winchester, clutching the rifle in a white-knuckled death grip. He half expected enemies to spring upon him from the darkness, but his ears picked up no sound besides the horses munching grass. He slowly pivoted, waiting for muzzle flashes in the shadows. But again, nothing happened.

Someone had visited the shed, unsaddled both horses, and then gone . . . where?

An ugly thought formed in his mind. Could it be Evan, going crazy as a goddamned bedbug? Had his mind fractured, somehow, to make him do things that he didn't realize in saner moments?

Or, worse yet, was he bent on infecting Ethan with his own bizarre insanity?

Frain mouthed a silent curse and pushed the thought aside. Evan was strange sometimes, admittedly, but this was simply too damned weird. If he was turning against Ethan, why not simply shoot him in the back, first chance he got?

And if it *wasn't* Evan playing stupid tricks, then there was someone else in Abaddon tonight. Someone who didn't want the twins escaping on horseback.

Warn Evan!

Ethan almost bolted from the shed into Main Street, but caught himself just on the threshold. One or more lawmen in town meant that the street would probably be covered. To be safe, he'd have to reach his brother by some other means.

Like what?

A shout along the street would simply tip the hunters that their game was up. Who could predict what they might do, in that case? There had been no gunfire yet, suggesting — even if it didn't prove — that Evan was alive. But weapons might be trained upon him, even now. A warning cry could mean his death.

Get moving!

Every second wasted now was lost forever. Ethan jogged back through the shed, past the distracted animals, and hesitated only for a moment at the rear exit. Outside, he anxiously retraced his steps back toward the Prairie Rose hotel.

And what would he do there?

Disjointed thoughts were scrambled in his mind, frustrating Ethan. He'd always been the cooler head, between himself and Evan, sketching out their strategy for raids, then trusting Evan for refinements. At the moment, though, he couldn't seem to think of —

Wait! He had it!

They were planning to burn Abaddon

before they left. Why not tonight, when it would do some good and force their enemies into the open? He would have to see the horses safely put away, but there was time for that. The breeze he felt was blowing from the north, away from the makeshift stable, toward the southern half of Abaddon.

Perfect!

He reached the back door of the Prairie Rose and eased inside, ready to fire at anything that moved or made an unexpected sound. A moment later, he was at the fireplace, leaning in to pluck out burning wooden slats and scatter them across the hotel's lobby.

By the time he stepped into the night once more, bright flames were leaping up the lobby walls, devouring all within their path.

Another narrow alleyway, this one between two shops on the east side of Abaddon's main street. Slade had been bold enough to cross at the north end of town, had drawn no fire, and thus encouraged he had set out to complete his circuit of the ghost town.

Somewhere on the way, he knew that he was bound to meet one of the Frains. Or both of them, perhaps, to speed the final moments of his manhunt.

Slade was considering a move into the street. Nothing dramatic, just a simple out-and-back to see if anybody took the bait. It was a risky move, but if it flushed his quarry out from under cover, it would serve his purpose.

That is, if their aim was poor.

It seemed unlikely to him that both twins would be on guard, but Slade had no standard for judging their behavior on the run. They'd staged one ambush for his posse, then allowed themselves to be surprised in camp with near-disastrous results. Slade searched for logic in it, but found none.

There were only three alternatives: two watchers on the street, one man on guard, or none at all. If the third option proved correct, then Slade could move about the town at will, as long as he was reasonably quiet. Otherwise, whether he faced one gun or two, sudden appearance and retreat would startle lurking snipers. If they didn't have his alley framed by gun sights — a coincidence which Slade dismissed as verging on impossible — they'd have to shift and aim at Slade before they fired.

Perchance to miss.

Slade braced himself, was pushing off toward open ground, when something flickered at the corner of his eye. Turning, he saw light showing through the downstairs windows of the Prairie Rose hotel. Not merely *some* light, but a glare of it, expanding, growing brighter even as he watched.

"Jesus!" he muttered.

The hotel was burning, and the fire was bound to spread. How long before the whole town was engulfed in flame?

Slade wasted no time pondering the nature of the fire, whether deliberate or accidental. Either way, its end result would likely be the same. After consuming the hotel, he pictured hungry flames devouring the western half of Abaddon. Whether it found a way to cross the street or not depended equally on wind and luck.

As Slade stood watching, fire raced through the ground floor of the Prairie Rose, bright tentacles extending to the second and third stories. The wood was tinder-dry and took no time at all to flare.

Still safe for now, Slade took advantage of the growing firelight to examine Main Street. Shadows leaped and capered without background music, reminding Slade that Abaddon was a *ghost* town, but he shrugged that off and concentrated on his search for human beings.

There! Was that a man emerging from the

darkness halfway down, along the west side of the street, moving toward the hotel?

Slade took another moment to confirm it, verifying that the figure he had seen was made of flesh and blood. Shadow obscured the face, but it could only be one of the Frains.

Slade raised his Winchester and drew a bead on the advancing target. He considered ending it with one clean shot across the street, rested his index finger lightly on the rifle's trigger, but could not go through with it.

Even cold-blooded killers like the Frains deserved a chance.

Not much of one, perhaps. But still . . .

Reluctantly, Slade let his rifle's muzzle sag off target, while the butt remained against his shoulder. Ready. He could call Frain out from where he stood, stay under cover, and command that he discard his weapons. If he tried to fight, then, all was fair.

Slade raised his Winchester again, drew in a breath for shouting —

And Frain stopped, appeared to see the Prairie Rose hotel for the first time, recoiling from the flames as if their heat had seared him. Stamping one foot like an angry child, the outlaw spat a curse that carried clear across the street to Slade's ears.

Then, he turned and ran.

Surprised despite his state of readiness, Slade lost his shot and saw his prey escaping, back into the shadows. Echoing Frain's bitter curse, he broke from cover, charging in pursuit.

Evan was shocked to see the Prairie Rose in flames. It had been his idea to burn the town, of course, but not while he and Ethan were *inside* it. And most definitely not when lawmen on the darkened plains beyond could use it as a signal fire to work out their location.

Evan realized that Ethan must have set the fire. His brother was too cautious to permit that kind of devastating accident.

But why?

He had to find Ethan, confront him in the short time that remained to them before the flames spread to —

The horses!

Evan felt a sudden, sickly rush of panic, picturing the tethered animals surrounded by a ring of fire. He imagined them emitting shrill screams like a woman's, as the blazing walls and roof collapsed on top of them.

And saw himself alone, on foot, running

across the endless flatlands with a posse in pursuit.

Frain glanced back toward the Prairie Rose, saw something else, and bruised his hip colliding with a hitching post that creaked and yawed under his weight. He stayed upright, arms flailing to preserve his balance, then dropped to a crouch, making a smaller target of himself.

Someone was stalking him.

At first, Frain thought it was a shadow cast by firelight, then he recognized the form and substance of a man. Not Ethan, whom he'd recognize by any light or none at all. A stranger, come to Abaddon for what could only be one purpose.

A lawman.

No sooner was the recognition made than Frain whipped up his rifle, aimed after a fashion, and squeezed off a shot that echoed in the street.

He missed.

The stalker ducked and dodged into a recessed doorway. Frain had no clear shot, but fired another anyway, hoping to score a lucky hit. If nothing else, the gunfire would alert his brother to the presence of an enemy.

Or did he know, already? Had the intruder gone for Ethan first, somehow resulting in the hotel fire? Was he already dead?

Impossible!

There'd been no shooting, first of all, and Evan was convinced that he would know when Ethan died, even if they were miles apart. Might even *feel* it, like a deathblow to himself.

A spray of jagged splinters from the hitching post stung Frain's left cheek. He heard the rifle shot as he recoiled, rolling across the sidewalk, seeking cover. Here, the shop doorways were not recessed, and he was forced to crawl across the planks as two more shots rang out.

One slug grazed Evan's hat, shoving it down over one eye, half blinding him. The other smashed a window overhead, somehow unbroken through the bygone years, and showered him with brittle chunks of glass. He wriggled through it, cursing as the wicked shards sliced through into knees and elbows.

At last, he reached an alley where the sidewalk ended and dark shadows beckoned. Evan pushed off with his boots and dropped a foot or more into the dirt, bruising his bloodied arms. Before he cleared the sidewalk, Frain's right knee collided with the sidewalk's edge and shot a paralyzing bolt of pain from hip to ankle.

Fairly sobbing, Evan dragged himself into the alley, braced himself against the nearest wall, and struggled to his feet. At first, he feared his right leg wouldn't hold his weight, but after several lurching steps he found that he could limp along at something close to normal walking speed, bracing one hand against the wall to keep himself upright.

Christ! Could it get much worse?

Damn right! You could be dead!

Small consolation, that, but Frain would take whatever he could get. Somewhere behind him, his pursuer would be bringing up the rear, delaying only long enough to verify that he was safe from an immediate ambush.

One and alone? Or were there more he hadn't seen?

It was the least of Evan's worries, at the moment. First, he had to find his brother, verify that Ethan was alive. Then reach the horses and escape, before his whole side of the street went up in flames.

The alley seemed to stretch for miles before him, though in fact it was no more than forty feet. When he had covered half its length, Frain reached the side door of a former dry-goods store. It wasn't locked — none of the doors in Abaddon were locked; he'd seen to that — and on a whim he ducked inside.

Why there?

Because the man who stalked him would've seen him duck into the alley, would assume that he'd pass through it to the rear, and then turn left or right from there. With any luck, the hunter would pass by and waste his time pursuing shadows, leaving Frain to make his way along Main Street to reach the horses.

Where was Ethan?

Would he fall back to the makeshift stable, as they had agreed in the event of an emergency, or run off chasing sounds of gunfire in the night?

Holding his breath to keep his fear in check, Frain stood and waited in the dark, ears straining to pick up on footsteps from the alleyway, outside.

Slade dashed across Main Street with shoulders hunched, Winchester clutched against his chest, expecting gunfire from the shadows. It surprised him when he reached the sidewalk on the west side of the street without a single shot in opposition.

Slade was fairly certain that he'd missed his man during their first exchange of fire. Ethan or Evan, take your pick, had come within a foot or so of winging him. Not bad, under the circumstances, but the pressing question on Slade's mind did not pertain to marksmanship.

He'd seen one of the twins. Where was the other?

Four rifle shots, the Prairie Rose hotel in flames, and still one of the Frains was missing. Had he gone to ground, preparing cover for his twin's retreat? And if so, why wasn't he shooting?

Slade considered that there might have been some accident at the hotel, disabling one of the Frains somehow, before the fire blazed out of control, but he didn't believe it. None of them had ridden all this way to die from stupid accidental causes.

No.

Both of the twins were waiting for him, somewhere in the heart of Abaddon, but with the fire starting to spread along Main Street, any surprise they might have rigged for him was now in jeopardy.

The alley was a black hole waiting to devour him. Slade knew he would be framed in silhouette the moment he entered it, an easy mark for any sniper lurking in the shadows. But what choice did he have? The only Frain he'd glimpsed so far was slipping through his fingers while he crouched against the wall of an abandoned shop, stalling.

Slade lunged around the corner, once again expecting to be cut down in his tracks — and once again, no shot exploded from the darkness. Pressed against another wall, holding his breath, he listened for retreating footsteps and heard none.

What now?

Slade judged the alley's length by those he'd already traversed, guessing that all of them were more or less the same. Faint starlight overhead and at the other end did nothing to illuminate the pitch-black tunnel, while the firelight at his back — ever expanding, growing brighter by the moment — tried to rob Slade of his night vision.

Get on with it, while you can see at all.

Slade fought the temptation to shuffle his feet, eschewing any noise that might betray him to his enemies. As a result, he took exaggerated steps, raising each foot well off the ground and placing it precisely, then repeating the procedure, navigating through the alley by his shoulder's contact with the nearest wall.

Slade reached the other end at last, delayed another moment just in case, then risked a glance in each direction, north and south.

Nothing.

Slade trembled with frustration, felt the anger turning sour in his stomach. He could play this stupid game of hide-and-seek all night, while Abaddon burned down around him, and have nothing more to show for it come morning than a pile of stinking ashes. He was stalking men who knew this place, who'd sought it out when they were hunted far and wide. They knew the battleground; Slade didn't. If he meant to stop them here, he had to take advantage of their only weakness.

They were running out of time and cover.

The advancing fire would see to that.

And they would need their horses to escape.

Sooner or later, he would find them at the makeshift livery. Whether the horses he'd untied were there or not, the Frains would come back looking for them.

Wouldn't they?

Unless one of them had already found the animals untethered and retrieved them. Saddled them again and led them somewhere farther from the fire.

Slade only knew of one way to find out, but there were two paths he could take to reach his goal. Retrace his steps along the backside of the threatened west-side buildings, or go back to Main Street.

Let himself be seen. Hell, flaunt himself for anyone who cared to take a shot at him.

And what? Pray that they'd miss?

No praying, Slade decided. *But a little hope can't hurt.*

Less careful of his noise this time, Slade turned, retreated through the alley to Main Street. The Prairie Rose was bright with flames from roof to lobby, blotting out the sky with acrid smoke, starting to sag as its support beams were reduced to fragile, blackened sticks. The fire had spread in both directions, setting light to shops on either side of the hotel, bridging the passageways between them with a rain of sparks and smoldering debris.

How long before the whole west side of Main Street was consumed? Two hours? Less?

Whatever, Slade knew he had no time left to waste.

Swallowing fear and tightening his grip on the Winchester, he emerged from hiding and stepped out into the middle of Main Street.

18

Ethan Frain stood in the recessed doorway of a shop on Main Street's east side, watching flames ravage stores on either side of the Prairie Rose hotel. Another moment, and the taller building's roof caved in, collapsing through the third and second floors in turn, with a sound like the roaring of African lions he'd seen in the Dallas Zoo.

In place of the hotel, a tower of flame rose skyward, hot air rising as nature intended, spewing white-hot coals and sparks as if the Prairie Rose were a volcano spitting lava. The night wind caught those embers, wafted them across rooftops, then shifted to the east and carried more across Main Street.

Frain tracked them for a moment, knowing that their bright trails spelled the final death of Abaddon, and realized he didn't give a damn. As long as he and Evan made it out alive, nothing else mattered.

But where in this dilapidated man-made

Hell *was* Evan?

Rifle shots had lured Ethan back down-
town, not exactly a long hike to start with,
but the fuss was over and the shooters
vanished by the time he reached his present
vantage point.

One of them must be Evan. Where had
any of them gone?

Three structures all ablaze left nineteen
former shops or office buildings still intact
on Main Street, waiting for the flames to
reach them and complete the work of dis-
solution that had started when the settlers
pulled out . . . what? How many years ago?

Frain didn't have a clue and couldn't have
cared less. Finding his brother and escaping
from the conflagration was his first priority.
Killing their enemies remained a distant
second. Gunshots in the street told him that
enemies were there, but Ethan would've let
them roast, in lieu of wasting time on them
while flames raced closer to the horses and
his only hope of leaving Abaddon alive.

He thought again of calling out to Evan,
but it felt too dangerous, and now the snarling fire would likely drown him out, in any
case. Sore throat for nothing, aggravated by
inhaling clouds of ever-shifting smoke.

He felt no inkling of regret for having
torched the Prairie Rose, and by extension,

all of Abaddon. He trusted Evan to be smart and stay out of the fire's way as it spread, but was he being overoptimistic? Would his brother's mind be caught up in the blaze, somehow, and swept away?

Perhaps. But he supposed it made no difference whether Abaddon was burned tonight, tomorrow morning, or two days from now. If Evan's mind had reached the breaking point, Ethan had no control over the end result.

"Somebody step out, now," he muttered to himself.

A hot wind brushed across his face like dragon's breath, driving him back, deeper into the recessed doorway. When his shoulders met the wall and he could go no farther, Ethan stood his ground against the heat.

He wondered if it felt and smelled like this in Hell.

And, if such a place existed, who'd be waiting for him when he got there. Friends and enemies alike, many dispatched by his own hand.

Meanwhile, he had to look out for his brother and himself.

Frain was about to make a move himself, try anything to break the logjam of frustration, when a figure stepped out of an alleyway across the street and four doors south of where he stood. Shadows concealed the tall man's face, but Ethan didn't recognize the hat or clothes.

One thing he knew for damned sure was that his Evan wouldn't have a tin star glinting on his chest.

Frain raised his rifle without thinking twice about it, sighted on the lanky figure, and was well into the squeeze before his target moved. Not dodging, but *advancing.*

Still, it was enough to spoil his aim. He couldn't stop the shot from cracking out, a whiplash cutting through the roar and whoosh of hungry flames, its echo battered back and forth between the Main Street shops.

And that was all it took.

His target bolted, firing from the hip. The bullet missed Frain by a foot or more, but still made him recoil instinctively, spoiling his second shot. Frain caught himself in time, before jerking the trigger, and tried to recover by leading the runner, sending a slug out to meet him as he ran headlong across the street.

It almost worked.

Frain focused on his rifle sights, almost to the exclusion of the sprinting lawman, calculating how far he should lead the runner with his shot. He couldn't say, in retrospect, whether his target stumbled or deliberately dropped into a shoulder roll and thereby saved himself.

In either case, it had the same result. Frain missed a second time, pumping the lever action on his Winchester and trying to recover while his man rolled over twice, then sprang erect and cleared the rest of Main Street, leaping to the sidewalk on the east side.

Lost to sight.

Frain swallowed a spasm of nervous excitement and willed himself to stay cool. One cop was nothing, when he'd dealt with ten aboard the *Katy Flier* and God knew how many more in other skirmishes. A badge meant no more to him than the bull's-eye on a target.

But he couldn't hit a target that he couldn't see.

Frain was the hunter now, eager to find his prey.

Slade wasn't sure, in retrospect, exactly how the first shot from the darkness missed him. Dumb luck worked as well for him as any other explanation. Afterward, when he was running, triggering a wild shot at the sniper, he had seen a glint of firelight from his adversary's gun barrel and dropped in time to save himself. Rolled twice and came up running hard, as if his life depended on it.

Which it did.

Slade lurched across the wooden sidewalk, hearing boards groan underneath his weight, then plunged into a doorway where he thought — or hoped — the sniper couldn't see him. That cut both ways, though. Slade couldn't see his enemy, either, without risking a bullet through his head.

It could have been a standoff, if the odds were level, but Slade had a second adversary drifting somewhere through the ghost town. Every minute he spent cornered in the doorway gave the other Frain more time to creep around his flank and find a roost from which to pick him off.

He had to move, but stepping back into the street was tantamount to suicide.

Which only left one choice.

Slade turned and tried the shop's door. Felt the knob turn in his hand. The rusty hinges creaked, but Slade trusted the nearby crackling flames to cover that small sound. He cleared the shop's threshold, sweeping the silent shadows with his Winchester, then eased the door shut at his back. He tried the lock, found that it worked, and gratefully secured it.

It would not protect him from a bullet or delay a zealous enemy, but anyone who breached the door would have to make some noise, thereby alerting him.

Next problem.

How in hell, Slade thought, *do I get out of here?*

He guessed there had to be a back door, and the firelight helped him find it, moving through the empty shell of what had once been someone's business, maybe with their home upstairs.

The back door offered no resistance, but Slade hesitated prior to opening it. What if this was what the sniper had in mind? One shooter drives him under cover, while the other waits for him to slip out through the only exit left?

It made no sense, of course. The rifleman who'd fired on Slade had been on that side of the street. Not herding him, but trying to prevent Slade's crossing over. Even if he'd planned to miss, which seemed absurd, how would he know which shop Slade would select for shelter?

Answer: it would make no difference, since a gunman placed behind the shops could watch a block of doorways, all at the same time.

Slade shook off the encroaching fear that tried to paralyze him. His *real* danger, as he saw it, was remaining where he stood until the shooter from the street had time to run around behind the east-side shops and find a nest from which to gun him down as he emerged.

Go now!

Slade bolted through the door, remembering to crouch and make a sharp turn to his left, Winchester leveled toward the shadows there. He was not greeted by a muzzle flash or bullet ripping through his torso, but he didn't linger. Didn't want to give his enemies a second chance.

Should he go back to Main Street, trying to surprise the sniper, or push on along the back side of the shops and flank him? Either course was perilous, and Slade decided on a compromise. He'd move north, skipping three or four shops, then pop out somewhere *above* the sniper.

If all else failed, at least he'd have a different view of Main Street as it burned.

And he'd be closer to the makeshift stable, when his quarry tried to flee.

It was a challenge, moving both swiftly and silently, pausing repeatedly to listen for his would-be killers closing in. Aware that he might be rushing toward danger, rather than moving away from it, Slade counted four back doors on his left before he tried another and felt it yield to his touch.

No locked doors in this ghost town.

And what would be the point of locking them?

Inside another dusty, vacant shop with nothing to distinguish it from any other in the dying town, Slade moved with cautious strides toward Main Street. Firelight cast long, leaping shadows through the window frames devoid of glass.

The pain in Evan's banged-up knee was easing, barely forcing him to limp as he prepared to leave the store where he'd concealed himself. The lawman hadn't found him, and in fact seemed to have doubled back, based on the shots he'd heard from Main Street.

Frain had been too slow to get in on the action there, but he had glimpsed his brother on the east side of the street, retreating from the spot where he had fired and obviously missed his target.

No corpse in the street. No shout of exultation for the kill.

And good news. No more strangers rising from the shadows to pursue Ethan.

Could it be true that only *one* lawman had

followed them to Abaddon? It seemed unlikely. Who would be that foolish?

Still, Evan had known a few who wouldn't quit once they had scented blood. They were like hunting dogs, entirely single-minded until someone scattered their obsessive thoughts with lead.

Frain flexed his leg and balanced on it for a heartbeat, proving to himself that he was fit to go. He couldn't see the lawman, and he'd lost his brother now, but lingering among the shadows didn't suit his mood.

Nor would it save him from the spreading flames.

One thing he'd always treasured about Abaddon had been its deathly silence. That was gone, now, given over to a hissing, crackling, roaring sound that grew in volume as it neared him, steadily devouring whatever lay before it.

As he eased out of the shop's front door, Frain saw that embers blown across the street had started small fires on at least two east-side rooftops. Those would spread, and more were bound to follow.

Abaddon was dying, more spectacularly than the first time, right before his very eyes.

Evan felt privileged to witness it.

He scanned Main Street, seeking a target, then decided he'd be wise to fetch the horses and remove them from the shed that stood imperiled by advancing flames. They had a while, yet, but it would be doubly difficult to move them once they panicked and began to rear against their reins.

And if he chanced to meet a lawman on his way, so much the better. Solving two problems at once.

Moving north along the sidewalk, Frain suppressed another urge to call out for his brother. Now that he'd glimpsed Ethan, had at least a rough idea of where he was, it didn't seem so urgent. Having laid to rest the fear of Ethan's death, the numbing thought that he had somehow missed it, left him free to act.

If only he knew what to do.

Frain wished that he'd remained with Ethan, so that they could frame a plan and face the enemy together, but if Evan hadn't gone off on patrol alone, they wouldn't know there *was* an enemy in Abaddon. Not until the bastard crept up close and shot them from behind.

They had a fighting chance, this way, but Evan loathed the separation from his brother in a time of crisis, when their lives were riding on the line.

He'd covered half the distance to the shed-stable when movement on the other side of Main Street caught his eye. Frain hoped it would be Ethan, *needed* it to be him, but instead he saw a stranger peering at him from the vacant window of the one-time feed and tackle shop.

He saw the lawman register Frain's recognition, start to bring his rifle up and into firing posture. Evan got the jump on him, triggered a wild shot from the hip, and wobble-sprinted for the nearest cover he could find. The shot that cracked across Main Street in answer to his own missed Evan by at least a foot.

Frain reached another shop with shattered windows, leaped over the sill, and dropped into a huddled crouch, glass crunching underneath his knee, just as another bullet whispered past him.

Closer.

Frain returned fire, three quick rounds, doing his best to make them count. He'd used up half his rifle's load, at least, without scoring a hit so far, and that would have to change. He'd left one box of ammunition at the Prairie Rose — long gone, by now — and had no more to feed the Winchester until he reached his saddlebags.

But something told him that the lawman wouldn't let him slip away so easily, this time.

And when in doubt, Evan's first instinct always told him to attack.

Rising, facing the darkened windows of the barber's shop, he fired another shot across the way, then hopped over the windowsill again, his sore knee snarling at him, and ran hell-for-leather toward the east side of Main Street.

Coming, you bastard! Stop me if you can!

Slade had his target framed, was taking up the trigger slack, when someone, somewhere to his left, called out a hoarse and frightened, "Evan! No!"

Slade knew who he was facing, then. The brother marked for Leavenworth, who'd never see the inside of another prison cell. Slade squeezed the trigger, felt the rifle buck against his shoulder — and the goddamned guy was gone.

Somehow, Evan had heard the warning shout and acted on it. Dropped, rolled, fired another shot, all in a crazy thrashing motion that had saved his miserable life while Slade's bullet whined off into the prairie night.

Before Slade had a chance to cock his Winchester again, a bullet struck the window frame immediately to his left — coming from Ethan down the street, it had to be — and stung his neck with splinters. Slade recoiled, cursing, and fired another wasted shot at Evan's scrambling form, before his target reached the sidewalk, cleared his field of vision, and was lost.

The brothers had him boxed now, damn it. If he didn't move, and quickly, they could sew him up and finish it.

Slade moved. Out through the back door that he'd used to enter, braced for gunfire as he cleared the threshold, hardly daring to breathe with relief as he made it unscathed. No time to waste, he realized. The Frains wouldn't be idling, granting him time to improve his position.

He could almost hear a trumpet playing "El Degüello" — the cutthroat song — as they closed in upon him. No quarter asked or offered.

It was getting on toward dying time.

Leaving the shop, Slade saw a flight of wooden steps rising immediately to his left. They ended at a second-story landing, where another door awaited him, standing ajar. Slade knew that neither of the Frains could be above him, lurking in the shadows there. Which meant that he could claim the higher ground, himself.

He took the steps two at a time, rushing but trying not to make any ungodly racket in the process. Any edge he had depended on surprise, and that was hard enough to manage when his enemies were closing in on him from either side.

Slade reached the second-story platform, eased the door a little farther open, and concealed himself within its shadow. From his place there, he could see both ends of the alley below him, along with a small slice of Main Street. A target passing by the alley's mouth would not be visible for long, but if he was prepared, he might get lucky.

Waiting, Slade was stricken by a sense that he'd forgotten something. That the twins could read his mind somehow and knew what he was planning for them. They could cross the street unseen, reclaim their horses, leave him standing there to face the steadily advancing flames while they rode out of town. Slade half imagined he could hear them laughing somewhere in the night. Beyond his line of sight. Beyond his grasp.

He almost missed it, then, when one of them — it should be Evan, coming from the northern end of Main Street — crossed the alley's mouth. Slade glimpsed his target just in time to fire, but heard his bullet splinter wood and knew it was another wasted shot.

How many left?

Slade hadn't counted, but he knew the Winchester would soon be running low. That left his Peacemaker and thirty rounds of ammunition slotted on his gunbelt. Plenty, for most situations, but it might not cover a protracted game of tag.

Of course, the fire would hasten things along. When there was nothing left of Abaddon but smoke and ashes, anyone still living would be forced into the open, where it all came down to do or die.

One of the Frains popped back into the alley's mouth and fired a shot up toward the second-story landing, but Slade was already descending the staircase in leaps and bounds. To hell with the noise, now that he had revealed his position. He fired once, on the move, and was rewarded with a yelp that might have indicated pain or mere surprise.

Don't count on anything.

Slade hit the ground moving and looking for cover. The next shop in line to the north sheltered him, as another shot slammed down the alley and missed him by inches. He skidded on gravel, then regained his balance and sprinted along to the next alley down.

Get the horses, he thought. *Let them know they're afoot.*

If the brothers believed they were trapped between fire and a long, lonely walk on the prairie, perhaps they would try something desperate. Give Slade the chance that he needed to take one or both of them down.

Not much of a plan, he acknowledged.

But now, it was all that he had.

He's going for the horses, Ethan thought. The lawman wouldn't know that he had doubled back to move them. Now, he felt a plan of sorts begin to take shape in his mind. It would be better if he had Evan to back his play, but calling on him now would only tip the lawman to what Ethan had in mind.

Instead, Frain broke from cover, checked the street, then dashed across it with his head down, focused on the opposite side-walk. He knew the spreading fire made him a target, framed against its glare, but no one seized the opportunity to drop him.

Huddled at his destination, Ethan stole a moment to look southward, noting that approximately half that side of Main Street was on fire now, radiating heat that put an oily film of perspiration on his face. He couldn't feel the cool night breeze, now. Just a searing draft that could've issued from the gates of Hell.

Too close for comfort, but he wouldn't let it sap his nerve. Frain was already one up on the lawman, and his target didn't know it yet. When he — whoever *he* was — reached the stable-shed, a shock was waiting for him.

Ethan had already moved the horses and their gear, although there'd been no time to saddle them before he went in search of Evan and the lawman. They were waiting at the far end of Main Street, behind the former feed store, which had struck Frain as appropriate.

Less than a hundred yards to go, but every step of it was perilous. It only took an instant for a bullet from the darkness to complete its work and still his beating heart forever. Such a death was virtually painless, Frain supposed, but he would put it off as long as possible.

That is, if he was given any choice.

Passing a long-closed lawyer's office, Ethan saw a sudden movement on the far side of the street. He spun in that direction, saw a figure leveling a rifle from the hip, and fired on instinct, willing the slug to find its mark.

And so it did, smashing a window that had captured his reflection, raining jagged glass onto the sidewalk over there. A quasi-suicide that cost him nothing — but he had to rethink that, as a muzzle flash winked in the darkness, not far from the window he'd shattered.

The slug grazed an earlobe, his left, with a sting like a sparrow-sized hornet's. Ethan yelped with pain and lost his balance, toppling over backward in a sprawl that sent him crashing through the long-gone lawyer's door, taking it down hinges and all.

The tumble saved him, showing nothing but Frain's boot soles to the lawman as he rolled away, clearing the shooter's line of fire. Warm blood spilled down his neck, beneath the collar of his shirt, its feel making his skin crawl.

Half an inch or less from death. A fraction farther to the left, and that shot would have opened up his throat, clipping the jugular and the carotid artery. Letting him bleed out on the lawyer's dusty floor.

That close.

Instead of brooding over it, Ethan felt energized by his near-miss. He had survived the law dog's best shot. Now, he was prepared to turn the tables.

Ethan had lost his hat when he went down, and he did not retrieve it before scuttling to the office's front window. Letting one eye peer around the frame, he scanned the east side of Main Street by firelight, looking for the man who'd nearly killed him.

Several of the east-side shops were burning now, though none could match the blaze he'd started when he torched the Prairie Rose. It would require a bit more time for Abaddon to finally consume himself, but drifting clouds of smoke already challenged his attempt to spot the lawman.

Unless . . . Was that him? Creeping through the shadows past the old gun store, on toward the blacksmith's?

Yes! Despite the smoke, he knew damn well that wasn't Evan's hat.

He watched the lawman cutting glances toward the building where he'd gone to ground, obviously looking for a target, but the smoke and glare defeated him. At the same time, though, Ethan couldn't beef the marshal with a clear shot from his window, fearing he might only wing his man or miss entirely.

What he needed was a clear view, something upwind from the steadily advancing fire. If he could get ahead of the lawman, somehow, without exposing himself too soon —

Why not?

The lawyer's office had a side door, fronting on another alley. In the past, he'd wondered whether it was placed to let selected clients come and go in secret, doing dirty business, but it was convenient for him now.

Staying well back from the office's window, Frain made his way to the side door and out. The alley's darkness cloaked him as he stalked his prey.

Slade knew that he was being shadowed by the time he'd covered half a block. It was a gamble, stepping out that way, when he knew one or both Frains had him spotted, but he had to force their hand before the town burned flat and left them stranded on a field of scorched earth.

If it worked, Slade knew he'd be rewarded soon.

If not, then he'd be dead.

Who'd hunt the twins, in that case?

Not my problem, Slade decided, as he took another peek across the street. And this time, there was movement.

Not a lot of it, but Slade could hardly fail to recognize a rifle barrel rising from the shadows into firelight. He was still at least five walking paces from the nearest decent cover, and Slade knew he couldn't trust the Prairie Rose's noxious cloud to save him.

Acting casual, as if he hadn't seen the gun,

Slade held his pace for two more steps, then broke into a studied trot. He hoped to spook the sniper, force his hand and spoil his aim at the same time.

A shot rang out behind him, and Slade stumbled, clutching at his side. He let his legs go rubbery but kept them moving, lurching toward the open frontage of a one-time blacksmith's shop. The old brick forge remained in place, and Slade collapsed beside it, sprawling on his left side, legs extended toward the street.

This was the all-time gamble, knowing there were four ways it could go. First up, the sniper, thinking Slade was wounded, could proceed to riddle him with bullets from a distance, making sure.

Another possibility was that the twin, whichever one it was, would be content with dropping Slade at last. Go off and leave him where he was, to roast when the advancing flames devoured the blacksmith's shop.

A third denouement had the shooter crossing over to confirm his kill. Appreciate his handiwork up close and personal. In that case, Slade would have a chance — however slim and risky — to complete part of his job.

The final and most dangerous conclusion, Slade's true preference despite the peril it involved, saw his would-be assassin calling for his brother to come celebrate the kill. The two of them crossing Main Street together, granting Slade one desperate chance to drop them both.

At last, he heard footsteps approaching on the grit of Main Street, barely audible above the sound of flames gnawing abandoned dreams. One person walking, by the sound of it, though Slade couldn't be positive.

It made a difference, of course, but only seeing could confirm it, and a twitch right now could turn his make-believe wound into something fatal. Slade would have one chance to do it right, and one chance only.

Any minute now.

The footsteps paused. Slade couldn't guess the shooter's distance from the blacksmith shop, with so much background noise, but he supposed the man who meant to kill him was no more than twenty feet away. Beyond that, with the fire raging, Slade didn't think his footsteps would be audible at all.

A little closer.

Every step in Slade's direction helped. Unfortunately, when the shooting started, it would be a help to both of them. For all Slade knew, the outlaw's weapon would be leveled at his head or heart in steady hands, before Slade tried his move.

In which case, all that he could hope for was a quick, clean death.

But if his adversary was a little cocky, if he let his guard down just a little, Slade might have a fighting chance.

Just might.

Slade didn't dare to hold his breath, not knowing how long he'd be under scrutiny. He kept his breathing slow and shallow, guessing that he wouldn't have to be a total goner for the gunman to approach him. Thinking of Hec Daltry and Creed Sampson at the outlaw camp, what seemed like years ago.

More footsteps, now. Closer. Slade tried to gauge the prowler's position. Behind him, of course — the only way into the shop — and now circling around for a look at his face. Nothing hasty, but closing the distance by cautious degrees.

Slade twisted like a striking rattler, glimpsed a Frain's face lapsing into shock and fury as he fired his Winchester at point-blank range. He pumped the lever action, fired again, and saw his second bullet strike before the tumbling form touched down, a lifeless sack of meat and bones.

They were alone . . . almost.

Somewhere down range, from the direction of the fire, Slade heard a rising howl of pain wafted away on hot air, off into the night.

Evan Frain recoiled from echoes of gunfire, wailing as a double bolt of pain lanced through his body. One leg buckled under him and left him kneeling by a water trough that had been dusty dry for years on end.

There was no doubt in Evan's reeling mind that he had lost his brother. How Ethan had allowed himself to be cut down remained a mystery, but there was no question of Evan misinterpreting the agony that racked his frame. It felt as if a red-hot knife blade had been thrust between his ribs, then twisted brutally for maximum effect.

Slowly, by small degrees, the moment passed. Frain found that he could breathe again, but only filled his lungs with wood smoke when he inhaled mightily, and wound up a patient in the final stages of consumption.

Finally, when an uncertain period of time had passed, Frain struggled to his feet, using his rifle as a prop, and slowly shuffled through a full circle, surveying the demise of Abaddon. The flames had nearly reached him, swaying toward him as the wind shifted, and he could feel his eyebrows crisping from the heat.

Time to move on.

Frain had to find his brother first, and then the man who'd killed him. Nothing else was real to him, or would be, until he had tasted vengeance. Raw and red, he craved it, like the roaring in his head.

Ignoring any risk of sniper fire, Frain moved along Main Street, exposed to the blind windows of surviving shops on either side. He took his half out of the middle, daring anyone to fire at him. He felt both wounded and invincible, a contradiction that had no impact upon his seething rage.

Ethan was laid out at the entrance to the blacksmith's shop. Hatless, he lay where he had fallen, dark blood soaking through his shirt and vest where he'd been heart-shot, also spilling from another wound beneath his jaw. Killed twice, it seemed to Evan, when he thought one bullet should've been enough to do the job.

He thought of dragging Ethan out into the street, clear of the flames, but changed his mind and did the very opposite. Gripping his brother's boots, Frain hauled him farther back, inside the blacksmith's den. Incineration meant no scavengers could creep around and feed on his remains. It was the best Evan could do, under the circumstances.

Nearly done, he palmed Ethan's .41-caliber Colt and jammed it down under his gunbelt, in back. The extra weight was a reminder of his loss, but he felt balanced by it. Looking forward to the moment when he pulled it on the lawman who had killed his brother, let the dirty bastard stare into its yawning muzzle, then put one between his eyes.

Or somewhere.

Evan hoped that he could make the law dog's dying last a while, but that might not be up to him. He had to find his adversary, first, by which time the encroaching fire could have something to say about how much time Evan had to spare for sweet revenge.

What did it matter, really, after all? A minute or an hour, it was all the same to him. As long as he left Abaddon with fresh blood on his hands, in honor of his brother's memory.

Where would he go from there?

Australia had a sour taste about it, now, after he'd laid the travel plans with Ethan. What good was it sailing to the far side of the world and seeing wonders never dreamed of when he had no one with whom to share them?

There was always Mexico. Or California, where his face would be unknown. Losing a twin reduced his risk of being spotted by a stranger to the neighborhood of zero.

Looking on the sunny side.

The blacksmith's shop revealed no clue as to the lawman's whereabouts. Frain wondered why he hadn't simply waited there for Evan to arrive and finish it. No guts, perhaps.

Or was it something else?

What would a manhunter be thinking, when he had one target left and no idea exactly where to look for him? His first thought, Evan reckoned, would be closing any avenue of escape from the ghost town.

The horses!

Christ! How had they slipped his mind?

Losing a brother unexpectedly would do that, he supposed. But now that he'd remembered, Frain was forced to give the tethered horses equal time and thought, along with Ethan's slayer.

He could play it both ways. Make a bold walk to the stable-shed, giving the lawman ample opportunity to do the manly thing or snipe him from the shadows, as he might prefer. In either case, Frain's enemy would be exposed.

And if the lawman meant to take the

horses and hide them somewhere to prevent Evan's escape from Abaddon, he still had time to frustrate that endeavor.

Ticking off the time in minutes while the ghost town burned around him, Evan Frain returned to Main Street and began to walk his long, distorted shadow northward, toward a rendezvous with Fate.

His or the lawman's?

At the moment, Evan didn't give a damn.

Slade pulled up short as he entered the shed and found no horses there. He had expected them to wander, but a quick run through the shed and out its other open end revealed no animals.

No saddles, either, when he checked the corner where he'd dumped them earlier. That ruled out any notion of the horses fleeing on their own and told him that the Frains — or one of them, at least — had foxed him.

One of them.

He'd just killed one, who obviously hadn't saddled up and ridden out of town. But why not, if the twins together were prepared to run?

Somehow, Slade had to figure they'd been separated when the first one spotted him and started shooting. Then came fire, chaos, and death. Unless the second twin had fled without his brother — always possible, but something Slade discounted as highly improbable — then that survivor must still be lurking somewhere around Abaddon.

Hunting for Slade? Or seeking his brother?

If one found the other dead, all bets were off. Slade didn't know his quarry well enough to say if the remaining twin would panic and escape or stay to seek revenge. His own experience with Jim's death was irrelevant, since they'd been years apart and neither was a criminal facing a noose if captured by the law.

Sniffing the smoky wind, Slade knew he had to *do something.* But what?

The variables stumped him. If he'd killed the twin who moved the horses on his own, the other might show up at any moment to retrieve them. If the living twin had taken them, he had no reason to return — unless he thought that Slade, expecting to find horses in or near the shed, would double back to cut off their retreat.

Choices.

Slade checked his Winchester and found that he had two shots left, before he had to fall back on his Colt. Not much, for an extended hunt, but roughly half of Abaddon now either seethed with flames or lay in glowing ashes, and the rest would follow soon enough.

It was too much to hope that fire had claimed the other Frain. Coincidence and luck would never stretch that far.

Move out, then.

Slade was turning back toward Main Street when a voice spoke from the shadows at his back.

"You wouldn't leave without me, would you?"

Turning toward the sound, he saw a tall man cast in silhouette, holding what Slade assumed to be a rifle at his hip.

"I was afraid I'd missed you," he replied.

"Where are my horses?"

"I could ask the same," Slade said.

A silent moment passed, before the shadow-figure laughed. The sound was harsh. It set Slade's teeth on edge.

"That Ethan always was a joker," said the man who must be Evan Frain. "I wish he'd let me in on it, this time."

"Maybe he didn't have a chance."

"Because you killed him."

"That would do it."

"Was it worth all this, lawman? The blood spilled?"

Was he crazy?

Slade said, "You and yours spilled most of

it, if you recall. I'm cleaning up your mess."

"My *brother*," Evan hissed, "was *not* a *mess*. He was a part of *me!*"

"You've got a choice to make," said Slade. "Lay down your guns, or join him."

Once again, that haunting laugh.

"I've got another choice in mind," said Evan Frain.

Slade threw himself to one side as the outlaw's rifle fired, squeezing his own Winchester's trigger while he was in midair, plummeting. He saw the shadow figure jerk a bit, recoiling, but the twitch could have meant anything.

Slade hit the ground, rolling, pumping his rifle's lever action one last time. A pistol shot echoed inside the storage shed — was his adversary's rifle jammed or empty? — and the bullet rattled past him, pushing little shock waves through the air.

Slade fired back at the muzzle flash and heard a grunt of pain this time, but Frain stayed on his feet, advancing, squeezing off another shot that spat soil into Slade's face.

Cursing, Slade pushed up to one knee, palmed his Peacemaker, and fanned off three quick shots from something less than fifteen feet. His target lurched and stumbled, dropped the smoking six-gun, and collapsed facedown.

Slade checked the body for a pulse, found none, and told it, "Now we're done."

It took ten minutes for him to locate the tethered horses at the far north end of Main Street. Slade untied them, mounted one, and led the other on a wide circuit of Abaddon, back toward the point where he had left his roan. Inside his head, the dead voice echoed.

Was it worth all this? The blood spilled?

"Some of it," he told the night. "Some of it was."

The employees of Thorndike Press hope you have enjoyed this Large Print book. All our Thorndike, Wheeler, and Kennebec Large Print titles are designed for easy reading, and all our books are made to last. Other Thorndike Press Large Print books are available at your library, through selected bookstores, or directly from us.

For information about titles, please call:
   (800) 223-1244

or visit our Web site at:
   http://gale.cengage.com/thorndike

To share your comments, please write:
   Publisher
   Thorndike Press
   295 Kennedy Memorial Drive
   Waterville, ME 04901